I0782290

iii

CURSED BLACK

Ed J. Thompson

DEDICATION

To the memory of Karlianne Short, a seventeen-year-old girl from Syracuse, New York, who was killed outside a convenience store when she was shot in the back nine days after her high school graduation.

October 15, 2005 – July 4, 2023

It is for freedom that Christ has set us free. And do not let
yourselves be burdened again by a yoke of slavery.
-Galatians 5:1 NIV

We use God's mighty weapons, not worldly weapons, to knock
down the strongholds of human reasoning and to destroy false
arguments.
-2 Corinthians 10:4 NLT

Prologue

Copiah County, Mississippi 1923

Liza ran as fast as she could as the afternoon sun mercilessly bore down. Her heart raced steadily in her chest as her feet moved gracefully over the dry, hard ground. She was strong for a nine-year-old, and she was barely out of breath when she reached her destination—a small two-room shack located a mile away just off the main road. She pushed the door open and rushed inside.

"Gal, what's wrong?" Mama Duke turned and asked with a startled look on her face.

"Mama say come quick," Liza blurted out.

"Why? Somebody hurt?"

"It's Chester Lee!" she exclaimed. "He got a root."

"A root?" Mama Duke flinched. "Ah, no, he's probably just got a little sickness. A lot of folks are ailing. It's the heat. What does it look like?"

"He started coughing and coughing and couldn't stop. Then he fell down on the ground and started crawling about like a snake."

"A snake, you say?"

"Uh-huh," Liza insisted. "He looks something frightful."

"When did it start?"

"Not long. He just came back from the tomato field."

Mama Duke looked perplexed.

"All right, let me get my bag," she said and headed to her corner where she kept her medicines. "Go tell George I am going to see about Chester Lee. He's around back."

"Yes, ma'am."

Mama Duke walked with purpose along the path, but she refused to run. At the ripe old age of forty-five, she was too old, too big, and too proud to run. Besides, it was too hot for all that. Liza easily caught up to her and Mama could tell that the youngin wanted her to move at a faster pace. But she ignored the girl's silent plea. She figured that this is what Chester Lee gets for chasing every tail he sees.

Mama Duke was born and raised in New Orleans. She moved to Mississippi after she married her husband George at the age of fifteen. Her mother was a "conjurer," and she taught both of her daughters everything she knew about the craft before she died. Now Mama Duke was renown throughout the county for her supernatural abilities.

There was a small crowd of people gathered outside of the modest dwelling when they arrived. Word of the cursing must have gotten out. Although most everyone was terrified of having a root put on them, they also couldn't resist witnessing a spectacle. The truth is that Mama Duke loved the attention.

The crowd spontaneously moved to the side to allow Mama Duke to pass by. She didn't acknowledge any of them. She only hesitated momentarily to order Liza to stay outside.

"Thank you for coming!" Sarah exclaimed.

Chester Lee was backed into one corner by his father and his brother. He was face down on the broken up wooden floor, with both hands supporting his muscular frame as he arched his back and neck upwards. When anyone moved in his direction, he raised his head in preparation to strike out. His eyes were darting back and forth in his head, and he was breathing hard as he opened his mouth wide, exposing his tongue, much like a cottonmouth snake.

"What happened?" Mama Duke demanded.

"We don't know," Sarah replied. "He just come in from the tomato fields and started acting strange-like."

"Can he talk?"

"He ain't said a word. He just keeps making noises and trying to bite people."

Mama Duke walked up to Chester Lee to get a better look at him.

"Get me a bucket of water," she directed. "We got to get him to drink some of my tea!"

"How we supposed do that?" Curtiss asked. "He won't let anyone get that close to him."

"Get some more men in here to help hold him down," she ordered.

Curtiss immediately turned and walked out. He was only gone about a minute before returning with two big men and a metal bucket. Mama Duke was standing at the small wobbly table in the middle of the room mixing some kind of concoction in a small wooden bowl. She worked as fast as she could. Afterward, she emptied the mixture into the bucket of water.

"Y'all ready?" she asked. "Hold him down on his back! Don't let him bite or scratch you and try not to look him in the eyes!"

A brief struggle ensued. Mama Duke spoke some strange-sounding words over Chester Lee while Sarah prayed quietly to herself and called upon the name of Jesus. Chester Lee fought hard, but he was no match for four grown men. As soon as they were able to pin him to the floor, Mama Duke pounced and began to pour her tea from the bucket onto his face and into his mouth. Most of it ended up on the floor. Chester Lee moved his head side to side, coughed, and made choking sounds. Eventually, he calmed down and soon appeared to lose consciousness. The sweating men relaxed as the tension in the room began to subside. They smelled like hard work.

"He should be fine now," Mama Duke remarked after several minutes of prolonged silence.

Sarah quickly moved in for a closer look. Her clear concern was readily apparent on her tear-stained countenance.

"Thank you for saving my boy," Johnny Ray remarked.

"Yes, thank you kindly," Curtis said.

'Thank you," Sarah echoed through her tears.

"You're welcome," Mama Duke said. "Don't move him at all. He should sleep for a while before he comes to himself."

"Anything else?" Johnny Ray asked.

"Just watch him for any signs that the spirits are still in him. Come get me if you see anything."

"All right."

"I have to get back and finish making dinner before George has a fit of his own," Mama Duke said with a slight laugh. "The man is helpless, I tell you."

"I'll see you out," Sarah responded.

The two women walked out together. There were only a few young children still gathered there along with Liza. They immediately stopped talking to gawk at Mama Duke. The sun had gone down a little, and the humidity had eased some.

Sarah decided to walk with Mama Duke a spell. Both women were quiet while they entertained their own thoughts. Sarah looked older than her forty years. She had four children, not to mention the same number of miscarriages. She was a God-fearing woman.

"Thank you again," Sarah finally spoke. "I was so

scared. Don't rightfully know what we would have done without you."

"Frankly, I was surprised that you sent for me, Sarah. I thought you said you didn't believe in the magic?" Mama Duke challenged.

"I don't," Sarah admitted. "Johnny Ray wanted you."

"Then how do you explain what you just saw with your own two eyes?" Mama Duke pressured. She threw her head back and put both of her strong hands on her wide hips.

"I don't have to explain it," Sarah defended. "I still don't believe that God's people can be cursed. But most of us don't know that. You better believe Chester Lee don't know it."

"I know that's right," Mama Duke answered with a reluctant grin and a chuckle. "Excuse me for saying, but everybody around these parts know that boy of yours got his nose wide open, and he ain't thinking about nothing but his nature."

"You better know it," Sarah agreed and nodded. "Got that honest straight from his daddy."

"Surely you could see the power of the curse in your son's eyes," Mama Duke pressed.

"What I saw was evil, and it scared me half to death," Sarah confessed. "God had nothing to do with cursing my boy. Now they got us cursing our own kind. Ain't that some trick!'"

"Who you talking about?"

"White folks have been cursing us for as long as we can remember," Sarah responded in a huff. "Maybe not with a root, but just the same. They do it with evil and hateful words too. They have called us everything but a child of God just to keep us down."

"We are colored people in the white man's world," Mama Duke reflected. "What do you expect? We will always be down in this life. They freed our bodies, but not our souls."

"But it's all a big lie," Sarah argued. "Magic is poison fruit only pretending to be good- it's enticing for sure."

"Maybe so, but most folks in these parts don't see it your way."

"That's the problem," Sarah insisted. "If you believe the lie, then it becomes just like the truth to you."

"So, you think it's as simple as closing our eyes to what we see when we look at ourselves in the mirror?"

"All I know for sure is that all people are made in God's image—colored and white people both. We can't let hateful words get in our heads and crush our souls."

"How we supposed to do that?"

"Resist the devil and he will run away," Sarah asserted. "Or risk busting hell wide open when we die. You can't serve God and the devil both!"

"You saying that I serve the devil?" Mama Duke contracted her eyebrows, clearly expressing her disdain.

"No, but you use his power and his words just the same," Sarah contended. "I know what I heard too and that didn't sound nothing like God's word you was reciting."

"I don't put curses on folk!" Mama Duke objected. "I help folk get out from under them!"

"But it's not what you do; it's how you do it," Sarah challenged. "God said we supposed to use his weapons to fight the devil."

"What do you care about how I do it?"

"'Cause God won't be mocked."

"Ain't nobody mocking nobody," Mama asserted.

"The bishop said a few Sundays back that we have been saved from all curses by *the blood of Jesus*."

"You don't say?" Mama Duke scoffed. "Tell me this then, where was the bishop, or your Jesus, when your boy was out of his mind and crawling around with his belly pressed against the ground like a serpent in the Garden of Eden? Maybe you should call one of them next time!"

Chapter 1

My name is Sam Hicks. I was born the proverbial statistic. That is, young Black men and teens made up more than one-third of the homicide victims in the United States, and Black kids were thirteen times more likely to be shot than white kids. I knew I was Black, and I knew I was poor. To me, they were the same thing—like two sides of the same coin. I didn't know any rich Black people. Running hard against both the odds and the clock was all consuming. But I had no other option. Nobody wants to die young.

My two younger sisters and I were raised by our grandmother in Utica, New York, a small upstate rural town located 240 miles northwest of New York City. Mostly due to the extreme poverty, Utica had a higher crime rate than most cities of its size. Although it is a city steeped in both American and African American history, it fell into hard times in the mid-twentieth century and never recovered from the economic decline. In the 1950s, the city was known for having rampant organized crime, earning the nickname "Sin City of the East." Only about 11 percent of the cities approximate 62,000 population in 1990 was Black or African American.

We lived in a crime-ridden neighborhood in the center of the city known as "Cornhill." My mother was a teen mother who lacked any ability to care for her children or herself. She loved the street life and wasted her youth pursuing mostly her carnal desires and the things that gave her immediate gratification. By the time she got married and settled down enough to even pretend that she wanted us, I was in junior high school and flat-out refused to live with her and her fake gangster husband. We stayed with our grandmother and saw our mother sporadically throughout the years.

I never knew my father. Although his name is on my birth certificate, I don't have his last name. I only know that he was much older than my mother when they got together, and he was married. He also was in and out of prison. Nobody ever talked about him, which was fine by me because I resented the very idea of him.

Tonya and Tasha, my sisters, were fraternal twins and shared a different father than me. He made the occasional appearance in their lives when the mood hit him. I looked after them a lot when they were really young. I was almost three years older than them, and the three of us shared a bedroom for years. My mother was better with the girls than she was with me.

Our grandmother was our saving grace. *Mama*, as we called her, worked as a cook at Utica Free Academy, the public high school we attended. She somehow managed to give us everything we needed, and some of what we wanted. I knew that it was hard for her having to provide for us by herself, but I never heard her complain. She somehow seemed to be very accepting of her lot in life and had no real expectation or hope for a better tomorrow.

However, she didn't hold back when it came to my mother or my aunt, both of whom were selfish to the core and mean as snakes. My mother never really worked as far as I was aware. Aunt Joyce was a strung-out prostitute, but at least she worked. The two of them were always fighting with Mama, and each other, and it got pretty ugly at times. I never understood why either one of them ever bothered to come around at all and I, for one, hated it when they did.

Although Mama had the occasional gentlemen caller, we never had a positive male role model in our lives. Understandably, her opinion of men, in general, wasn't too high. I felt guilty that she didn't have someone to share her life with. She was clearly lonely. But she always seemed more beleaguered than bitter.

Occasionally, Mama took us to church when we were very young. Dressed in our Sunday best, we went to New Bethel Church of God in Christ, a small, raggedy corner church that was located close enough to our house that we could walk to it. Although I enjoyed many aspects of attending church, such as the music and the histrionics associated with "the move of the spirit," there was no spiritual awakening on my part. I believe that we were considered "members" of the church, but I rarely attended after I got into high school.

I was a quiet kid and kept mostly to myself. I had a few friends. I was just average-looking, and I grew to just shy of six feet with a medium build. Never particularly personable and completely devoid of game or street creditability, no girl was ever interested in me in school, at least not that I was aware. I preferred to just blend in with the crowd anyway, and I never sought attention from anyone of the opposite sex.

I never wanted anything to do with the hardcore street life either, and I avoided the troublemakers like the plague. When crazy stuff started happening, I somehow always managed to leave the scene just in time to avoid being part of something horrific, such as where someone ended up getting shot or killed. But I was mostly just lucky.

Two guys my age, who lived across the street from us, never saw their seventeenth birthdays. I used to hang out a lot with one of them, and I was just with him the day before he was killed. His name was Freddie Jackson, and he was a good kid with a great sense of humor. To my knowledge, he was never involved in anything illegal. I just remember feeling a rush of anger when I heard the news. That was the first funeral that I ever attended. Unfortunately, there would be several others over the years. I never cried at any of them.

Although I never actually saw anyone get shot, I heard gunfire many times. It was a regular occurrence, especially at night during the summer months. Mama never really let me hang out too late. I was always home by midnight, and I think that helped me to miss out on a lot of trouble. Freddie was shot at 2:38 a.m.

However, I was by no means immune from acting like an idiot. There were several mental lapses along the way stemming from foolish choices I made in the moment, such as smoking marijuana with guys on the block and being talked into doing things that were out of character for me. That's how I started drinking alcohol at fourteen. That's also how I lost my virginity at the age of seventeen to a big girl from the block, to whom I wasn't even the least bit attracted, and who we all shared that night.

Most regrettably, there was this one time that I hit this kid so hard in the face that I broke his nose and his eye socket. I don't even remember exactly why I did it. I know he said something to me that I didn't like, and I hauled off and punched him repeatedly in the face with everything I had. My deep-rooted anger was often hard for me to suppress. Fortunately, there were no lasting implications from these youthful indiscretions.

I was very different from my sisters, and we were never close. For one thing, they were much more attracted to the dark element than I ever was. Initially, I tried to look out for them, but they always resented whenever I tried to tell them what to do. Eventually, I had to leave them to their own devices. It's very hard to help people who don't want your help, or worse yet, don't know they need it. They had each other and were content with that. They loved the attention that their light skin and light eyes garnered, physical characteristics that I unfortunately didn't possess. I don't know, maybe I was a little jealous.

For as long as I can remember, Mama loved her coffee, which she drank all day long. She brewed it in the old shiny metal coffee pot that was always on top of the stove, and which we were told, under penalty of instant death, to never touch. But I loved the smell of it, and its intoxicating aroma was the first thing we experienced every morning. Although we would ask for it sometimes, Mama never let us drink it.

"Na baby, coffee ain't for kids," she would say. "Coffee makes children black."

<hr>

I don't ever remember opening a book or studying anything in high school. I just listened in class and took the tests. I accepted whatever grade I earned. Otherwise, I didn't care. Neither did Mama, who never went to any parent-teacher conference for us or considered our report cards.

One day, Mr. Roberts, my eleventh-grade guidance counsellor, called me into his office. He was a Black man who appeared to be in his mid-thirties. I had only spoken to him a few times before.

"Sam, I'm just wondering about your plans after high school," he began.

"Plans?" I asked.

"Most kids in your position are thinking about what they want to do after they graduate," he asserted. "Do you know what you want to do?"

"Uh, no. I don't have plans," I sheepishly replied.

"Do you think you might want to go into the military? College maybe?"

"College?"

"You have decent grades. I could see you going to college."

"I do?" I questioned.

"Yes, you do," Mr. Roberts stressed. "If that is something that you are interested in, then I can help you with that."

I was speechless. I seriously didn't have a clue what he was talking about. I'm not sure that I even knew what college was exactly. I thought it was where white people went to become rich, and Black guys went to play basketball and football on television. I didn't personally know any Black person who had gone to college other than the teachers at school. I just agreed to the idea of college right then so that Mr. Roberts wouldn't know that I was totally brain dead when it came to stuff like that.

—•●•—

Outside of school, I didn't really know any white people. Although there were a few non-black families living in Cornhill with us, I can't say that I ever interacted with them. We also had a white doctor and a Vietnamese dentist. I saw police driving through regularly too. Mama didn't have a car. I pretty much never ventured outside of our neighborhood during my entire childhood. I knew white people mostly from television and from what I heard others say about them, much of which was negative.

But it's not fair to say that I hated growing up in Cornhill, because I didn't. I basically knew everybody who lived on Kemble Street, and there were many good times. In the summers, there were barbeques, where maybe a hundred people or so would be in attendance. We played music in the street and danced well into the night. There was a genuine sense of community in that it felt like we were all the same, and that it was us against the world.

After high school, I went to Mohawk Valley Community College for two years before transferring to Utica College. I earned a bachelor's degree in criminal justice. Thereafter, I attended Western New England Law School in Springfield, Massachusetts. I received my law degree in 1990.

More than anything else, higher education introduced me to the stranger living inside of me. I was never introspective before. Obviously, I was aware of my feelings of insecurity and anger, but it never once occurred to me to examine them, or heaven forbid, to challenge them. College forced me to at least take a closer look at myself and reframe my thinking about the world and my place in it. In the end, that turned out to be a very hard thing to do.

My mother just happened to stop by the house when I was home for spring break a few weeks before my law school graduation. Foolishly, I mentioned, in passing, that I was nearing the end of my studies.

"You probably really think your stuff don't stink now, huh?' she mocked.

Like my college graduation before, no one came to witness me get my law degree. It wasn't a big deal for me because I never really expected that anyone would be there anyway. Mama hated to travel, and my sisters were too busy chasing after the wild boys to care about me. My matriculation pretty much went unnoticed by those closest to me.

Kevin Fritz, my white study partner for the bar exam, went to Europe, a graduation gift from his parents. In contrast, Mama made me a German Chocolate Cake. I don't want to sound ungrateful—I really did appreciate her making the effort. Growing up, she was the only person in the whole world who even pretended to give a damn about me—and German Chocolate cake was my favorite. Even so, the contradiction left me more than a little angry and bitter-- feelings I knew all too well

In hindsight, the biggest thing lacking in my life growing up was vision. I literally had no sense of self-worth. As far as I knew, none of us did. Even self-centered people like my mother had given up on life completely. Not only didn't I have any dreams for my future, but I didn't even know that was a thing. I never wanted to be a doctor, or a lawyer, or even an athlete or an entertainer. I just thought that life was about responding to whatever bad thing happens to us next. So, I taught myself to always be on guard. And while I didn't want to get shot or die, I had no idea how to live—or what to believe about myself. I only knew about survival—like a wild animal in the African rainforest.

Chapter 2

New attorneys in the Oneida County Public Defender's Office in Utica were assigned to Utica City Court. There were three city court judges. They were each middle-aged white men. The judges rotated monthly; one presided over the criminal term, one handled traffic matters, and the other had trial term. It was a busy court, especially morning arraignments. Felony cases were transferred to county court after the arraignment. Misdemeanor cases stayed in city court.

I never wanted to be a public defender. Believe me when I say that I have never been quite that noble. Besides, I'm not sure that this was really anybody's dream job— low pay, long hours, and no respect. Who in their right mind would sign up for that? The fact is, unlike most of my law school classmates, I didn't have a job lined up upon graduation. I had gone on several interviews around the state, but I didn't have any luck. This was the only job that I could land— probably because no one in their right mind would choose to live in Utica either. The starting yearly salary was $18,900—less than $1,000 per month take home pay. Reluctantly, I went back home.

Mama was disappointed that I didn't want to live with her. Both of my sisters were living in Rochester with their babies' daddies, and she was by herself. She was starting to have some minor health problems, and she looked every bit of her sixty-six years. I wanted her to come live with me in my new apartment in North Utica, but she refused.

"I ain't going nowhere!" she protested loudly.

"I don't see why not," I argued. "You have so many locks on the doors now that I'm worried about you if there is an emergency like a fire or something. How are you supposed to get out in time?"

She laughed.

"Mama, seriously aren't you tired of all these fools shooting up everything?"

"Nobody is gonna bother me," she insisted. "I need to stay with the people I know."

"But I don't understand why?" I appealed. "You know that doesn't make any sense. Why keep doing this to yourself?"

"'Cause I'm not trying to be fooling around with all these other folk," she argued. "They don't mean us no good."

"But it's only like five or six miles from here," I maintained. "You can still see people. I would feel better knowing that you aren't living in this war zone by yourself."

"I thank you kindly, Sam, but you don't have to worry about me. I suspect that after all these years, I know how to take care of myself."

"But you are not getting any younger," I pressed. "And unfortunately, the world is getting worse, not better."

"I know that's right," she conceded. "But it's a blessing to even get to my age. Tomorrow ain't promised to nobody, especially now."

"Now you really do sound like an old woman."

"I'm old enough to know what I ain't gonna do," she resisted. "You can best believe that!"

I knew that it was a waste of time to argue with her when she had made up her mind about something. But it really did bother me to leave her there. They told me at work to expect to get threatened from time to time by a client. I was especially concerned that someone might try to get back at me by hurting her. I was the first Black attorney in the history of the public defender's office, which meant that my presence wasn't going to go unnoticed. Despite all of her tough talk, she was an easy target.

Obviously, a lot of the poor people who were assigned to be represented by the public defender were from Cornhill. That meant that I needed to live separate from where I worked. I had no desire to rekindle any old friendships or to socialize with anyone who I might end up having to represent in court the next day. It seemed too risky and that lines invariably would be blurred and crossed.

I met Judge Dominic Berrettini on my first day. He was doing pre-trials in the county courthouse. The public defender's office was located on the fifth floor, opposite the district attorney's office. I was nervous as I was led into the courtroom on the first floor by Mike Cantone, the assistant public defender who was assigned to Judge Berrettini' s court that day. Mike was thirty years old and married with two small children. He told me that he had been with the office for four years.

We walked past a sea of mostly black faces gathered outside the courtroom waiting for their names to be called. Most of them looked like they forgot that they had court today and had just rolled out of bed with no time to get dressed properly. I didn't see anyone that I knew, but I really didn't look that hard.

"Good morning, Judge," Mike said as we walked into chambers.

"Good morning," Judge Berrettini replied without looking up.

He was seated at his desk in what was a small-nicely decorated office reading a magazine.

"Judge, this is Sam Hicks. He is the new guy in our office."

The judge lifted his head slowly. His expression never changed as he looked me up and down like I was a slave on the auction block.

"Oh, they're gonna love you!" he finally exclaimed.

Mike laughed nervously.

The judge continued to stare in a way that left me feeling really uncomfortable.

I was motionless. I knew what he meant; I just didn't know what to say. Mike quickly broke the awkward moment with a question about one of the cases that was scheduled to be pre-tried that morning. As they engaged, several other people came into the office. They all appeared to be lawyers. In less than ten minutes, the room was completely full of idle chatter. I felt completely out of place.

Right away, I was introduced to Susan Kramer, an investigator from the public defender's office. She was a conservatively dressed white woman in her late fifties. I appreciated her warm smile. I really needed to see a kind face.

I also met Matt Collins, the assistant district attorney ("ADA"). He was about forty years old, tall, and blond.

"Welcome to the zoo!" he said.

"Thank you."

"You from Utica?"

"Yes I am."

"Then I don't have to tell you to just keep your head down," he advised. "You got to be a little crazy to do this work."

He gave me a fist bump.

I mostly just shadowed Matt and Susan all morning. Near the end, I stood up with one client while Judge Berrettini took his guilty plea to a negotiated reduced charge. He was a young Black kid who had stolen some food items from a gas station. It was an interesting feeling being a part of that for the first time, a bit unsettling for sure.

I met the rest of the public defender staff that afternoon. They all seemed nice. I could already tell that they were a cast of characters. They were loud and kept talking over each other. There were five attorneys altogether, two investigators, one secretary, and one receptionist. The office was one-third the size of the district attorney's office.

The public defender was a woman named Teresa Keys. She was a Republican, appointed to the position by the Republican-led county legislature. She was short and stocky and appeared to be in her fifties. My impression of her during my initial job interview with her was that she seemed tough as nails, like a truck driver. She was a chain smoker, who swore a lot. It turned out that her husband was one of my professors at Utica College.

I was given a tiny windowless office. I immediately noticed that there was a slight hum that came from the lights when you turned them on. The off-white walls were stained in places, and there were nail holes evident from items that had been previously hung there. An old wooden desk took up most of the room. It was clear on top, except for a big black phone on the right-hand corner. There was a small file cabinet forced into the far corner of the room and a metal trash can on the floor. It was hard to imagine a humbler beginning.

A big part of me questioned what I was even doing there. Although I majored in criminal justice in college, and while I strongly believed that the criminal justice system was patently unfair in its treatment of the poor and minority groups, there wasn't even an ounce of me that wanted to do my part to help make it better for my people. I fully accepted that the most I could ever hope to be was a cog in a broken justice wheel rapidly spinning out of control. I was very much a realist. I wasn't looking to change the world. I just needed a job.

Indeed, I had student loans that I needed to pay back. I also wanted to maybe have a family one day… maybe. This was the career path that I had chosen—no one forced me. I just wanted to learn as much as I could about the practice of law in general and see where that took me. Hopefully, I didn't embarrass myself too much in the process.

Surprisingly, I found the work to be more interesting than I had imagined. Every day was something different. Every criminal case that was prosecuted by the district attorney in Utica began in City Court, even the ones where the defendant had his own attorney. I was there every day, taking it all in. Routinely, we dealt with ignorant people, mean people, and plain-old-scary people—you name it, and I experienced it firsthand. It definitely was an acquired taste.

Right out of the shoot, I was regularly interacting with hardcore offenders. I was often the first person that the newly arrested felony suspects in Utica spoke to other than the police, and I represented him or her at the arraignment. I felt completely out of my league. It was crazy!

I thanked God for Susan Kramer every day. Not only was she an excellent investigator, but she was also a good teacher. I quickly learned that plea bargaining was our friend because most cases were plea bargained down. There simply weren't enough resources available to try every case. The key was being able to evaluate a case quickly and adequately, then know how to talk to the ADA about it, and then, most importantly, how to present the deal to our clients. A good public defender is only as good as his or her ability to negotiate a deal, and thanks to Susan, that's the part that came easiest to me. It was a gift I never knew I had.

However, the Bible says that people who live by the

sword die by the sword. About plea bargaining, it was a double-edged sword for us in that oftentimes the offers coming from the district attorney's office were harsh and mean-spirited. Generally, the better the case the ADA thought they had, the worse the plea offer. I never liked that approach much because it didn't necessarily take into consideration the seriousness of the crime and the harm caused. Just because a crime was committed didn't mean that anyone was actually harmed. Believe me, it was hard enough to get our people to accept a plea when the deal was a fair one. It was nearly impossible when it wasn't. Hence, there was always a large backlog of cases waiting to be tried in both county court and city court.

To my chagrin, a lot of people were interested in the new Black attorney in the public defender's office. There was an interview with the local newspaper, the *Observer Dispatch*, that Teresa forced me to do and that they ran twice. I was absolutely mortified. Thereafter, local attorneys began regularly introducing themselves to me, and I got to know everyone in the clerk's office. I soon realized that I needed to just put on my big boy pants, swallow my pride, and take everything that came with this job in stride.

One part of the job that I didn't much care for was night court. There were a lot of small towns and villages in Oneida County that regularly held court at night at least once a month. Most of the cases were petty offenses or traffic infractions, and most of the judges were not lawyers or formally trained. Every attorney in our office was assigned several courts to cover. I always had five or six-night courts. They typically started at 7 pm. Most never lasted more than an hour or two, but believe me, after a full day in City Court, the last thing I wanted was to have to go back out into the night, especially in the winter.

The first time I went to night court, the judge there thought I was a defendant. I arrived just before 7 pm, and

I had been sitting in what was an empty room for several minutes when the judge opened a side door, peeped out at me, and disappeared back behind closed doors. As he turned away, I heard him mumble something to himself about the public defender being late. I stood up, walked to the door, and softly knocked.

"Excuse me," I said. "My name is Sam Hicks, and I'm from the public defender's office."

"Really?" replied a middle-aged white man dressed in a flannel shirt and jeans. "I saw you sitting there, but I didn't take you for no lawyer."

"Well, I am a lawyer," I answered.

"Did you know?" he asked the ADA who was sitting there.

"No idea," the ADA responded.

———•●•———

My colleagues and I used to regularly meet at a local bar on Wednesday nights after court. We jokingly called these "staff meetings." It was just an opportunity for us to unwind and to share our daily frustrations. Oftentimes, one or two ADAs would join us. I was never much of a bar person, but I enjoyed the fellowship.

Unfortunately, some of us liked it more than others. It caused a bit of a scandal when Ross Scalisi, one of our older attorneys, was arrested for driving while intoxicated ("DWI") after leaving one of our "meetings." Teresa was furious at us all. Notwithstanding, we were a good group, and we got along quite well considering we were all different in many ways.

I became good friends with one attorney in the office. His name was Larry Simpson, and he was a little older than me. But we quickly discovered that we shared the same sense of humor. It goes without saying that many of the people who we represented were obnoxious and impossible to deal with. Almost all were guilty of something, if not every charge in the criminal complaint or indictment. But that didn't seem to matter, and typically neither they, nor their families, ever appreciated having free representation. We were unfairly stigmatized as being inferior somehow to private attorneys. At times, the disrespect, along with the pressures we faced, weighed heavy. So, we needed the medicine of laughter. It helped us maintain our own sanity.

— • ● • —

I won my first jury trial. Jerry Sawyer, my white client, was arrested by a New York State Trooper after he was found walking on the shoulder of a highway one afternoon drinking a can of beer and carrying three more cans in his pocket. When the trooper discovered that Jerry had left his car a quarter of a mile back stuck in a ditch, he ordered him to submit to a breathalyzer test, which he refused to do. The trooper then charged him with DWI in Floyd Town Court. The ADA, Paul Roberts, was near retirement age and mean as a bear. He refused to reduce the charge, so we had no choice but to go to trial.

Jerry testified that he was driving too fast on his way home from work and failed to properly negotiate a curve in the road. He hit the edge of the roadway and slid down into the ditch and got stuck. Because his brother only lived about a mile away, he decided to walk there. Jerry further testified that he only opened the can of beer after he got out of the car and set off on foot. The six-person jury only deliberated for twenty minutes before finding him not guilty of DWI and guilty of possessing an open container of alcohol, a minor violation and not a crime. He was sentenced to pay a $50 fine and a small surcharge or tax.

Unfortunately, the poor guy still lost his driver's license for six months stemming from his initial refusal to submit to the breathalyzer. It was a mandatory civil penalty. Nevertheless, I was very happy with this outcome. It was a good start for me.

Chapter 3

The two other City Court judges were Marco Fratangelo and Tony Cipolla. They were basically clones of each other—Italian-American crusty grandfathers. I never had a problem with either one of them. Although both men could be grumpy from time to time, especially when court lasted too long, and they were late for lunch or something, they were both harmless. Believe it or not, I ended up liking Judge Berrettini the best because at least he always spoke his mind and wasn't overly bothered or offended when we attorneys did the same.

I was a fast learner, and I pretty much knew what I was doing after a couple of months. Honestly, it wasn't that hard. It wasn't exactly brain surgery. The worst part was witnessing all the pain in the people.

However, the biggest surprise for me was discovering that most of our Black clients preferred to be represented by anyone who wasn't me. Initially, I thought it was because I was new, and they thought I didn't know what I was doing. And then I reasoned that it was because they had figured out that they couldn't snow or intimidate me. But it turns out that neither theory was correct.

It was during one of my weekly jail visits that I was set straight.

"Mr. McDuffie, have a seat please," I directed.

Carl McDuffie closed the door and sat down. He was

wearing an orange jail jumpsuit. He was a forty-eight-year-old Black guy with an extensive criminal record, including having served time in state prison for attempted murder. Fortunately for him, he was only charged this time with a misdemeanor assault related to an argument that he had with his girlfriend. He only looked at me briefly before focusing his attention on something over my shoulder.

"How are you?" I asked.

"Do I have to keep you for my public defender?" he bluntly inquired.

"Technically, you are being represented by our office, not by me," I explained. "Can you afford to hire an attorney?"

"Where's Garin? He represented me last time."

"That was for a felony charge in county court. You are only charged this time with a misdemeanor. He's in a different courtroom."

"Look, man. I don't know you. I want Garin again." He laughed sarcastically and rolled his eyes.

"I'm sorry, but it doesn't work like that," I explained.

"What do you mean? Mr. McDuffie fussed. "The other public defender's get better deals than you do, and everybody knows it. I'm not trying to be in here any longer than I have to!"

"I don't think that's true," I argued.

"It is true," he disputed. "Separate but equal was never equal."

"What?" I scoffed. "You don't even know what you're talking about!"

"Yes, I do," Carl replied and snickered. "These judges are never going to listen to you. You can't even talk like they do. It's a private club, and they take care of their own. You ain't no different than me."

"Yes, I am!" I asserted strongly. "We aren't the same."

"Yo, bro. It don't rub off. You black just like me. Is that what they told you in college? That it comes off?"

He repeated his menacing laugh.

"At least I went to college, bro!" I fired back. "If you know so much, then why are you sitting here in an orange jumpsuit and I'm not?"

"I don't care. I don't want you trying to represent me."

"Then I suggest you bring that up with the judge at your next court date!"

"I will!" he maintained.

He didn't. However, it turns out that what Carl said to me carried a measure of truth with it. That is, the black men and women in the jail gave me mixed reviews at best. It took me a few minutes to fully grasp what was happening. Thereafter, I became a little more accepting of this reality because a part of me understood where they were coming from. The way I saw it, this mindset was just a manifestation of both their self-hate and jealousy. They thought less of themselves, so they naturally thought less of me and any service I could provide them. I told myself that I shouldn't take the rejection personally, which admittedly was easier said than done.

Interestingly, most of our Black clients insisted upon calling me by my first name. But they typically didn't do that with the other attorneys in our office. In contrast, almost all the white clients, including those who were much older than me, called me "Mr. Hicks." The fact is that many of them seemed to prefer me over the other public defenders for some reason.

Truthfully, that's the part that surprised me the most. Don't get me wrong: the disrespect we experienced as public defenders was across the board in that it came from all races, sex, and colors. But our white clients were clearly more willing to give me the benefit of the doubt than my own kind was. The implications were troubling. So much for Judge Berrettini' s prediction regarding my popularity with the Black clientele.

I always got along with the police personnel in city court. Most were friendly enough and appropriately deferential, at least to my face. We talked mostly about sports, our families, or some crazy thing that just happened in court. I routinely cross-examined officers from the Utica Police Department ("PD") at felony examinations that were designed to determine whether the police had probable cause to arrest my client, and although I often pushed hard, I never felt like any of them ever held it against me later.

But I was no fool. I knew that they acted differently with me than they did with other people of color they had cause to interact with in another setting. Without a doubt, I had experienced enough personal interactions of my own with police officers on the street to know that they couldn't always be trusted to do the right thing any more than we could be counted on to handle ourselves in an upright manner. That's why these encounters were always fraught with peril.

While I didn't know any Black officers on the Utica PD, there were a few Black deputy sheriffs and several Black state troopers I ran into from time to time. We were cordial, but I never got to know any of them personally. We chose to keep it professional. It was just easier that way.

But I have to say that I was always suspicious of the deputies at the Oneida County Jail ("OCJ"), who appeared to be a little more over the top, and who also seemed to enjoy telling me what to do a little too much. I generally just followed their direction without question. I had nothing to gain from going there and acting like a jerk.

On one jail visit, I happened to encounter an

administrator who apparently didn't know who I was. The deputy at the front desk had buzzed me in like normal and directed me to go to the attorney's room and wait there for my client to come out. I was dressed in typical business attire, including a suit and tie, and I was carrying a briefcase. I had made it halfway down the hall when I heard someone yell from behind.

"Excuse me, what are you doing?"

I turned around to see a red-faced, bald, white man dressed in plainclothes. I stopped as he approached me.

"What do you think you're doing here?" he yelled again.

"I'm going to the visiting room to…"

"Who let you in?" he barked. "You're out of place, buddy!"

He stepped closer with the clear intention of threatening me by invading my personal space. I held my ground. We were face to face.

"Is there a problem, Mr. Hicks?" a uniformed deputy asked in a loud voice as he hurried in my direction.

"Yes, there is," I replied calmly.

"Why don't you just go to the attorney's room?" he directed. "Your client knows that you are here. He'll be there in a minute."

I stepped around the crazy dude and walked away. I was flustered and angry inside. But I managed to pull myself together, and I met with my client for about an hour without incident. As I proceeded to walk back down the hall, the dude approached me again.

"Hey, I just need to explain what happened earlier," he began. "Whoever let you in this area without an escort violated procedure, and I intend to get to the bottom of it. This is not regular visiting hours, and I had no way of knowing who you were or that you are an attorney. I was just doing my job. I hope that you understand."

I didn't say anything. I just shook my head and walked

away.

I reported the incident to Teresa at work the next day. I wanted her to hear about it first from me in case it got twisted somehow. She said that she would take care of it. I don't know if she did or not, but I never had a problem at the county jail again.

———————•●•———————

That first year flew by for me. I got some really good experience. I lost some trials, but we basically always lost as the deck was stacked against us. Very few young lawyers get into the courtroom the way I did. They mostly just did research and carried the briefcases of the more senior attorneys in their firms. I was in court every day, getting hands-on experience. I liked that part of it.

Whenever possible, I would sit in on the trials of the more experienced attorneys in town in order to learn as much as I could about the art of trying a case. I watched them as closely as I could, hoping to discover exactly what it was about them that made them so effective. In so doing, I was surprised to discover that I had some hidden talents I didn't know I had. Nobody knew.

Mike Cantone unexpectantly announced that he was moving to Buffalo and resigned from his position in our office. It took about a month for Teresa to hire a new attorney. His name was Greg Meyers, a socially conscious older man coming out of retirement. As the new guy, he took my spot in Utica City Court, and I was moved up to County Court, which meant that I was going to be handling felony cases with the big kids.

Chapter 4

There were two county court judges: Tom Mazur and Joseph Lombardi. They were okay, I guess. Both were conservatives and had pretty good temperaments. They mostly treated the attorneys who appeared before them with respect, including the attorneys from our office. They were somehow able to separate us from our causes—meaning, the people we represented, about whom they were not overly sympathetic.

But they were both slow, and cases often moved at a snail's pace. It was especially hard for us to get good results in Judge Lombardi's court because he was obsessed with his public image and desperately wanted to portray himself as tough on crime. That was clearly his driving force. I just thought he was self-centered and lacked compassion for broken people.

Once, in the middle of picking a jury in an assault case, Judge Lombardi directed the attorneys to approach his bench. My client, John Brown, was a young Black man, and he was charged with first-degree assault stemming from a bar fight where he allegedly stabbed another man in the chest during an argument over a woman. He was sitting next to me at the defense table. Just as I stood to go up to the bench with the ADA, he asked me if he could go to the bathroom. I told him that he had to wait for an official recess before he could leave the courtroom. We had been huddled at the bench with the judge with our backs to the crowd of approximately fifty prospective jurors for several minutes, when someone from that crowd spoke out.

"Excuse me!"

We stopped talking and looked out.

"I don't know if you guys know, but he just left."

That's when we notice that John had left the courtroom.

"Oh, Judge, I think he just went to the bathroom," I interjected. "He told me earlier that he had to go."

"Well, Mr. Hicks, I suggest that you get *that SOB* back in the courtroom, pronto!" the judge ordered out loud in an angry tone.

"Yes, Judge," I replied and immediately turned away.

John and I soon returned to our proper places. I warned him not to do that again. Now I had a problem. I needed to make a motion that I knew wouldn't be well received.

"Judge, before we go any further, I'd like to ask to go on the record outside of the hearing of the jurors on a matter."

Judge Lombardi already wasn't happy. He had been short-tempered all morning. He shook his head, dropped his pen aggressively on his desk, and reluctantly ordered a ten-minute recess. I ignored his childish protest.

"Your honor," I began. "Prior to the recess, you inadvertently referred to my client in a derogatory manner in the presence of the entire jury pool. It is our position that that reference has tainted the entire panel. Accordingly, I am asking that we begin jury selection all over with a new panel."

Judge Lombardi's eyes shot open wide.

"What derogatory word did I supposedly use?" the judge challenged.

"You called Mr. Brown an 'SOB.'"

The Judge began stewing.

"I don't recall using that reference," he lied.

"It's not just what you said, it is also how you said it," I pressured.

"How was it said?"

"Not respectful," I described. "These people already know what you think about my client. I don't see how they can be rehabilitated."

The judge stared at me. He clearly was caught off guard and didn't know what to do. He was seething just below the surface.

I appealed to the ADA, a nice guy who I always found to be fair minded, "Tim, did you hear it?" I asked.

"No," the ADA quickly responded. "I never heard anyone say that."

"Your request is denied, Mr. Hicks," the judge said defiantly with a scowl on his face.

His nostrils were flared and his jaws tense.

"Anything further?" he challenged me.

"No, your honor," I answered.

The thing is that I get that John should not have left the courtroom without permission. But he wasn't in custody any more than any of the perspective jurors were, and no one had been explicitly barred from using the facilities as needed. Turns out that a lot of these judges had what we called "black robe disease," meaning they were always threatening to take their ball and go home when the game didn't go their way.

I ran into that same ADA the next morning in the hall before court.

"Hey, Sam, I just wanted to talk to you about what happened yesterday."

"What about it?" I blurted out.

"I want you to know that I really didn't hear what Lombardi said about your guy."

"Well, he said it," I stressed. "You are probably one of

the few people in the courtroom who didn't hear it."

Tim raised both of his hands in surrender. "I believe you, but there wasn't anything I could do."

"Okay, if you say so," I relented.

"I don't think that it was that big of a deal anyway," Tim maintained. "There was no way Lombardi was going to dismiss all those people. The commissioner of jurors would have lost his mind if he had to replace the entire panel!"

"Yeah, we wouldn't want that to happen," I mocked.

Undeniably, most of the poor people we defended were uneducated and socially inappropriate, among other things. It really was quite embarrassing at times. I cringed every time one of our clients asked to address the court themselves. I rarely knew what they wanted to say, and, in the end, it rarely went well.

Regardless, the point is that those individuals who represent the public as part of the criminal justice system, such as judges, lawyers, and especially police officers, needed to take their oaths of office a lot more seriously. We must be held to a higher standard. Justice is supposed to be fair, equal and color blind. And we are supposed to be the guardians of the keys to the kingdom as public servants. It's no wonder that we were struggling as a nation and moving in the wrong direction.

———— • ● • ————

I learned very quickly that I wasn't going to make it if I was easily offended by what transpired in the courtroom. For instance, there were numerous times during jury selection that perspective jurors told us in open court that they didn't think that they could be a fair and impartial juror in a case with Black defendants because they didn't like or trust Black people. And it wasn't just what they said, but also the way it was said it- with such spite and contempt. It wounded me every time. Judge Mazur told me one time after an older white man expressed his racial bias in court in front of me that he thought that the only reason that people kept saying that was because they didn't want to be selected to be on the jury in the first place, and they figured that this was a sure-fire way to get excused. I respectfully disagreed with the judge concerning this matter.

—•●•—

My whole life was my job. I used Sundays as my sabbath rest day to allow my body and my mind to recover from high stress situations. But I didn't attend any church services. Mama tried to get me to go to church with her a couple of times, but I refused. I thought she just wanted to show me off. I just wanted to be alone and not have to deal with people and their stuff. Sometimes I never even got dressed. I stayed in my pajamas all day watching movies. I preferred comedies and avoided watching crime or legal dramas altogether.

There was a social worker I met in city court who was temporarily assigned to help us do intake and screening of individuals for possible mental health diversion. She was only there for a few months, but I liked her. She was single and really nice. Before she left, she gave me her phone number. I was very tempted to ask her out, but I never did. I was afraid to call her because she was white, and I couldn't see how that could work.

During a routine physical examination, it was discovered that I had had latent tuberculosis infection. Basically, while I didn't have active tuberculosis or any symptoms, test results revealed that I had been exposed to the disease. My doctor suspected that I probably encountered someone at the jail—where ventilation was poor—who was sick. He explained that there was only a very small chance that I would ever develop active tuberculosis. He just wanted me to be watchful about developing symptoms.

Additionally, my blood pressure was slightly elevated. Not a condition typically found in people under thirty. As far as I knew, no one in my family suffered from hypertension. But that's part of the problem; I actually knew very little about my family history. I didn't know anything about my father or his family, which meant that half of my history was lost. Unfortunately, a rather high percentage of African Americans find themselves similarly situated—incomplete.

Chapter 5

"Judge, you wanted to see me?"

"Yes, Sam. Come on in," Judge Mazur coaxed.

He was a heavy-set, gray-haired man in his early sixties. His large office smelled like cigars. There were a lot of photographs scattered around the room and on the walls. It appeared that he had a hundred grandchildren.

"How are you doing?" he asked.

"I'm good," I replied.

I had no idea why I was there.

"I thought that was a good plea your guy took today," Judge Mazur said. "Not sure where you were going with that kind of video evidence."

"Well, I can only play the hand that I am given."

"Ain't that the truth. But you guys are a good group. You seem to hold your own."

"Thank you."

"Anyway, I wanted to tell you something," he began. "We were at this shindig the other night, and my wife introduced me to this really lovely gal. She is new in town and just took a job at one of the television stations. I told her about you."

"*Me?*" I recoiled.

"Yes, I think that you might have a lot in common. You'll like her. I think you should call her. Here's her card."

"Uh, thanks, but I don't know," I hesitated.

I took the business card and only pretended to look at it.

"You're not seeing anyone? Are you?"

"No, but…"

"Call her!" the judge barked, "Her name is Carla Jenkins. What do you have to lose?"

"Okay, maybe," was all I could force myself to say.

"Sammy, you're too serious. You need to lighten up. I tell my grandson that all the time. You young guys don't know what's important."

I was not happy. I didn't want, nor did I need a matchmaker. My life was already stressful enough. I got hit on by women from time to time, even by some of our female clients. But I never took the bait—ever. I didn't feel like I was ready for all that. I was determined to stay on point. Upon return to my office, I immediately tossed the card in my top drawer with the rest of my miscellaneous items.

• ● •

I was sitting at my desk when Teresa walked in.

"Hey Sam, did you hear that we are getting a new murder case?"

"No. I haven't heard."

"I just got off the phone with Greg. He just finished the arraignment. You want it?"

My heart nearly jumped out of my chest. "Are you serious?"

"Yes, I am," she said. "You have been here almost two years now. I think you're ready."

"Okay," I replied cautiously.

"You sure, because I could assign it to Frank?" she pressed. "It will be his third one this year."

"No, I can do it," I entreated.

"Okay, then it's yours," she decided. "It's a drive-by shooting by a teenage kid. Greg said that the felony hearing is scheduled for tomorrow morning. You need to touch base with him."

"Do you know who the judge is?'

"Berrettini, I think."

"All right. I'll see Greg. Thank you."

"Don't thank me too soon," she warned. "These things are the worst."

She just stood still, thinking. She had a pained look on her face.

"Are we having fun yet?" she finally asked and sighed loudly.

I didn't respond because I wasn't quite sure what to say.

She slowly turned and walked out without waiting for my answer.

According to Greg, our client was arrested, along with two other teenagers, within days of the shooting. All three were "bad guys" and apparently gave written statements to the police. Berrettini set no bail, and they were all in jail. Greg and I agreed that we would waive the felony hearing if the DA gave us copies of all the signed written statements now. Otherwise, we would force them to go through the effort of holding the hearing, which although provided for in the law, was a complete waste of time in most instances.

That night, I met up with the gang after my night court at a bar in New Hartford. As we stood around the bar, all I wanted to do was talk about my new case.

"I think you'll be fine," Larry reassured. "At the end of the day, these cases are all the same."

"I don't know," I admitted. "I think Teresa just gave it to me because she didn't have anybody else to give it to."

"I don't think that's true," Larry maintained. "Besides,

what difference does it make why she gave it to you?"

"I just don't want to get second-guessed later. I'm still pretty new at this."

"Second-guessed by who?"

"By the fourth department on appeal when my poor client later claims that his conviction should be overturned because I was too young and didn't know what the hell I was doing."

"I think you worry too much," Susan interjected. "You're more than ready. Just think of it as just another case."

"Yeah, just another case where the guy is facing twenty-five to life," I asserted.

"Well, it's not like this case is going to actually go to trial," Greg said and shrugged his shoulders. "He signed a statement admitting to firing the gun out of the car. He's got to plead guilty to something. I agree with Susan. Just do what you normally do."

"I just don't want to screw it up worse," I repeated soberly.

"It's already screwed all the way up," Nick Garin spoke in earnest. "The entire system is a lesson in disfunction."

— • ● • —

Ronnie Walker died. I knew him from high school. He was the funniest guy I ever met. He kept us in stiches. I always thought that he should have been a comedian. But I lost track of him after I graduated. Apparently, he never married and struggled with drugs and alcohol. He was shot and killed by a teenager on a Utica Street corner in an apparent dispute over drugs.

I went to the calling hours at the funeral home. I had to take Mama, or else I probably wouldn't have gone at all. I hated those things. Fortunately, the funeral home wasn't in Cornhill. It was in North Utica, not far from my apartment. Ronnie's sister Courtney Walker-Thomas had done well for herself and was employed at City Hall as an auditor. My guess is that she paid for the funeral.

There were quite a few people in the receiving line when we arrived at the funeral home. It took longer than I had anticipated to get through it. I wasn't expecting so many people to show up. I knew a lot of them. Because the funeral was scheduled to follow immediately, Mama talked me into staying.

The funeral lasted less than an hour, that's counting the reading of the obituary, two eulogies, and two songs that were sung mostly off key by three young girls. I counted seventy-five people sitting in the chairs. Most of the people were casually dressed, many of whom were wearing shorts and t-shirts. I felt overdressed in a blazer and khaki pants.

The minister who officiated, Reverend Titus Strickland, wore a suit and tie. I had never heard of him. He was short with a medium build. He appeared to be in his fifties. He seemed unprepared and mostly talked about the need for people to get saved because "nobody knows when death was gonna come knocking at the door." He prayed hard for Jesus to deliver us from "all of this earthly pain."

At the close of his sermon, he expressed his frustration at all the senseless killing and said that the police needed to do more to protect us. Overall, it wasn't an overly emotional affair. I didn't see anybody shedding tears. Nobody got saved that day that I saw. The death of males under the age of forty was a regular occurrence in the hood. We had somehow learned over time to temper our response to black-on-black crime.

In contrast, the death of a Black person caused by police tended to hit a much bigger nerve. There was almost always an immediate loud outcry in the minority community when a police officer shot and killed a Black man. It didn't seem to matter whether the victim was armed or unarmed or was engaged in criminal activity or was an innocent bystander at the time of the shooting. The swift response from community leaders and advocate groups typically called for police reform and accountability. In the end, these demands mostly fell on deaf ears as nothing really changed. Fortunately, deaths caused by police didn't happen a lot in Utica.

I never pretended that I had all the answers. I didn't. And I never felt that being Black or poor somehow made me an expert on these unbelievably complex issues. Specifically, I never thought that my dark complexion necessarily gave me greater insight on the causes and cures of our societal ills, such as police brutality and ending racism. I only knew what it felt like to be a victim of many of these sins. Unfortunately, the little I knew, I knew very well.

Chapter 6

A jail, or a prison is a place where condemned individuals are confined and denied a variety of freedoms under the authority of the state as punishment for a crime they have committed. During the formative period of American history, that crime often was being born Black. Today, the modern prison in the US looks strikingly similar to the plantations of old—a throwback to a more primitive stage in our evolution when our government actively preached and indoctrinated the citizenry with the lie that black skin is the very mark of inferiority and servitude. A rather large percentage of the people incarcerated today in state prisons are Black or people of color. Almost all of them are poor people. I used to think a lot about that whenever I made my weekly jail visits.

———— • ● • ————

I waited patiently in the attorney's room at the jail for them to call out my client. His name was Marcus Williams. He was from Cornhill and just seventeen years old. He had a rather lengthy criminal record that included several arrests for misdemeanor level assault, larceny, and drug possession. His rap sheet showed only one felony drug conviction two years ago that had been sealed by the court because of his status as a youthful offender ("YO"). He had been in the system since the age of twelve.

He walked in and stood in the doorway. His orange jumpsuit was too big and hung off of him like an old bathrobe. His sneakers had no shoestrings. He looked like a boy who should have been at home studying for his history test.

"Come in," I said. "Have a seat."

He plopped himself down and slouched over.

"Hi, my name is Sam Hicks. I'm from the public defender's office. I am going to be representing you."

He didn't say anything and remained expressionless.

"You have been charged with the crime of murder in the second degree. They say that you shot and killed Travis Peyton last Saturday. I don't want to talk about that just now. We have plenty of time to go over what happened. Your bail will be set high, so you are going to be here for a while."

Marcus just stared at me. He almost looked bored. But my sense was that he was confused and intimidated and that he had gone to his default, which was to check out emotionally.

"Are you sick or hurt or in pain? Do you need a doctor for anything?"

"No," he replied.

"Do you have any medical condition that requires you to take medication on a regular basis?"

"No."

"No diabetes, heart condition, or asthma?"

"No."

"Can you read?'

"Nah, man...," he admitted as he cast his eyes downward.

"Do you remember talking to the police about the shooting after you were arrested?"

He nodded.

"Did you sign a piece of paper telling them what happened?"

"Yeah."

"Did you read it before you signed it?

"No."

"Did someone read it to you before you signed it?

"No."

"Why did you sign it?"

"Because they said I had to."

"Who told you that?"

"I don't know them."

"Did they threaten you in anyway?"

He just shrugged his shoulders and looked away.

"Look, I need to know what they said to you," I pushed.

"They just told me that I had to sign it, okay?"

I could see that he was getting annoyed with me. I didn't care.

"Okay. Marcus do you have any family here in Utica?"

"Yeah."

"Who?"

"My moms and my sisters."

"Where do you live?"

"We stay on Canal Street."

"Is there anyone that you want me to call for you?"

He shook his head no.

"Do you have any questions for me? Anything at all?"

"Can you get me 'YO'?"

"You mean youthful offender status?"

"Yeah, I'm seventeen."

"Yes, I know," I replied. "It looks like you were already given YO once before. But we can definitely try for it again. Do you have any other questions?"

"No."

"We don't have your next court date yet," I said. "They

have about a month to indict you. Until then, we just have to wait. I don't want you talking to anybody in here about your case. Nobody here is your friend, and they will sell you out in a second if they think that it will help them with their case. I mean don't say anything to anybody!"

"I know," he whispered.

"I hope you do," I lectured. "You're just a baby compared to all of these tough guys in here who think they know it all. They are gonna see you coming a mile away, so don't trust anyone."

Marcus sat up in his chair. He was perspiring a little in his face. I saw fear in his eyes.

"Do you understand?" I asked firmly.

"Yes. I mean, okay," he mumbled.

"Here take this," I directed as I stood to my feet. "It's my card with my name on it. Tell the deputies here if you need to see me."

Marcus took the card and stared hard at it for a second before slowly standing to his feet and walking out of the room with his head down.

I took a deep breath and sat back down. I needed a second to process what had just happened. That had gone pretty much like I thought it would, and still I was deeply saddened. My stomach felt a little off too. I was beginning to understand what Teresa was trying to tell me before when she assigned this case to me. Representing this kid wasn't going to be a walk in the park.

"You need to see anybody else?" the deputy standing at the door asked.

"Uh, no. I don't think so," I whispered. "Thank you."

"You don't look so good," he commented while giving me a quick once over. "Can I get you something?"

"No, I'm good," I said and began gathering my stuff.

It was important to me that I always maintain my game face. That's what I was taught to do in law school, and that's clearly what every attorney in our office had already learned to do. I was still struggling with that. I'm not saying that it was harder for me because I am Black. That wasn't it at all. It's just that this is a tough business, and it takes time to make the necessary emotional adjustments to survive the daily grind.

We used to talk about it all of the time. The people who worked in our office genuinely believed in the cause. But if we got too close or let it get too deep inside, then we risked losing ourselves completely and/or becoming completely ineffective. Remaining objective was a necessity. No one wanted a burned-out lawyer.

But I did think that it was a little different for me. Some things can't be fully explained; they have to be felt. Marcus and I danced to the same beat. I basically knew how it felt to be him without ever having spoken to him before. This meant that I knew deep down that it could have just as easily been me walking around that jail with an empty heart and scared to death that someone would figure me out. I doubted any of my colleagues ever felt that way.

Obviously, the same negative conditions prevalent in the general population today are multiplied in the minority community. We found that a high percentage of our clients suffered from some type of undiagnosed mental illness, such as depression, anxiety, obsessive-compulsive, and bipolar disorders. The root cause was poverty, which is like a cancer. If left untreated, it will spread throughout the body, or in our case, throughout the entire community until it eventually kills us all.

———•●•———

I saw a lot of people get beat up as a young person. To some extent, I grew numb to it. There were fights almost every day when I was in junior high school. And the girls were worse than the boys because they fought like they really wanted to kill each other over a boy. It seemed like the police were called to the school several times a week. While I personally never got in any fights on school grounds, I don't recall any negative stigma associated with having been in one. In fact, it was just the opposite—most of the bullies liked that everybody knew who not to mess with, which meant that the fighters enjoyed almost celebrity-like status among our peers.

— • ● • —

I stopped by to see Mama on my way home from the jail. I didn't trust that she would always call me if she needed help with something. This time, for some reason, I paid closer attention to the Cornhill neighborhood as I drove through. I saw the broken-down, dilapidated houses and unkept yards. I saw the boarded-up buildings with debris thrown about and the broken sidewalks and roadways. People of various ages were huddled together in front of the corner convenience marts doing absolutely nothing but wasting time. And beneath the setting sun, I clearly saw the dispirited look on the faces of the people as the demon forces moved about freely. It all played out in real time in black and white in my head, like a nightmare.

My visit with Mama was good. She was well. But I had a screaming headache by the time I got home at 6:30 that night. I ate a small dinner and then drank almost an entire six pack of beer. It helped me to settle down and sleep, or so I told myself.

— • ● • —

I heard her before I met her. I was sitting at my desk, and I heard a loud voice yelling something that I couldn't understand. Amy, our receptionist, rushed in.

"Sam, there's some crazy lady out here asking for you."

"Me? What's her name?"

"Trina Williams. She says that you are representing her son."

"Okay," I replied. "Tell her I will be right there."

"You need to hurry and get her out of here," Amy pled. "I'm not in the mood today. I told her to wait for you out in the hall."

Amy was from a small farm in Ilion, New York. She was tough as nails and was the perfect person to deal with our troubled clientele.

"All right, I'm coming," I responded. I was hesitant because the parents were often the worst. But dealing with them was part of the job.

And she was a sight! When I got there, she was sitting in the hall by herself. She was wearing a long sleeve yellow blouse with fur around the neckline and wrists, jean shorts and silver slippers. On her head was a white satin cap. As I approached, it appeared that she was either having a seizure or practicing her dancing moves. It was hard to tell exactly which one it was. She was very young, probably barely in her thirties.

"Can I help you?" I asked.

"You Sam Hicks?"

She looked disappointed.

"Yes I am."

"You my son's public defender?"

"Who is your son?"

"Marcus Williams. They got him locked up out there at the OCJ."

"And your name is…?"

"Trina Williams."

"Hi, Trina. Nice to meet you," I said. "Yes, I am representing Marcus."

"Well, I need to know what's going on with his case'" she stated emphatically.

"I just saw him on Saturday," I began. "We are just waiting for the case to make its way up here to county court. He hasn't been indicted yet."

"What that mean?'

"He's charged with murder, which is very serious. It just means that his felony case has to be presented to the grand jury before it can be heard in court."

"How much time is he looking at?'

"I don't know," I hedged. "A lot."

"See, hell no!" she objected and twisted her neck and head about. "I ain't gonna let ya'll do him like that. Marcus didn't even shoot that boy. He don't even have no gun. Where was he supposed to get a gun from? He don't got no money. There was a bunch of people in that car, right? Pick another brother! This is a set up from the start!"

"Maybe, but you weren't there," I said. "Neither was I. So, we don't really know what happened, do we? We have to just wait and see. It's still very early in the process."

"I wasn't there, but I know Marcus," she shot back. "He's not like that!"

"Listen, I am going to do everything I can to help your son," I explained.

"'Cause it ain't gonna go like they think," she maintained.

"Is there someone who knows him who I can talk to? Like a teacher or a counsellor who can vouch for him?"

"No, he don't go to school."

"Why not?" I wondered.

"How come he can't come home now?" she pivoted. "Don't make no sense for him to sit in jail for something he didn't do. Can't you do something? What kind of public defender are you anyway?"

"I know that it's frustrating because you really care about him," I asserted. "But like you said, he doesn't have any money so he can't get bailed out of jail. There is nothing that anyone can do about that. I'm very sorry."

"They just came and took him away," she lamented. "That's my only son. He's… my heart."

"You can go see him," I suggested.

"I ain't got no car."

"He can call you."

"Ain't got no phone either," she informed. "Do me a favor: tell Marcus to call me at Tiffany's house. I go over there a lot."

"Okay, I'll tell him."

Wackiness aside, I gave Trina Williams a lot of credit. At least she made the effort to do something on her son's behalf. That is, that morning she somehow managed to get herself out of bed and get dressed and then walk to the courthouse to see me. That was a lot. Most of the parents of our clients didn't want to know anything, and honestly, I'm not sure that we can really blame many of them. These kids pretty much came out of the womb looking for trouble, which unfortunately wasn't that hard to find. Even the most engaged parent will eventually reach a breaking point.

Every kid I knew when I was young got spanked or hit. Some were physically abused. Historically, Black people in this country have never shied away from beating our children. Even the Bible arguably condones corporal punishment. The institution of slavery began with brute force and was supported and defended by unimaginable cruelty. The lesson to us has been that violence works and is a viable option to get what you want.

However, Mama never really hit us. Occasionally, she swiped at us with the back of her hand, but she mostly just fussed and made threats. I can honestly say that we were never really afraid of her. But the threat of violence was always there.

Regardless, the undeniable truth is that not everyone is cut out to be a good parent. Take my mother for instance, she never should have had any kids. There was not an ounce of maternal instinct in her entire body. And I'm not sure how much of that was her fault. It is simply impossible to give what you don't have or to teach what you don't know. But I resented her just the same.

Occasionally, when representing some young person, we came up against the helicopter parent or an overzealous spouse or family member. These people tended to constantly call the office, be rude and insulting to staff on the phone, and make threats against us. Their biggest threat was to file a grievance with the bar association or to call a reporter at the *Observer Dispatch* and expose us. I generally avoided the family members as much as possible. They didn't value the services we provided because they weren't paying for them. I simply refused to be anybody's punching bag.

———•●•———

In addition to everything else, I was struggling financially. I was in dire need of a new car. I was still driving the same beat-up Ford Mustang that I bought in law school. It had nearly 120,000 miles on it, and there was always something wrong with it. I needed a reliable car to get back and forth to my night courts. My salary had increased by a few thousand dollars, but I was still basically living hand to mouth. Apparently, I was destined to struggle regardless of how hard I worked or how many degrees I earned.

I admit that I have always tended to feel sorry for myself. As a child, I remember wanting some of the things that I saw other kids had, but I always knew that it was never going to happen for me. Simply stated, Santa Claus didn't come to Kemble Street. It's one thing to have to accept that you can't have something right now and that you just need to wait, and something altogether different to believe in the deep recesses of your mind that those things are forever out of reach for you. Like so many others before, it was a critical blow with potentially life-long implications when I was still just an adolescent.

Chapter 7

The arraignment in county court was uneventful. It took less than ten minutes. Marcus, alongside two slighter older kids, and their assigned attorneys, formally entered his plea of "not guilty" to the crimes of murder in the second degree and criminal possession of a weapon in the second degree. He never said a word and kept his head down the whole time. At the end, I whispered to him that I was planning to come see him on Saturday.

Joe Bartolotta was the ADA assigned to the case. We could have done a lot worse, or so I thought at the time. Joe was a couple of years older than me. He had reddish-brown hair and pale skin. His nickname was Bobby B because he looked like Bobby Brady from the *Brady Bunch*, only older and heavier. I thought he was nice enough, and we had one or two cases together before without incident.

For some unknown reason, I looked for Trina Williams in the crowd. But I didn't see her. I sent a letter to her residence last week letting her know the date of the arraignment. But I honestly never thought I would ever see her again. I knew she was unpredictable.

"Hi. How are you?"

"Good," Marcus replied and immediately slouched down in his seat.

"Can you sit up, please?" I asked.

He complied.

"I spoke to your mother. She wants you to call her at Tiffany's number."

"That number don't work!" he barked. "She knows that!"

He rolled his eyes and crossed his arms in front of him.

"I just think that she's looking for some kind of way to talk to you," I offered. "She is your mother."

Marcus didn't respond.

"Can you read at all, or just a little bit?"

"A little."

"When were you last in school?"

"Last year?"

"What grade were you in?"

"8th grade."

"Were you in special education?"

"I think so."

"Do you take any medication for anything?"

"No."

"Here is a copy of the statement you signed. Can you read the first sentence out loud to me?"

"No."

"Why not?"

"Come on, man! I already told you."

"How come you dropped out of school at such an early age?"

"I didn't have time for all that, man," he articulated. "I wasn't learning anything that I needed to know."

"You need to know how to read. How are you ever going to get a job?"

Marcus leaned back in his chair and sighed loudly.

"Okay, okay. I'm sorry," I apologized. "Besides your mother and your sisters, do you have any other family in Utica?"

"Yes, I have a whole bunch of cousins and people like that."

"Has anyone of them been here to visit you?"

"No."

He looked slightly dejected.

"Okay, these are very serious charges you are facing," I announced. "The murder charge could send you to prison for a really long time. I'm talking twenty or thirty years. You're not even twenty years old yet. So, this is no joke. Do you understand that?"

"But I didn't do it, yo."

"You didn't do what?"

"I didn't shoot that dude."

"Who did?"

Marcus was silent again.

"Who did?" I asked again.

He just shrugged his shoulders. "Not me."

"Look, you have to talk to me," I said. "I am the only person in the world who is trying to help you now."

"Man, just tell them that I didn't do anything, all right," Marcus spoke. "It's all some bull... Look man, I didn't shoot that dude. I been trying to tell you."

"It doesn't work like that, and it doesn't matter if you are the one who fired the gun," I presented. "According to the law, everybody in the car at the time of the shooting is guilty of causing the death of this kid."

Marcus slouched back down in his seat again and closed his eyes. He clearly had enough of my questioning.

"Why were you there?" I pressed.

"Business," he replied and shot open his eyes before transitioning into a cold, hard stare.

"What kind of business?"

"*My* business."

"I don't know what that means," I insisted.

Marcus refused to respond. He just acted as if he hadn't heard me.

"In the statement you signed, you said that you guys were looking for Travis Peyton because he owed you money?"

"I don't know him."

"So, what you said here isn't true?"

"Nope."

"Well, you told the police that you shot him from the passenger side window. And now he's dead. What do you say to that?"

Marcus just continued to stare at me.

"What do you say?" I asked again in a more forceful tone.

He mumbled something under his breath.

"I'm sorry," I said as I leaned into him. "I didn't hear what you said."

Marcus just looked away again.

"Somebody died," I pointed out. "Don't you care?"

"C'mon, man, I told you I didn't do it!" he shouted.

"Who did?"

"Like I said, not me," he insisted.

"But you were there," I argued. "You admitted it."

"They can't prove anything without the gun."

"Who told you that?"

"Nobody told me."

"Well, they might not have a gun, but they do have a dead body with a bullet hole to the side of the head and another in the center of the chest. Kinda hard to argue with that, wouldn't you say? How do you think the jury will react when they see those pictures?"

"Get out of here, man," Marcus erupted.

"No, I really want to know," I persisted. "Please tell me what you think will happen when the jury hears that you were in the car where the shots came from? Do you really think that they are going to care which one of you Black guys actually pulled the trigger? Is that what you think?"

Marcus closed his eyes again and appeared to be doing everything he could to block out the sound of my voice.

He had gone to a place deep inside where he could hide from the world. I knew because I had one of those places when I was his age.

"And then they have the other two clowns in the car with you telling the whole world that you were the one who fired the shots at Peyton." I charged ahead. "It's a lot of evidence against you. They have made you the bad guy."

There was complete silence in the room, with the faint, muffled sound of voices coming from people down the hall. Marcus sat motionless as if he was trying to hide from me right there before my eyes.

"Who are Thomas Martin and Tyrell James to you?" I insisted.

"Nobody," he spoke harshly.

"Then why are you protecting them?" I asked.

"We weren't doing anything," Marcus lied.

"Who had the gun?"

"What gun?"

"Okay, I think I'm through with you," I declared and threw up my hands in frustration. "You can go now."

Marcus abruptly stood to his feet. I could tell that he couldn't care less that I was annoyed with him. He was just relieved that he could finally leave my presence. I could have sworn that I saw an ominous half-smile on his face. It was annoying and I was offended.

"Let me tell you something, Marcus," I implored. "These jailhouse lawyers in here don't know what the hell they are talking about. Like I said before: I'm your only friend. If you keep listening to them, you will be an old man when you get out of prison. Please try to remember that."

He marched out of the room without hesitation, leaving me there simmering. One of the guys in our office coined the phrase "felony stupid." We used it all the time when referring to those clients who were charged with felony offenses and were too thuggish and/or hard-headed to be of any assistance in their own defense. It wasn't a reflection of IQ necessarily, rather a commentary on one's ability to listen to his lawyer. Marcus was felony stupid.

Every jail is full of these guys who like to tell everyone what they should do with their case. Some go as far as to charge for their advice. Typically, they knew just enough to be dangerous. They were critical of real lawyers and offered up advice that was full of holes and lies. It was a constant battle to get our people to think rationally and to make the right decisions about their own lives, and these false prophets were a big part of the problem.

———————— • ● • ————————

I had to subpoena Marcus' school records from the Utica school district. Just as I suspected, he suffered from a learning disability, and he was in special education. It was an easy call on my part because we knew that a higher percentage of Black and minority students in this county were identified and labeled as such. I'm not an educator, so I didn't really know why that was the case, but I'd say that Marcus's story was a common one.

Indeed, his attendance at school had been sporadic at best, and he was often disruptive and violent when he was there. One school psychologist suspected possible autism and attention deficit hyperactivity disorder ("ADHD"). I couldn't tell if he was ever prescribed any medications. Apparently, his mother, Katrina Williams, was also on the autism spectrum. Their address was listed as "unknown" and "homeless."

Contrary to his assertions otherwise, Marcus had pretty much disappeared from school altogether in the sixth grade. I suspected that he was essentially raising himself on the Utica streets, which meant that prison was virtually inevitable for him. In some respect, it might have even been an upgrade for him. At least there, he had a bed to lay his head at night and three-square meals.

Interestingly, Marcus's IQ was in the lower normal range. That meant that he was capable of learning, he just didn't want to. This is the reason that these kinds of test are of limited value. They only measure potential. Everyone knows that there are plenty of men and woman in prison today who are bright, talented, and full of promise. But unrealized potential is just a wasted asset that eventually rots away or disappears altogether as if it never existed.

To that point, I wonder how many NBA championships rings Michael Jordan or Lebron James would have if the only basketball courts they ever got to play on when they were young were inside a juvenile detention center. Physical gifts alone are just a small part of it.

Obviously, character is much more important than any physical attribute or skill set one might possess. The fact is that a physically gifted specimen of a man could be playing basketball before a sellout crowd in Madison Square Garden on Christmas Day and still be a tortured and defeated human being inside. Ultimately, the kind of good character to which Dr. Martin Luther King Jr. was referring in his dream speech is developed over time in the minds of *free* people, who act like they know that there are no longer any shackles on them.

Like many of us who were struggling just to make it through, most of our clients were completely lost souls. They weren't inherently bad or prone to violence. But they were oppressed and caught in a web of lies perpetuated on them by a society that has never respected them as human or quite figured out what to do with them. To know them was to fear and despise them. Worse yet, most of them didn't know what to do with themselves.

Chapter 8

I hurried over to Judge Mazur's court. He was doing a sentencing in one of Larry's cases. His client was Travis Boyd, a twenty-year-old Black man who had pleaded guilty to manslaughter in the second degree. It was another drive-by shooting. The victim, Jaquan King, was a star player on his high school basketball team. There was a large public outcry at the time of the killing.

There already was high energy in the courtroom, which was filled to capacity with mostly anxious Black people. I could see the news cameras in the back of the room. There was some light chatter as people huddled together in groups. I took a seat near the front in the section that was reserved for attorneys.

Larry was seated at the defense table with his back to us, waiting for them to bring in the defendant. Tom Ryan, the ADA, was sitting at the other table. He was hunched over while he was reading something. There were five uniformed police officers standing on the right side of the judge's bench.

One of the court attendants walked to the front of the room. He was an overweight, balding white man in his sixties. He looked serious.

"Please listen up, everybody," he began. "We are about to begin. There will be no talking permitted by anyone in the crowd while court is in session. You must remain seated at all times. Only those individuals recognized by the court may address the court. Anyone who speaks out of order will be removed from the courtroom and possibly arrested. Please remember that you are in a court of law and that you must conduct yourself in a respectful manner at all times. This is your only warning!"

There was no response from the crowd as the attendant finished wasting our time and walked back to the side. This was going to be a show of epic proportion, and everyone knew it. I didn't like that Judge Mazur allowed cameras in his courtroom for sentencing. It could only make matters worse.

I'm not sure why anyone ever thought allowing victims to address the defendant at the sentencing was a good idea. It was hardly therapeutic. It only served to allow people to vent uncontrollably, almost like a second funeral. A victim's impact statement was always included in the presentence report that was prepared by the probation department for the court, and it was sufficient for our purposes. Admittedly, however, a video feed of black people screaming and yelling in court did make for a great lead for the local news channels to broadcast that night.

Travis was escorted in from a side door by two deputies. He was wearing street clothes. Both of his hands were handcuffed in front of him, and one of the deputies seemed to struggle a little getting the handcuffs off. He looked very young, but he also had a hardened look on his face—like a brooding toddler in timeout.

There was always something a little unsettling about seeing another person in restraints, even a bad one. It was something that I never got used to fully. Whenever one of our jailed clients had an outside appointment, like to a medical provider or a funeral, we always tried to have the sheriff deputies bring him or her into the office or building through a back door or a nonpublic entrance to avoid causing needless trauma to the public and embarrassment to the prisoner. Although clearly necessary in many instances, forced incarceration is dehumanizing, no way around it. Men were created to be free.

Larry stood to his feet and began whispering in his client's ear. They both sat down at the same time, and the deputies walked away. The quiet stir of the crowd added to the ominous atmosphere.

I almost laughed aloud when Judge Mazur walked in and took his seat at the bench. He had slicked his hair to the side and was completely clean shaven. He looked like a caricature of himself. He seemed to be on edge too, and he didn't look out or acknowledge the crowd in any way. But now that everyone was in place, the drama could unfold naturally.

Travis had already entered a plea of guilty to manslaughter in the first degree with the understanding that he would be sentenced to fifteen years to thirty years in state prison, which meant that he could be eligible for parole in fifteen years. He admitted earlier that he had fired twice into a crowd of people standing together and that he had missed his intended target, killing Jaquan King. He refused to say in court why he was shooting at the other kid, but it had something to do with an ongoing feud of some kind. In response to the judge's question, both attorneys agreed that sentencing could proceed.

"It goes without saying that the events that led us here are particularly tragic," the ADA began. "A young man has lost his life as a result the senseless act of violence on the part of this defendant. He will never have the chance to fulfil his great potential. Worse yet, the defendant has not shown even the slightest bit of remorse. Without a doubt, he represents an extreme level of risk and danger to this community. Despite his young age, he has shown that he already possesses a depraved mind, and that he is without a conscience, not to mention having very little socially redeeming value. We need to clean up our streets and this individual should never be permitted to walk freely among us ever again. Sadly, he represents the worst of humanity. Accordingly, it is the position of the People that he be sentenced to the period of incarceration previously agreed upon at the time of the plea allocution."

"Mr. Simpson, do you have anything?" Judge Mazur asked.

"Yes, your honor," Larry said as he stood to his feet. "First, let me say that Mr. Ryan is not correct when he said that my client has no remorse for his action. The presentence report accurately reflects that Travis stated emphatically in his interview with probation that he is very sorry for what happened. The way I see it, my client is a victim too. Data shows a clear connection between poverty and violent crime. Travis was born and raised in poverty. This was not a choice that he was given, nor the result of a decision he voluntarily made. He literally came into the world that way. Gun violence is a public health crisis, and it seems to me that we are losing the fight for our children. We all have a part to play. Haven't we've grown tired yet of antiviolence rallies and vigils when children keep dying or they are being locked away for most of the prime years of life? Something has got to give. Everything about this seems wrong and I just want to say that Mr. Boyd is not a depraved animal. He's just a broken man who never really had a fair chance to succeed in life or to pursue the American dream of life, liberty, and happiness."

"Okay, thank you both," the judge said. "I understand that there are two victims who have requested to speak today," Judge Mazur continued. "I'm going to permit it. Where is…Ramika King?"

"Here," answered a woman sitting near the front.

"You can come up to the podium and address the court," the judge acknowledged.

She rose slowly and walked even slower. She was a short, small-framed Black woman in her late thirties. She wore a New York Knicks hoodie, jeans, and sneakers. She had a piece of paper in her hand and began to read from it.

"Um, I just want to say that I have been really messed up since they told me what happened to my son," she whispered.

"Can you speak up, please?" the Judge interjected.

"Yeah, I'm sorry," she responded nervously. "My son was everything to me. Ever since he was a baby all he cared about was being close to me. You can ask anybody; he followed after me wherever I went. It used to drive me crazy a little, but that was just his way of showing how much he loved me. All he ever wanted was for me to be happy, and he used to tell me all the time about all the things he was going to buy for me when he made pro. He was a really good person, and I miss him every day. I think that this boy here who killed my son should get the death penalty. I really do. I know that he won't, but I think they should change the law about that. And I don't understand where all the guns keep coming from. Those people are to blame too for selling these here guns to our Black boys in the first place. It's a shame before God. Um…that's all."

She turned slowly and walked back to her seat. There was complete silence as everyone watched her, and the air in the room was thick.

"Thank you," Judge Mazur said. "Venita King, please come forward."

A young girl stood up. She looked to be about fifteen or sixteen. She was heavy set, and she was wearing a white t-shirt depicting the face of Tupac Shakur, black leggings that were too tight, and flip flops on her feet.

She was clearly fighting her nerves too. She also had prepared written remarks and chose to focus her attention on what was written there.

"Jaquan was my older brother," she began.

She spoke in a much louder voice than her mother.

"Like my mother said, he was a good person. All he

ever did was play ball, listen to beats, and hang out with his friends. He never hurt nobody. I'm really mad about what happened. This piece of garbage shot Jaquan over stupid stuff! Because some dude owed him ten dollars! You mean, my brother died over ten dollars? Are you serious? This is just stupid stuff, and all these guys out here are all idiots 'cause they just don't care about anybody or anything, not even their damn selves. My whole family is ruined, and we will never be the same without my brother."

She suddenly stopped reading, lifted her head, and turned to the right slightly to look directly at the defendant like a venomous snake preparing her attack.

Everyone sensed the shift in the air pressure in the room and watched with bated breath.

She spoke from her broken heart, "Travis, I want to tell you to your face how much I hate you. I hope you die in prison. I hope you rot there, punk! You ain't no man! You're an animal! Prison is too good for you. I hope you live a long time and one of those guys in there gets ahold of you and turns you out and takes everything from you until you wish that you was dead."

She was screaming, shaking, and crying now and pointing her finger toward Travis.

"I'm gonna keep track of where they send you and when you finally do die, I'm gonna go to your grave and spit on it!" she struck out again with reckless abandon. "That's a promise! That's how much I hate you!"

The crowd began to stir.

"You're going to die the most painful death!" she further cursed. "And after you are dead, like you killed my brother, I hope you go straight to hell and burn there forever!"

"Young lady, you need to calm down," Judge Mazur ordered.

"Sit your black ass down!" someone yelled from the gallery.

"Go to hell!" she shouted back.

The crowd erupted and people stood up and began shouting out. The deputies rushed in from the sidelines. They were yelling at the crowd to be quiet and to get back in their seats.

"Order!" the judge demanded and hit his gavel repeatedly. "Please return to your seats now!"

It took several minutes before the officers were able to restore order. Two women, who were arguing, had to be forcibly removed from the courtroom. There were two officers standing at the defense table protecting Travis as he and Larry continued to sit there.

"I will not tolerate any more disruption!" the judge warned. "If any one of you say one more word, I will empty this courtroom. Do you understand? Not one word! Miss King, you can take your seat."

"Will the defendant please stand?" the judge directed. He looked anxious. His gelled hair was still perfectly in place.

Both Larry and Travis stood.

The judge cleared his voice loudly before he spoke, "Mr. Boyd, is there anything that you would like to say before sentencing is pronounced?"

"No," was the response. He put his head down and nervously crossed both hands together in front of his body.

"It is hard for me to fathom how any rational human being could fire a firearm into a crowd of people. It is nothing short of mind-boggling. Not only was it the act of a coward, but a sin against all humanity. You seem to be completely devoid of compassion for anyone except yourself. Now I don't know how you got that way, but I fear that there are many others just like you running around our fair city. I may not be able to prevent any of those senseless deaths that these predators may cause in the future, but I can make certain that you will not be in a position to shoot anyone else in the near future. It is the sentence of this court that you serve a period of incarceration of a minimum of fifteen years and a maximum of thirty years. You are hereby committed to the custody of the New York State Department of Corrections. You have the right to appeal this judgment of the court, and you should talk to Mr. Simpson about that. If there is nothing else, this court is adjourned."

The deputies handcuffed Travis and escorted him out. Most people got up and immediately headed for the exits. A few attempted to linger and huddle together; however, the court attendants were aggressively at them to leave. I waited for Larry, and we walked out of the courtroom together.

I told Larry later that I really liked what he said. I agreed with him that gun violence in this country is a public health crisis, just like the war on drugs or disease outbreak. Gun violence was the leading cause of death among Black teenage boys over fifteen. If we were going to break the cycle of suffering, then an entirely different approach is needed.

It was easy to place all of the blame on these juveniles and social outcasts who were not the least bit sympathetic. They have shown time after time that they will shoot each other dead over ten dollars. But we got here because of deliberate policy decisions reenforced over an extended time period that created segregated communities designed to keep the undesirable element locked in place. Larry was right: there was plenty of blame to go around, starting with immoral government.

The major difference between Black people who break out of the plantation mindset and those who continue to languish there is belief. The key is not what they say; it's what they do. Specifically, it's how and whom they choose to fight. Obviously, those who believe that they can shoot their way to freedom and respectability have fully accepted the lie about Black inferiority.

Interestingly, I had a friend in law school from Nigeria. His name was Obie Coker. He wasn't a law student. He was pre-med. His father was a urologist in Boston. He once said that he was very surprised at how much African Americans struggled with their own self-worth. His observation was that even his countrymen, who were living in abject poverty in Nigeria, possessed an inner belief in themselves that far surpassed that held by most Blacks in the United States.

———— • ● • ————

I decided to watch the evening news. I usually wasn't that interested, but I wanted to see how they covered the sentencing. As I suspected, Venita King was the breakout star. They showed her twice—once during the beginning introduction, and then again when the story ran. I'm pretty sure that no one asked her permission to splash her irreverent, grieving image before the entire community. I thought it was exploitive.

I also thought that the young Black woman who covered the last news story was breathtaking! My heart leaped inside my chest as I watched her, and I hung on her every word. I simply couldn't take my eyes off her.

———— • ● • ————

It took me a minute to remember what I did with the business card that Judge Mazur had given to me. I only hesitated slightly before I dialed the number. The judge had said that I had nothing to lose. Suddenly, he sounded like a genius.

"Hi, this is Sam Hicks. I'm an attorney in the public defender's office. I got your number from Judge Mazur."

"Oh, hi, Sam," she replied. "Yeah, the judge was telling me about you."

She sounded pleased to hear from me.

"Uh-oh, I hope that he didn't say too much."

"He said that you are a very good attorney."

"Well, I don't know about all that, but I do try hard," I replied. "That must be good for something."

"I'm sure you are just being modest. He seemed to really like you."

"I just hope that it wasn't too awkward for you," I said in earnest. "It's a little embarrassing."

"No, not at all," she offered and laughed. "I thought it was funny."

"He said that you are new in town?"

"Yes, I have been here just two months. I'm originally from Rochester."

"Well. you're not too far from home."

"No, I'm not, but I really don't know too many people in Utica."

"I was born here," I volunteered. "So, I know everything that there is to know about living in this paradise."

"Is that right?"

"Well, actually no," I admitted. "But it sounded good."

"An honest man," she stated with a laugh. "Where have you been?"

"Here in Utica," I said. "That's why you never heard of me. Nobody has ever heard of anybody from here."

"Well, it's refreshing to meet an honest man."

"What do you say we get together?" I urged. "I'd love to get lunch or something and really meet you."

"Ah, that sounds nice actually," she said. "Lunch is probably better for me since I work most nights."

"Me too. What about sometime this weekend?"

"Yeah, okay," she stated. "I can meet you."

I was excited. I hadn't had anything close to a date in a long time. I had put that part of my life on hold partly because I thought that I needed to focus on my career for now, and I didn't want the distraction. But the truth was probably just that I hadn't met anyone yet who motivated me enough to make the effort to climb out of my comfort zone. I had never been one of those guys who was looking to make conquests or who necessarily wanted to be in a relationship. My mother had really messed me up.

We met at this little Italian restaurant near the mall. I got there first, and from my seat I could see her out the window walking across the parking lot. She moved effortlessly, almost as if she were defying gravity. She was dressed to perfection. She wore a beige sleeveless dress that clung to her body in a way that captured my imagination. Her shoulder-length straight hair responded gently to the warm breeze. She was *smokin' hot,* and like a moth to a flame, I was drawn by the fire.

I stood as she approached the table.

"Hi, Carla," I said.

"Hi, Sam."

We smiled at each other.

"So, how are you?" I asked after we were both seated.

"I'm good," she said. "I hope that I didn't keep you waiting."

"Not at all. I'm glad to finally meet you."

"Me too," she replied. "I saw you once."

"*Me*? Really?"

"I saw you in court the first time I was there with a colleague. We stood in the back. You didn't see me."

"I wished I had," I remarked.

"You are an intense guy. I could tell."

"I told you I try hard."

"That must be exhausting," she surmised.

"Some things are worth giving your all," I replied with a sly grin.

"I bet you say that to all the girls."

"Nope, this is the first time." I admitted. "I swear."

I couldn't tell if she believed me.

She told me about her family and growing up in Rochester. She said that her father was an oral surgeon, and her mother was in real estate. She had an older sister and brother. After graduating from Syracuse University with a degree in communications, she landed a job in Rochester doing the weekend news. She came to Utica for job advancement.

Her fondest memories growing up were travelling with her family. It seemed like she had been just about everywhere. She glowed when she talked about all of the different places she had been. She said that her favorite city in the world is Paris. Apparently, she first went there when she was about three years old, and she has been there several times since. Her career aspirations included wanting to be a field producer or foreign correspondent. She said that she had always been interested in political, social, and economic events.

Like mine, her family wasn't overly religious. She said that her uncle was a pastor of an inner-city church in Rochester, but they never attended there because her father didn't like the location of the church. He thought it was too dangerous. She attended a Catholic high school, but she was never Catholic.

I was very impressed by her. She seemed well rounded, and I got the impression that she worked hard on maintaining her poise. She wasn't really like any Black woman I had ever met. The thought entered my mind that she might be a little out of my league. Clearly, she was a lot more worldly than I was.

But I wasn't intimidated by her. For some unknown reason, my personal insecurities never extended to the opposite sex. I told her the truth about my background, including the fact that I didn't really know my father. I readily disclosed that I had never travelled anywhere. I knew how it sounded, and I was a little concerned that she would turn and run from me as fast as she could. However, it was the fact that she was so different than me that had me intrigued.

"I don't understand how you can represent someone you know is guilty," she said at one point.

"You mean me personally or anybody?"

"Anybody, I guess," she clarified. "It would be hard for me to represent some child molester who I knew was guilty."

"On some level, I get that," I conceded. "But people do all kinds of things for all kinds of reasons. If justice is going to be done in a particular case, then everybody has a right to their day in court. My job is to represent my client to the best of my ability. I took an oath. The prosecutor's job is to prosecute people and be fair. The judge's job is to preside over the case and be fair. The jury's job is to listen to the evidence and be fair. Everybody has a part. It won't work if I decide that I want to prosecute too, or the judge decides that he wants to defend the case. I just stay in my lane. It's so much easier that way."

"But wouldn't it bother you if somebody got off on a technicality, and they were really guilty?" she asked.

"No. At least not the way you mean," I answered. "If the prosecutor can't prove his or her case, then the guy is supposed to get off. That is justice."

"I'm not sure if I agree," she contended. "Do you think a lot of people get off that way?"

"No, I think just the opposite is true," I advised. "I think that a lot of people in the system—like the police—break the rules because they feel that the person is bad and deserves to be punished regardless of whether they can prove it without cheating."

"Cheating?"

"Yeah, like forcing people to sign confessions or lying on the witness stand about what they saw or did at the time of the arrest or during the investigation. Most people don't get that until they, or someone they care about, gets targeted by the police. I find that poor people get railroaded a lot."

"Railroaded?" she repeated.

"Might be a bit of an overstatement, but I know that the police regularly take advantage of uneducated people like it's a game. That's all I'm saying."

"I give you a lot of credit," she said. "It's a tough way to make a living."

"So is running all over the world and reporting on other people's wars," I replied and teased her with a smile.

She smiled back.

"You got me there," she conceded.

We stared at each other for a few seconds without speaking. I was captivated.

We dined together for a little over two hours. The restaurant staff patiently waited for us to leave. It was easy with her. She was straightforward and confident. I also appreciated that she said what was on her mind. She didn't seem like the type who played a lot of games, and I was averse to a whole lot of drama. The time got away from both of us. We agreed to get together again soon.

———•●•———

Fortunately, I finally bought a reliable used car. That was a big relief as my old car was definitely on its way out. It would have been very embarrassing if Carla saw me driving that jalopy. Suddenly, I was more concerned about how I looked and how I dressed. Usually, I never paid much attention to stuff like that. To me, a suit was a suit.

As long as it was clean, I never really cared about the rest of it. That all changed with one look at her.

I didn't want to seem too aggressive, so I waited a couple of days before I called her. It was 10 pm. She seemed happy to hear from me.

"I have been thinking a lot about you," I admitted.

"You have?"

"Yes, ma'am, I have."

"I'm still not quite sure how to take you," she said.

"*Me*? Why is that?

"You seem guarded."

"I assure you: what you see is what you get."

"Men always say that at first," she noted. "Then you find out that he's some crazy narcissist with two baby mamas."

"Well, I can't speak for all men, but I'm from Utica, New York. We are not sophisticated enough here to hide our crap. And I can't even spell narcissist."

"I don't think you have to be able to spell it to think that the whole world revolves around you."

"I grew up with a lot of guys who acted like they thought that," I admitted. "But we lived in the hood. None of us had anything compared to the rest of the world. It was all an act."

"So, you are saying that guys who grow up poor can't run game on women?" she posed.

"Not on women who hold themselves in high regard and who are paying attention."

"See, that's what I'm talking about," she reflected. "You say things that sound innocent and honest, but they also cut to the quick."

"I told you I'm honest, but I assure you that I'm not innocent, in case you are wondering."

"No, I didn't think that you were," she disclosed.

"It's just that I have already experienced enough in my life to make me really jaded." I replied.

"That makes two of us."

"Some things can't be unseen or unlearned," I articulated. "I hope that doesn't scare you."

"You don't scare me," she commented. "It's just that I don't think that I have ever met anyone quite like you before."

"I'm going to take that as a compliment."

"You should, Mr. Hicks. It is a compliment."

"Then let me return the favor," I spoke. "For some reason, I'm very much at ease when I talk to you."

"Really?"

"I feel like I can trust you with my secrets," I expressed. "Can I trust you?"

"It's probably too early for you to fully trust me," she opined.

"Good to know," I said and laughed to myself. "I'll go slow."

"Me too," she followed.

I enjoyed the mental dance with her. She was bright and seemed to like our playful banter. This was new for me too. Of course, there were a lot of really smart women in college and law school. Back then I mostly followed my more carnal desires and the laws of physical attraction. I never looked deeper. It never even occurred to me.

Chapter 9

I decided I needed to change tactics with Marcus. Rather than talking *at* him, I needed to try talking *to* him, which was easier said than done. I doubted talking was his thing. But I really had nothing to lose.

"How's the food here?" I asked.

"All right," Marcus mumbled and shrugged his shoulders.

"Do you get any choices, or do you have to eat whatever they make?"

"It's mostly the same every day."

"Is there anything you really like?"

"No."

"Is there anything you definitely hate, like something that you can't even make yourself swallow?"

"Um…oatmeal."

"What about it don't you like?"

"Uh, you know how it's supposed to be kinda thick like?"

"Yeah," I encouraged.

"It's too thick, like mashed potatoes. It is hard to swallow."

"That sounds nasty," I commented.

"Some of these cats can eat anything."

Marcus shook his head back and forth in disbelief.

"Is there any kind of food that you are missing now?"

I wondered. "Something that you have been craving?"

"Um…chocolate chip cookies from Dunkin Donuts." He grinned wide.

"Really? I have never had those," I said.

"I used to have them almost every day with some *cold* chocolate milk."

"I have to check them out."

"I promise you, dog," Marcus said and grinned. "I used to tell everybody."

"They don't have chocolate chip cookies here?"

"They're store bought. They don't make 'em."

"Have you seen your mother?"

"Nah, she ain't coming out here," he answered matter-of-factly.

"What makes you say that?"

"'Cause she ain't."

"How does that make you feel?" I wondered.

"Mad."

"I get that," I offered.

"Why?" he asked.

"Let's just say I know what it feels like to not have a mother or a father."

"Oh," Marcus replied.

"Is there someone else who I can reach out to for you?" I followed up. "A grandmother or aunt maybe?'"

"Nah, man. I already told you. I ain't got nobody."

"I thought you said you have a bunch of cousins?"

Marcus just looked away.

"Okay, okay," I relented. "You haven't been talking to these guys about your case, have you?"

Marcus shook his head.

"You sure?"

"I ain't going out like that," he said.

"Good," I encouraged. "You ever hear the saying that there is no honor among thieves?"

"No."

"Trust me, you're doing the right thing." I assured.

I really wanted to ask him the specific details about his case. It had been almost a month since he was arraigned on the charge of murder, and I still didn't know what facts he was going with as a defense. One of my criminal law professors in law school drilled into our heads that we should never fully believe the people we represent.

"Your client will lie and deceive you!" Professor Hodges used to always say. "Expect it; accept it, get over it!"

His point was that as an officer of the court, we never wanted to lose our credibility with the judges or with the jury. Not only is it unethical for an attorney to use perjured testimony in court, but one's judgment is severely impaired if we personally buy into the lie. It makes it nearly impossible to see and evaluate the case objectively.

Some people have argued that perception is reality, so it's a mistake to care too much about what really happened. Some criminal defense attorneys never even ask their clients specifically to tell them their side of the story. Rather, they just lay out the prosecutor's whole case for the client before encouraging the client to respond creatively. It's like setting out a roadmap for them to lie.

But I always thought that was like playing with fire. I hated that people think that lawyers lie all the time. We are not supposed to, and most of us don't. I know that personally I would never sell my soul to protect my client or to win a case. In the end, the only thing that the devil has in his hand is a bag of lies and deceit, and anything built upon those things will eventually crumble and lead to spiritual death throughout. It's true for the individual, and it's also true for a nation.

The problem I had with Marcus was we didn't trust each other. Further complicating matters was his warped sense of reality stemming from the way he saw the world. His sense of right and wrong wasn't the same as the average person, and he was his own worst enemy. There was an unwritten code among incarcerated persons that mostly defied common sense. For instance, their aversion to incriminating their friends or "squealing" was mind-blowing, considering that the code was regularly breached behind closed doors.

This is the kind of stuff that kept me up at night. To be clear, I didn't believe that there was more pressure on me because I am Black. I specifically rejected the notion that I somehow owed our Black clients more because I knew their struggles firsthand. I'm sorry, but it was just too much to ask me to carry the weight of an entire race on my shoulders.

But there was a second there when I looked into Marcus's eyes, and I saw myself reflected. That doesn't mean that I knew what he was thinking because I didn't. Nor did I feel sorry for him exactly. It's just that I knew how abandonment and lack can eat away at the inner lining of a kid's heart like a cavity imbedded in a molar, a process that can be fully completed in adolescence. I definitely could empathize with that part of it.

The fact is that gun violence is concentrated in specific neighborhoods in cities. Typically, we find the lack of jobs, failing infrastructure and schools, and underinvestment in these communities. Historically, when the government has decided to improve or promote investment in one of these areas, the first step has been to remove the people living there. Therefore, it's clearly the people who are carrying the spirit rather than it being a product of the geography.

Indeed, generational poverty is an oppressing spirit and a curse that is *on* people, not *in* them. It affects people of all races and nationalities. The poverty mentality is taught and learned. Potentially, all affected people can overcome it, regardless of the neighborhood they live in or how much money they make.

Recently, something odd happened as I was leaving the barbershop one afternoon. This was the shop in Cornhill where I had gone my whole life. It probably had been a very nice private home at one time. But now, the foundation was cracked, and the floor was uneven. Also, the paint on the outside had mostly peeled off and the small side parking lot, where I had parked my car, wasn't paved, and had huge potholes. As I was slowly pulling my car out of the parking lot, a Black teen was walking aimlessly and crossed on the sidewalk directly in front of me. I came to a complete stop to allow him to pass by. Just then, he stopped and turned to face me. I was immediately taken aback by his zombie-like appearance. He glared at me with the darkest, coldest eyes that I had ever seen. It was like he was daring me to say or do anything, and I was completely caught up in the presence of devilry. The air inside the car was suddenly super-charged. I thought I was looking at a demon, literally, and my insides quivered and shook uncontrollably as I held my breath. Slowly, he turned and walked away. It was several minutes before I was able to settle down completely.

I told myself later that I read too much into that incident and the kid was probably just high. But I had seen a lot of people high before, and this was different. No one or nothing had ever made me feel like that before. It felt personal. Like it wasn't a chance encounter, and this kid hated me for some reason. I decided to consider switching to another barbershop, maybe something closer to my apartment.

———————— • ● • ————————

Carla was a very good cook. She liked to try different types of food, and she read cookbooks for fun. She blew me away the first time that she made me dinner at her place. The Cajun meal was delicious, and the presentation was perfect. She also introduced me to fine wine. I was a beer guy. It's all I knew. But she seemed to enjoy showing me to the finer things, and I liked learning from her.

In the end, I really did like that she wanted to take it slow. I wanted things between us to just develop organically without the added pressure of me needing to be somebody I wasn't. I figured that she already knew that I wasn't a player, and I didn't have game. I wanted her to know me for me.

The thing is I really didn't know anything about relationships. That is, there were very few healthy man/woman relationships in the hood that I saw. To the contrary, I saw a lot of short-term hooking up, and a lot of teen pregnancies. I also witnessed plenty of infidelity, physical abuse, prostitution, and homosexuality. While sex was everywhere in Cornhill, it was often dehumanizing, nothing like the mature love that I saw in the movies or heard people singing about all of the time on the radio. No, true love didn't live on my block.

Mama used to say that everything in Cornhill was broken. She was mostly talking about the apartments, the appliances, and the cars. But the truth in her statement was actually revealed in the people themselves and in the way that we treated each other. Strife, confusion, and brutality were all around too. It was just easy to take out our frustrations on each other.

Obviously, there were many good God-fearing people living there too. Poor people have the same feelings as everybody else, and there often was a real sense of comradery. Some people were capable of incredible acts of kindness and generosity, of which my own family was the beneficiary.

I remember one time, Mrs. Knox from across the street walked several blocks in the middle of a snowstorm to the drug store to get medicine that one of my sisters needed badly. She acted on her own initiative as Mama never asked her for help. And she paid for it out of her own pocket!

However, the people living there tended to also make some incredibly bad choices, all too often stemming from brokenness and despair. Lack is a harsh teacher. It's mean and relentless. We have all been tempted to go the wrong way at one time or another—even me.

———•●•———

I was desperate for Carla to want me too, and I didn't want to do something stupid to mess it up. One day at the office, I reluctantly asked Susan for her opinion. She was surprisingly honest in her response.

"Sam, I think that you have it all wrong," she replied. "Relationships are hard for everybody, not just Black people."

"I know, but I just think it's harder when you don't even know what a healthy relationship looks like."

"You really like this girl, right?"

"Yes, I think so."

"Then just be yourself," she encouraged. "You're a good-looking, straight man with a job. That means that you are halfway there. You're also smart and sensitive. Don't sell yourself short. You are a hot commodity, and I'm telling you that this woman knows it."

"It's not that simple," I admitted. "I have a lot of stuff from how I grew up. We are very different and…"

"Yes, it is," she interrupted. "Listen to me, your lady has stuff too. Everybody does. The way I see it: either you are right for each other, or you aren't. Only time will tell."

At that moment, I wasn't sure if Susan understood the deficit that I was dealing with. She had a good rapport with our clients, but I figured that was just because she was a nice lady who was very professional. I seriously doubted that she fully understood the widespread ramification of the bondage that people in the hood were under every day for their entire lives. I say that not because she was white, but because she came from a somewhat privileged background.

But I really appreciated what she had to say. Confiding in others wasn't my strong suit. I was taught at a young age to keep my thoughts and feelings mostly to myself or face being ridiculed by the others in our house. So, this was new ground for me. It felt weird, like I was exposed. However, I saw the benefit of it. If nothing else, she gave me something to think about.

Carla and I were also on opposite schedules. I got into the habit of calling her at the station on most nights right before I went to bed. Unless I had a late night out with my friends, I tried to be in bed by eleven. She was a night owl and slept in late every morning.

"Hey, you," I said from my bed.

"Hi, yourself," she replied. "I was hoping you would call."

"How was your day?"

"Busy. I'm working on a new piece now. I'm hoping to pull it together by the weekend."

"What's it about?"

"All the new immigrants moving to Utica. It's about the problems they face."

"Like in jobs and housing, you mean?"

"Yes, somewhat," she answered. "I feel bad for a lot of their kids who don't speak English, but they are still required to go to school."

"I remember kids in school who barely spoke English," I reflected with a chuckle. "They got better grades than some of the Black kids did who were born here."

"Eventually they do, but not right away," she answered. "It's asking a lot from the kids."

"Yes, and from the teachers too I would imagine," I offered.

"I'm trying to get someone from the district to go on air talking about the immigrant influx."

"Sounds right up your alley."

"My producer wants to see something by tomorrow and so far, I can't get anybody from the city to call me back."

She sounded frustrated.

"Oh, that reminds me, are you still interested in going to the new play at the Stanley?" I asked.

"Yes, I want to go," she said and perked up. "Pick a Sunday if you can. I can pay for my ticket."

"No, I got it covered."

"You sure?"

"Yes, I'm sure."

"Thank you," she said. "Oh, it's getting late. You better go to bed."

"Are you trying to rush me off the phone?"

"No, I just happen to know how much you need your beauty sleep," she joked.

"Yup, I'm just not as naturally gifted in this area the way you are."

"Aw, you all right." she responded.

I laughed.

I always slept better on the nights when I got to talk to her. My overall mood had changed immensely since I met her. I still completely owned my Type-A personality, but little thoughts of her crept into my consciousness from time to time and lifted me up to a better place where the world didn't seem so bad after all. Life was suddenly bearable and worth living.

I finally told Mama that I met somebody. I was hesitant to say anything to her at first. I thought that she wouldn't be supportive. She wasn't exactly a believer in the virtues of true love.

"Is she a lawyer too?" she wondered.

"No, she's a reporter."

"What kind of reporter?"

"She does the news on TV."

"What does she look like?"

"She's very classy," I bragged.

"I knew she was pretty," Mama responded. "You didn't have to tell me that if she is on the news. You better be careful though cause the really pretty ones have a whole lot of devil in them." She laughed to herself.

"She Black?" Mama wondered.

"Yes, she's Black," I said. "Does that matter?"

"You crazy? Of course, it matters. Can't no white woman love a Black man like a Black woman can."

"I'm not sure that is true," I argued. "That's just something Black women say because they don't like seeing Black men with white women."

"No, it's not," she disagreed. "Black men are peculiar, like a wild horse. If you don't know what you are doing, you're likely to find yourself half-killed."

"Oh, yeah, Black women are a piece of cake!" I countered. "Most of the women out here are buck-wild. Worse than the men."

"They got that way chasing after some piece of man not worth a damn," she fussed. "It ain't easy loving a Black man."

"You don't say," I questioned with all the sarcasm I could muster.

"You best listen to me, Sam, if you know what's good for you," she admonished. "If you find a Black woman who really loves you, then you are really into something because she will follow you to the end of the earth."

"And if she doesn't?"

"Find one who will!" she stressed. "There are good women everywhere just praying for someone good to come along. But I don't know too many good men myself."

Mama was never married. She had several relationships over the years but nothing for long. She used to go out sometimes at night to the bars and clubs when we were younger, and she occasionally brought someone home with her. But he was always gone when we woke up.

There was this one man she liked when I was in high school, and she would stay over at his place every now and then. Tony Monk was his name. I don't know what happened there. I just remember her being sad a lot after it ended. It must be demoralizing to be physically attracted to men she knew she could never really trust or respect. Like so many other Black women I knew, her pain had shaped her worldview.

But the conversation with her about Carla went better than I thought it would. I had to tell her. She was always asking questions about what was going on with me. She would have been all over me if she found out that I was hiding this from her.

Everybody knew that I was Mama's favorite offspring. Some of it was just because I was the only boy. She would do things for me that she wouldn't do for the girls. And she was better with me, less aggressive. She regularly asked me what I wanted for dinner, whereas no was else was given the choice. Even my mother was jealous of me in that regard. But the real difference was that I always listened to Mama when she said things, even if it turned out in the end that she was just barking at the moon. I think I was the only one who ever really listened to her, and in the end, that was the one thing she really needed.

———— • ● • ————

I was excited about the prospect of falling in love for

the first time. This may sound strange, but I didn't know that that was even a possibility for me. I had long accepted the fact that there were many things in the world that probably were not in the cards for me. For example, growing up, I never thought I would fly on a plane or swim in the ocean. Even though by most accounts, I had already broken through the chains of my past in many respects, I still was learning what that meant as a practical matter. It was for me a slow awakening.

"Do you want to be a public defender your entire career?" Carla asked one night during one of our phone calls.

"I don't think so. I never really wanted to do this in the first place. I was as surprised as anyone to discover that I'm pretty good at it."

"But do you like it?"

"Uh, I don't know," I said. "Sometimes I think I hate it."

"*Hate* is a strong word."

"I know it is," I reluctantly agreed.

"Do you think that what you like is helping people who are completely hopeless?"

"I like proving I can do this job."

"Proving to who?" she inquired. "The world or to yourself?"

"Ah, probably a little of both. But it also feels like there's something else trying to hold me back by making me second-guess myself."

"I don't know what you mean," she pushed.

"It's hard to explain," I said. "But I'm not crazy. I know it's real. I'm just trying to stay on point."

"I wish you could just let your guard down a little. You don't seem to know how to be happy."

"I'm trying to get there."

"How?" she inquired.

"You make me happy," I flirted.

"How do I do that?'

"When you smile."

She was quiet. I knew right away that my feeble attempt at flattery had missed badly. Carla told me more than once that she thought I was too guarded. Honestly, I always thought the same was true for her, maybe even more so. I just never said anything because I didn't want to challenge her about anything related to our relationship. Three months in and we had yet to be intimate physically. I was crazy about her, and I wanted to be with her in every way. But whenever we got too close, she just pushed me away. I never forced the issue. I just figured that she needed more time.

Chapter 10

Joe Bartolotta came to see me. He had an offer for Marcus.

"He pleads to the murder, and I'll recommend twenty-one years," Joe said.

"He's seventeen years old," I replied. "That's longer than he's been alive."

"I know but it's out of my hands."

"How's that?"

"Following orders," Joe explained.

"What is the offer for the other two guys?"

"Seventeen-and-a-half years."

"Why more for my guy?"

"Because he's the shooter," Joe answered. "They all three said that in their statements."

"You got anything else that shows that Marcus was the one with the gun?" I pushed.

"You know we don't have the weapon."

"Or a positive identification on the shooter," I asserted.

"I don't need either. C'mon Sam, you know that. I can make the other two testify if you want to push the issue."

"I know that Marcus insists he never touched the gun."

"Good luck convincing a jury of that," Joe spoke. "He's cooked. We both know it."

"Hmm...I'll talk to my client," I conveyed. "But I'm telling you: I think it's too much time."

"All right, let me know," Joe requested without any expression. "I got your motions. If you make me go through with the suppression hearing on his statement, then the offer is off the table."

"I figured as much, but if this thing ends up going to trial, then you will have to try each defendant separately," I contended.

"Probably just yours. The cops tell me that your guy is young, but he's hardcore. His name has come up in several homicide investigations."

"Then it's probably a good thing that they finally got him," I replied flippantly.

"No, I just mean that he is no angel; more like the angel of death."

Joe had a point. The state is obligated to protect its citizens from domestic threats, even if the threat is coming from a teenager who is barely out of puberty. Whatever the reasons, we all knew that these young Black kids were not just more likely to be killed, but they are also more likely to kill. There are many street corners in the inner-city where nobody in their right mind would dare walk by at night unarmed. To pretend otherwise is to just perpetuate the lie. Until we address the root causes of poverty, innocent people of all economic levels need to be protected.

But he also missed an important truth. Most likely, we will never know for certain who the actual shooter was, regardless of what Marcus or his friends say. We can't believe anything they supposedly told the police. Regardless, the prosecutor has the burden of proof, meaning the state needs to be absolutely correct if it is wanting to send anyone to prison for twenty-one years. The integrity of the system should be of utmost importance.

Moreover, what the police thought happened was irrelevant. They tended to believe that which was most convenient for them. Here, they created an artificial distinction between the defendants at the expense of my client. Ultimately, punishments must be just, not to mention tempered with compassion.

—•●•—

I decided to make a midweek visit to see Marcus at the jail since I had plans with Carla for the weekend. He had no idea I was coming, and he was surprised to see me.

"Let's just get to it," I began. "The ADA came to see me yesterday and made us an offer. He wants a plea to the murder charge in exchange for a twenty-one-year sentence. Do you understand?"

He looked disheveled. His hair had grown longer, and it looked like it had been a while since he had put a comb through it. He had no facial hair except for a small shadow of a mustache.

"No. How can I get so much time if I'm YO?"

"You are being tried as an adult, not a juvenile. You are facing twenty-five years to life if we go to trial and lose. We talked about this."

"But I didn't do it?"

"You told the police you did."

"That's because I thought I could get YO," he disclosed.

"Who told you that?'

"Everybody said it."

"Did the police tell you that?"

"Yeah."

"Who?"

"I don't know his name. The short one with the glasses."

"What did he say?"

"I asked him about YO, and he said that he would do

what he could as long as I told him everything."

"And you told him that you are the one who fired the gun out the window?"

"Man, I just told him what he wanted me to say," Marcus complained. "But I didn't shoot nobody. Thomas shot that dude, man. It didn't have nothing to do with me."

"Then why did you tell the cops that you did?"

"Cause I could get YO! Both Thomas and JT, they can't get it."

"Well, you can't either," I rebutted. "The ADA is now looking to send you away for a long time. Even longer than your two friends."

"But that's not how it went down. I swear to God, man. I was in the back seat. Thomas was in the front, and JT was driving."

"Well, you better tell me something then." I stressed.

"Like what? That's all I know."

"Where's the gun?"

"I don't know. Thomas sold it."

"To who?"

"I don't know."

"How do you know he sold it?"

"He told us. He said he sold it to his cousin or somebody."

"Why do the police want you so bad?" I questioned further.

"I don't know, but you gotta help me man," he complained. "This is messed up!"

"Messed up how?" I pushed. "There is probably a mother out there whose heart is broken into pieces because her son was gunned down on the street for no reason. It was just *business*, right? Well, the whole world hates you guys because of what you did!"

"That's not me, man!" Marcus shouted.

"Not you?"

"No!" he shouted in a loud voice. "Leave me alone!"

"I'm sorry, but I can't do that Marcus."

"No, let me go! Get off me, man! Step…. off!"

"You have to talk to me!" I demanded. "It's now or never!"

"No, let me go! I wanna go!"

Marcus suddenly jumped to his feet. He grabbed his chair and threw it as hard as he could up against the wall. His eyes were aflame, and he was hissing and moving his tongue in and out. He began to wail uncontrollably, and his face was quickly covered with a mixture of his tears and the mucus coming from his nose and mouth.

"Marcus, you have to calm down!" I directed.

Instead, he did the opposite. He started shadow boxing the air with upper cuts and jabs in rapid succession. He was out of his mind. He looked possessed, like that kid I saw on the sidewalk outside of the barbershop that day.

I just sat there. I wasn't afraid for myself. Somehow, this seventeen-year-old skinny kid without a weapon was not that menacing. I was more concerned about what the corrections staff would do about all the commotion. It took longer than I thought for someone to appear, but two deputies finally rushed in and cornered Marcus.

"Up against the wall!" they ordered. "Do it now! Do not move!"

Marcus did not resist them. His chest and face were flesh up against the wall as the deputies were both leaning hard against him. He was completely out of breath.

"He's okay!" I shouted. "He's okay!"

"Are you sure?" one deputy questioned. "It doesn't look that way to me."

"Let him go," I said calmly.

They let up and stepped back. Marcus eased up and slowly turned to face us. He began wiping his face with his hands. He looked raving mad.

"This meeting is over!" the deputy declared. "I'm sorry, counselor, but you have to go."

"I just need one more minute alone," I begged. "Please, just one minute."

The two officers looked at each other for a second and then slowly started walking toward the door.

"One minute," one of them said. "We are just outside."

"All right, listen," I whispered as I stood to my feet. "I'm going to tell the ADA no deal on the twenty-one years. He's not going to like it because it's going to mean a lot more work for him if we act like we want to go to trial. I'm going to try to get you less time, but I can't make you any promises. But you have to trust me and only me!"

Marcus just looked at me oddly. He was still heavy breathing.

"Say something!" I insisted. "I need to know that you understand."

"Yeah," was all he said.

He looked me directly in the eyes for possibly the first time.

I felt the weight of them.

"Okay," I replied. "Hang tight."

—•●•—

I duly reported to the ADA that Marcus declined his generous offer. Joe looked bewildered and frustrated. He shook his head.

"Okay, but it's not going to get any better for him," he said. "I already told you."

"Yes, I know what you said," I responded bluntly. "But it's probably worth the gamble for him at this point, don't you think?"

I turned and walked away.

I always thought that the attorneys in the District Attorney's Office had it a lot easier than we did. They wore the white hats in the eyes of the public, and they had almost unlimited resources when it came to the management of their cases. The entire Utica police force was literally at their disposal, and the judges sided with them most of the time.

Moreover, they made almost twice as much money as we did, even though we were all county employees handling the same cases in the same courtrooms. They didn't have to deal with whiny, difficult clients or make jail visits or lack the ability to hire expert witnesses. And they almost always won their cases. Neither job was a walk in the park for sure, but what we did was harder, no doubt about it.

— • ● • —

Carla and I finally made love. It just happened naturally one night after one of our dates, and it was all that I had hoped it would be. More than anything, however, I was just happy to know that she wanted me too in that way. I wasn't sure before. However, although we were now closer than we had ever been, it wasn't like we were magically transported onto a new level of commitment. But it was definitely a step in the right direction for us as far as I was concerned.

Chapter 11

I lost six felony trials in a row in the year-and-a-half since I moved up to county court. I gave them all my best efforts, even though I knew from the start I was going to lose all of them. I tried not to take any of the losses personally because nobody could have won them. For me, it was an excellent opportunity to learn my craft—another thing I kept telling myself.

The last one was an assault case. My client, a white guy, had beat up his girlfriend for about the tenth time. This time he also stabbed her in the arm with a paring knife. She wanted to drop the charges before trial, but the ADA explained to her that that wasn't her choice to make. My client didn't think that he should have been charged at all because she had apparently stabbed him in the back last year, and nothing happened to her. It's just crazy how some people live.

He also didn't believe that she would show up for trial and testify against him. He was wrong. She testified for about two hours. The jury only deliberated about an hour before finding him guilty. It was public humiliation for me and all so disheartening.

"I'm glad you lost that case," Carla expressed during our late-night phone conversation.

"Wow, that really hurts," I replied jokingly.

"I'm sorry, but I have no sympathy for men who put

their hands on women."

"How do you feel about women who assault men?" I asked sarcastically. "'Cause that's the kind of relationship they have."

"I don't care about him!"

"That's really my point," I said. "Nobody has probably ever really cared enough about either one of them to go out of their way to help them. It's a mistake to ignore the people who are in pain because they generally turn around and produce more of it."

"You seem so forgiving of these people," she noted. "I don't understand it."

"It's not about forgiveness. It's about trying to understand their circumstances as a way of preventing it from happening again. I promise you; his girlfriend will be the one waiting to pick him up from jail the day he gets out."

"Then she's a fool!" Carla emoted.

"Hey, listen, I don't necessarily disagree with you," I replied calmly. "But most things aren't as black and white as we try to make them. It seems to me that there has got to be a better way. One of these two fools just might die next time. Jail is only a band-aid."

"So, nobody should go to jail?" she challenged. "At least jail keeps him away from her."

"Incarcerated persons don't stop committing crimes just because they are serving time behind prison gates," I explained. "They routinely torment and assault each other, as well as corrections staff. And most who get out are worse than they were when they went in— even less civilized, if you can believe that."

"You're probably right" she conceded. "I just don't know what the answer is. It all makes me crazy thinking about it."

"Now you sound like me."

Turns out that Carla was a Republican. I was not

political at all, despite having taken a ton of political science courses in college. I was a registered Democrat, mainly because every Black person I knew was a Democrat. I wasn't overly concerned about such matters. I never heard anybody in Cornhill talking about abortion or immigration. We called those "white people problems." I only voted once in my life, and that was because one of my college professors guilted me into it. So, it didn't bother me that our political affiliations were different. But I feared that she might not feel the same way.

We were spending more time together, which I really liked. Sometimes I stayed overnight at her apartment, but it wasn't a regular thing. Our schedules didn't permit it. She never stayed at my place. But she was clearly comfortable being herself around me and having me in her space. Just not too much of a good thing, I suspected.

I noticed that when she talked about her plans going forward, I wasn't necessarily a part of them. She was obviously very ambitious, and I knew that journalists tended to move around a lot as they chased after promotions. Occasionally, she voiced her desire to move to a bigger market as soon as she could. I never said anything in response that didn't sound supportive. We hadn't been dating that long, and we had agreed to take it slow.

Carla was turning into a bit of a small-town celebrity. Turns out that a lot of people had taken notice of the beautiful Black woman on the local news. People regularly walked up to her and told her that they were big fans of her work. She was always receptive and gracious. To her credit, she never seemed taken in by it. I thought it was nice, and I was proud to be seen with her.

We had gotten into the habit of shopping for groceries together on the weekends whenever possible. It started when she decided that she needed to teach me how to pick out fresh fruits and vegetables. I didn't get it. We were only talking about tomatoes or melon, or so I thought. We went maybe a couple of times a month.

On one occasion, we were in the produce section of a supermarket when we came upon a young Black woman arguing with a store employee. She was with another slightly older woman and two small children.

"I already told you that somebody else did it," she yelled. "My daughter didn't do that!"

"But I saw her do it," the balding, middle-aged white man asserted.

He was red-faced, and his voice was slightly elevated.

"That's a straight-up lie! You weren't even over here yet? How could you see her? I was just standing right here. I didn't see nothing."

"I could see her from our security camera," he snapped.

"No way!" she shrieked. "We just got here. You ain't seen nothing!"

"I'm telling you I saw her open two different bags of cherries and eat them," he maintained. "If she does it again, you will have to leave the store. I'm sorry but …"

"I wanna see you move me, bitch!" she dared. "I'll be the next owner of this mama jama!"

She glanced over at her friend who nodded in support.

"Don't talk to me like that!" he demanded.

"What are you gonna do?" she baited. "I'll set it off in here. You need to get out of my face before I make it rain in this joint!"

"Nice way to act in front of your children," he countered.

"You need to mind your own damn business!" she screeched and leaned in.

"People who steal from this store are my business!"

"I didn't steal anything! There you go accusing people again! You just target Black people, and we know this!"

"You must be kidding!"

He shook his head in disbelief.

The argument was all so painful to watch. All the other shoppers were gawking and looking distressed. Carla and I glanced at each other quickly and lowered our eyes. We didn't say anything. We had to maneuver our way around because they were all standing right in front of us. It was such a relief once we had gotten through that wreckage.

Obviously, I had witnessed similar encounters before. Many of the people I knew from Cornhill were quick to object to and resist any critical comment or question directed at them. It seemed that so many of us were either unable or just unwilling to be reasonable. In the end, it was a distinction without a difference because the best course of action probably was to just leave them to themselves rather than force the point.

Carla was very quiet on the drive to her apartment. I noticed it right away.

"Is something wrong?" I asked.

"*Me?*"

"Yeah, *you.*"

"No, I'm good."

"What are you thinking about?"

"Hmm…That woman fighting with that security guy," she disclosed.

"What about it?" I pressed.

"I thought that was really awful."

"I think that it could've been a lot worse," I suggested.

"Really?" she questioned. "Do you ever get embarrassed about…?"

"Being Black?" I interrupted.

"…Yeah, I guess," she hedged and laughed a little.

"It's hard not to. My grandmother used to say that Black people will always show out if you let us."

"But none of that had to be," she offered. "She could have just disciplined her daughter."

"That would have been too easy."

"But why? I don't understand."

"Because she has trained herself to always be ready to fight anything and anyone who dares to challenge her in any way."

"Is it just anger at the world in general, you think?" Carla inquired.

"Anger, bitterness, disappointment, pick one," I articulated. "All these unprocessed emotions working together—a kind of not-so-perfect storm."

"Hmm, I think a lot of it is sadness too," she added. "A heart can only be broken so many times."

"Probably," I echoed. "It's not easy to make it in the jungle where the predator can so quickly become the prey."

"Women have always been preyed upon!" she stated emphatically.

"I know."

"We have to be strong, or we won't survive at all."

"It's hard. I know," I agreed.

"She reminds me of Rita, the woman who does my hair. She has her own shop on Genesee Street. She has got to be the most unprofessional person that I have ever met! She is never there on time. She's rude to her customers, and she talks on the phone the whole time that she's supposed to be working on my hair. That means that I am there twice as long as I should be."

"Why do you go to her?" I asked. "That would drive me crazy. Just go somewhere else."

"There is nowhere else to go," she explained. "I have asked around. This is the place where the station told me to go."

"See, she probably could have a thriving business if she just applied herself a little," I offered.

"Yeah, well I have had enough of her," Carla complained. "I'm seriously thinking about going back to this lady I know in Syracuse. At least then I won't have to put up with all this foolishness."

I was still trying to figure out exactly where Carla was coming from a lot of the time. She often was very critical of poor people, especially the ones I represented, who were charged with a crime. But at the same time, she also seemed to understand the struggle. Thus, it was nearly impossible for me to predict what side she was going to come down on regarding any one person or topic.

———•●•———

Understandably, everyone in the courthouse was very interested in our love affair. Part of that was because Judge Mazur completely lost his mind when he found out that Carla and I were dating. He bragged to anyone who would listen about his foresight in knowing that we would be a good match and how he had insisted that I call her. He was exaggerating, of course. He didn't really know either one of us personally. He happened upon a single Black woman at a party and put us together in his head. Undoubtedly, I was the only single, professional Black guy he knew. But everyone seemed to like the story better the way he told it.

In contrast, I was careful not to talk about us too much. It wasn't just that I was a private person, which I obviously was. But I felt like we were still too new to reveal too much to the entire world. I also didn't want to say the wrong thing and risk Carla getting wind of it somehow. Utica was a very small town.

———•●•———

"How's it going with Carla?" Susan asked.
We were sitting in the break room drinking coffee.
"Good."
"She's beautiful. I see why you are so taken with her."
"I know she is," I agreed. "We are just taking it day by

day."

"A girl like that must have a lot of suitors," she surmised. "I hope you are not the jealous type."

"I don't know if I am or not. But so far, I'm not aware of any competition."

"Oh, I'm sure they're out there," Susan reflected. "Just waiting for an opportunity."

"Do you think that I should be worried?" I wondered aloud.

"Worried? No, worried is the last thing I think you should be."

"Then what?"

"Be confident," she stated emphatically. "Men who are confident are the most attractive."

"That has never been my strong suit," I admitted.

"Okay, then that's your thing to work on."

"I'm just being honest," I protested mildly.

"Sam, who are you kidding?" she disputed. "You have a lot of confidence. Remember, I've seen it on you in the courtroom. You just need to embrace it."

"How am I supposed to do that?" I questioned. "It's not the same thing."

"If Carla dumps you tomorrow for the richest and most handsome man in the world, then she will be making the biggest mistake of her life because no man could possibly be better for her than you."

I froze in place.

"How much different would your life be if you thought like that?" she challenged.

"But isn't thinking like that arrogance?"

"My ex-husband was arrogant," she disclosed. "So much so that he cheated on me behind my back every chance he got. He thought it made him a man. But all it really did was reveal his insecurities and that he is still a little boy struggling to overcome the impact of his father's alcoholism on his life. Believe me, you're not arrogant in the least. Just be the man you want to be and own it!"

I didn't know what to say. My thoughts were running wild in my brain like a group of toddlers on a waterslide.

She was quiet too as she pondered what she just said.

"We live our lives in stages," she continued. "If you don't like who you really are deep inside, then the most important thing you can do is invest all your efforts in changing the things that can be improved upon. Simply refuse to see yourself as a victim or let anyone treat you like you are one."

We were processing once again.

"How did you get so smart?" I teased.

"A whole lot of pain—and first-year psych," she said with a hint of a smile.

Chapter 12

Judge Mazur wanted to see me and Joe in his chambers. I told Marcus to sit still. We always met in chambers before starting a suppression hearing. The judges never liked doing them and always tried to streamline everything in an attempt to get them over as quickly as possible.

"Come in," the judge directed.

"Did you find some more grandkids?" I joked after glancing at the photo array all around.

Judge Mazur laughed. I sat down in the empty chair next to Joe.

"How many witnesses do you have, Joe?"

"One, possibly two, if necessary."

"Sam, how about you?"

"The same. Just two."

"Who are they," Joe asked.

"It's a secret," I toyed.

"All you had to do was ask," Joe gruffly replied. "I'm calling Scott Draper, who took the statement. Tony Sanzone is also available if I think I need him."

"I'm calling Maria Baez, and my client, maybe," I disclosed.

"Who is Maria Baez?" Joe asked.

"She has known Marcus for many years."

"What does she know about the taking of the

confession?" Joe pushed.

"Nothing," I answered. "Obviously, she wasn't there. Only Draper and Sanzone were there."

"Come on, Sam," the judge urged.

"She is a reading teacher with the Utica School District," I spoke up. "She will testify that Marcus is illiterate."

"He can't read at all?" Judge Mazur questioned.

I shook my head no.

"Not according to his IEP," I said.

"His what?" Judge Mazur wondered.

"Individualized Education Program," I explained. "It's a program for educating kids with special needs. My understanding is that all schools use them to best meet the need of children at risk."

The judge looked at the ADA.

"I don't believe that" Joe offered. "You never said anything before."

"You didn't ask me," I replied flippantly. "According to the IEP, my client has a disability that affects his ability to read. He's so embarrassed about it that he won't even try."

"Even if he can't read, that doesn't mean that he didn't make the statement!" Joe asserted.

"Right, but it does mean that he didn't identify and initial the eight corrections indicated on the two pages," I argued. "Or sign the acknowledgment at the end stating that he fully read and understood the document. I can't wait to hear Detective Draper explain how he pulled off that trick."

Joe face was turning white as the blood drained from his head. He was flustered.

"Sam, I don't know what your game is, but…"

"My game?"

"Yeah, your game!" he shouted.

"The only people who are playing games here are

Draper and Sanzone!" I defended.

"They are only doing their jobs!" Joe resisted.

"If their job is lying, then I'd say they are pretty good at it!" I jabbed.

"I suggest you be careful," Joe warned. "You're treading on thin ice."

"Oh, bite me, Joe!" I countered. "Those guys should go to jail themselves for what they're trying to pull here!"

"That will be enough, gentlemen!" Judge Mazur erupted. "I will have none of this! You hear me? Sam, you can step out into the hall. I want to speak to Joe alone."

I stood to my feet and walked out. I only pretended to be angry. Inside, I was laughing to myself. I sat there quietly for about five or ten minutes until Joe opened the door and told me to come in. I could tell that he wasn't very happy.

"Is there something you want to say, Joe?" the judge asked.

I remained standing.

"Um…Sam, I'm prepared to offer you the same seventeen-and-a-half years as the other two defendants."

"I thought you said no more deals for us?" I answered.

"Are you going to talk to him or not?" Joe barked and jumped out of his seat.

"Yeah, I'll talk to him, but my sense is that this offer is not good enough. I certainly can't recommend that he take it in good conscience."

"What?" the ADA fumed. "Are you kidding me?"

"I don't believe that I am," I answered arrogantly. "You wanted to play hard ball."

"You are out of your mind!" Joe fumed.

"Oh, really?" I lashed out. "Well, let me put it to you this way, friend. If you put either one of those fine detectives on the stand, I'm going to rip them a new one. And then I am going to order a copy of the transcript of me ripping them a new one and share it with the rest of the criminal defense bar in this county. Unless I'm way off, this will most likely be the last suppression hearing for either one of them. Ever! Tell your supervisors that!"

"I will do just that!" Joe yelled. "And we will remember this in all the cases that your office handles."

"Joe, will you excuse us?" the judge jumped in. "Please wait in the hall."

Joe immediately picked up his file and marched out the door like a teen being sent to his room for misbehaving.

"Sit down, Sam," Judge Mazur said calmly.

I immediately complied.

"You know, you are a real piece of work," he reflected and sighed heavily.

"He started it," I heard myself sound like a six-year-old.

"You have a lot of talent," he commended. "Good for you. You just played Joe like a fiddle."

"Thank you."

"How long do you think you'll continue swimming in this sewer?" the judge wondered. "You know what I think? I think you should marry Carla and move to some place where you can make some real money. Someplace like New York City or Atlanta."

"Maybe. Who knows?" I remarked.

"I'm going to adjourn this hearing to give you time to talk to your client," the judge advised. "We both know that you can't go to trial here even if you get the statement suppressed. That's too much to risk. So, you two fellas need to work it out. Hear me?"

"Yes, I hear you."

"You can go," the judge urged.

It wasn't hard to explain to Marcus exactly what was going on. I just told him that the judge wanted us to talk some more before having a hearing. The truth is that Marcus and I hadn't talked that much about the hearing. I had absolutely no intention of letting him testify so I never bothered to prep him.

Maria Baez was relieved that she didn't have to testify. She said that she was so nervous that she hardly slept last night. I thanked her profusely for coming. Upon my return to the office, Teresa walked out of her office and followed me to my desk.

"What happened today with your suppression hearing?"

"They gave us a new offer," I advised. "It got adjourned."

"I heard that you really got into it with Joe Bartolotta."

"Nothing I couldn't handle. Who told you that?"

"Did you really threaten to send the hearing transcript to all of the criminal defense attorneys in the county?" she asked suspiciously.

"Yes," I admitted. "And I wasn't bluffing."

She smiled a little.

"What made you think of that?"

"I don't know. Just came to me. You should have seen the look on Joe's face."

She chuckled to herself. "Well, you really pissed them off with that."

"I don't care," I said and shrugged. "All the stuff they pull on us all the time."

"Frank wants to meet with you tomorrow."

"What? The district attorney wants to meet with me?"

I sat up. I wasn't expecting to hear that.

"Yes."

"Why?"

"He says he wants to work out a deal with you himself."

"Really? What happened to Joe?"

"I don't know."

"I don't get it," I said. "Why did he call you and not me?"

"Because he wants to meet with me too. I'm going with

you."

"I don't want my mother going to school with me!" I resisted.

"First, I'm not your mother," she stressed. "Second, you don't have a choice."

"It makes me look weak," I whined.

"No, it doesn't," she advised. "I'd say this all sounds very good for you. I'm proud of you. I will only be there to support you. I told you that you were ready for this. Don't read too much into it."

"If you say so."

"Just remember though that this isn't our only case with them," she cautioned. "You don't want to burn any bridges."

------- • ● • -------

As soon as we arrived at the security desk at the district attorney's office, the officer just waved us in. I was nervous. I had only spoken to Frank Lloyd a few times. He had been elected DA three times. Prior to that, he was a long-time ADA.

"Come in, please," he beckoned. "Teresa, it's good to see you."

"Same here, Frank," she replied.

He was a balding, middled-aged man with gray hair on the sides. There was nothing about him that was at all outside of the norm. He looked exactly like every other Italian American man his age in Utica.

"Sam, how are you?" he asked and smiled.

"I'm good."

"Have a seat."

I was very uncomfortable. I felt like I had just been called into the principal's office.

"Well, Joe is out of the office today or he would be

sitting in," Frank explained. "I heard about what happened yesterday, and I just wanted to see if we can work this thing out."

"Work it out?" I questioned.

"Sam, I know that you and I don't really know each other that well. But I have always been a straight shooter. Teresa can tell you. We go way back."

"So, what do you have in mind?" I asked.

"You tell me, what will it take?"

"Fifteen."

"Done," Frank quickly replied.

"I have to check with my client."

"Of course," Frank said. "But I need your word that no one in your office will ever use or disclose anything associated with this case to anyone or use it against any of the law enforcement officers involved in the investigation. I want this thing settled for all time."

"That's not a problem," Teresa asserted.

"We got a deal, Sam?"

"I want an Alford plea," I interjected.

"That's really a decision for Judge Mazur, but we will not oppose your request that your client not have to talk about the circumstances surrounding the shooting during the plea allocution."

"Okay, but I need for the offer to the other two guys to stay at the seventeen-and-a-half. My client feels like they sold him out."

"Okay, we can do that," Frank assured. "We got a deal?"

I looked at Teresa.

"Deal," I said definitively.

"Great!" Frank replied. "I'll let Joe know."

<hr>

There was no real response from Marcus when I told him the new offer. I didn't really expect that there would be. Most of these guys are not afraid of going to prison. Especially, the young ones. So many people they know have been there. To be honest, we are only talking logistics with Marcus anyway. He was born imprisoned in his mind.

On the street, it is almost a badge of honor to have served time in state prison. This is why the idea of increasing the penalties for some offenses as a deterrent is seriously misguided. Not many of our clients ever thought beforehand that they could be apprehended. It's like a blind spot—a natural byproduct of being felony stupid.

I called Joe.

"Hey, I just want you to know that Marcus Williams will accept the offer."

"Okay, thanks," was his low-keyed answer.

"Can you let Judge Mazur know? I'm not sure if he will want to conference this again."

"I don't know."

"Can you reach out?"

"Yes, I will," Joe replied dryly. "Is there anything else that I can do for you, sir?"

He sounded spiteful.

"No, I think that's it," I said.

He hung up the phone.

Chapter 13

Apparently, my Aunt Joyce was arrested for prostitution again. She called the office looking for me. She indicated in her message that she wanted me to visit her at the jail. I knew what that meant right away. If she was in jail, then she had tested positive for a sexually transmitted disease. In New York State, prostitution is only a Class B misdemeanor, which is punishable by up to three months in jail and up to a $500 fine. Typically, everyone arrested for prostitution in Utica was tested for disease and immediately released from custody if they were negative. However, if they tested positive, then they had to accept treatment before being released back into society to sell their wares once again.

Joyce was a junkie for as long as I could remember. She was forty-seven-years old, a year younger than my mother. We got used to hearing about her name being in the newspaper, and we used to make jokes about her being like Julia Roberts in *Pretty Woman*. But it really wasn't funny, and we were all embarrassed by her.

As a teenager, she used to hang out all night and sleep all day. Mama kicked her out of the house when she was sixteen years old. After that, she would stop by periodically to shower and get a bite to eat before vanishing back into thin air. I had no idea what she wanted with me, but there was no way that I was going to go see her. I just hoped that she wasn't telling everybody in that jail that she was related to me.

——·●·——

I didn't know that Mama was regularly watching Carla on the news. She never mentioned it. She just announced one afternoon that she wanted to meet Carla. I knew immediately that it was a terrible idea. I wasn't ashamed of my grandmother, but I had never introduced her to anyone before. Only God knew how she was going to react. It was stressful to even think about.

A week later, we went to Red Lobster, which happened to be Mama's favorite restaurant. Carla was not a fan of chain restaurants. Mama insisted on sitting in the front seat next to me on the drive over. Carla didn't like sitting in the back because she got car sick easily. She also hated to be hot, and the first thing Mama did when she got in the car was turn the heat button to high. It was a miracle that we even made it to the restaurant at all.

"I sure hope they have the biscuits I like," Mama said as we were seated.

"I'm sure that they have plenty," Carla replied.

"Well, I like them hot. Not the ones that have been sitting around all day and got hard. They are not the same cold."

"Oh, I didn't know that," Carla said.

"I think they give Black people the cold ones on purpose."

"Why would they do that?" Carla foolishly challenged.

"'Cause that's what white people do," Mama insisted. "You mean to tell me that you don't know that?"

Mama had a major-league scowl on her face.

I was sweating.

"No," Carla replied. "I just meant that they want people

to come back again and again to this restaurant so it's doubtful that they would do that…"

"'Doubtful,' you say?" Mama confronted. "That's what you think, huh?"

"We can just tell the waitress to make sure that she brings us the hot ones," I interjected as fast as I could. "It's not a problem."

"Yeah, I know that's right," Mama responded. "Let 'em know upfront."

Carla looked annoyed. But she was trying, which was more than I could say for my grandmother.

"I really like your hair," Carla threw out at one point.

"It's a wig," Mama answered.

"I know," Carla followed. "It looks really cute on you!"

"'Cute'? See, that's what I'm talking about. I think young girls today spend too much time trying to look cute and not enough time trying to work out their own salvation like the Bible say. God don't care what we look like. It's about what's in the heart. Looks ain't everything."

"Carla's uncle is a minister in Rochester," I offered.

"Good for him," Mama said. "Did I tell you, Sam, that Reverend Tisdale died?"

"Yeah, you told me."

"They say that his wife already got a boyfriend. Can you believe that? The man ain't been dead but a minute, and she's already laying up with some scoundrel. It's a shame before God! That's cause she thinks she's cute."

Carla didn't say much after that. Mama spoke directly to me the rest of the evening, mostly about her minor aches and pains, all of which I already knew about. Carla pretended to listen attentively, but she was pretty much checked out. I was mortified.

Thankfully, the evening came to a quick end. I dropped Mama off at home. As she exited the front seat, she told Carla that it was nice meeting her. I couldn't pull away fast enough.

"Look, I'm so sorry," I blurted out as soon as I pulled off.

Carla began laughing hysterically.

"No, I'm so embarrassed," I declared. "That was bad, really bad. I don't know what got into her."

"Oh, forget about, Sam," she replied.

"I guess she's just a little jealous," I concluded.

"You think?" Carla asked sarcastically and giggled. "She thinks some young hussy is trying to steal her man."

"I'm not her man!"

"Yes, you are!" she maintained. "You're probably the only real man she has ever respected. It's *cute*."

We looked at each other and then both laughed aloud.

———— • ● • ————

One would think that being raised in an all-female household that I would have understood women a lot better than I did. But I never really understood what was going on most of the time. I can hardly remember one day growing up when they weren't fighting with one another or with someone else on the block. They seemed to like it and actively looked for reasons to be offended and have conflict with people. I felt surrounded. As the alpha female, Mama was maybe the worse because her word was law, and she was often mean-spirited.

I was drawn to the guys in the neighborhood who preferred to laugh and joke around more than smoking weed or finding girls. I was close to some of them. But we all eventually grew apart. I was one of the few who even graduated from high school.

"Sam?"

I heard the call from behind as I was getting into my car outside the county courthouse. I turned around quickly.

"Smitty?"

"Oh my God! Hey, Sammy! I thought that was you, man. How are you doing?"

We shook hands and hugged. He had the biggest smile on his face. I did too.

Ron Smith was probably my best friend when we were in junior high school. He looked the same, only a littler heavier. He had light skin and wore his hair in braids that extended down to the bottom of his neck in the back. We were about the same height. I hadn't seen him in probably five or six years.

"I'm good," I replied. "What are you doing here?"

"I need a copy of my birth certificate from the county building."

"How are you?"

"I can't complain, man," he said. "You know, I heard you were back in town. Look at you! I can't get over how good you look!"

"Thank you," I replied. "You don't look so bad yourself. What are you up to these days?"

"I moved to Newburgh."

"Newburgh?"

"Yeah, man. I followed my girl there. That's where she's from. I have five kids."

"Five kids! You're kidding."

"Nope. My oldest is thirteen."

"Whoa, good for you," I replied. "What do you do there?"

"I drive a bus for the city, man," he replied. "I don't know if you heard that both of my brothers got killed. Bobby and Philip both were shot to death out here on these streets. Both in the same year."

"No, I'm so sorry," I sympathized. "I didn't know."

"Yeah, man, I'm the only one left," he lamented and began to tear up. "Me and my sister Linda. It's been almost three years now. It really messed me up."

"That's unbelievable!" I declared. "I remember you and me and Philly walking home from school every day."

"Me, too," Smitty reflected. "Remember that time we went into that abandoned house on Albany Street looking for ghosts, and we heard something and started running, and Philly fell into the hole in the floor?"

I nodded and laughed.

"And we left him there," I added. "That's the funniest part."

"Yeah, yeah man!" he acknowledged. "We were so crazy!"

We were both laughing.

"I heard that you are a lawyer," he said. "That's really great! Couldn't be prouder of you, man."

"Thank you. I really appreciate it."

"Maybe you can do something about these young boys out here with all these guns. They are the some of the coldest cats on the planet! I swear to God. They ain't got no conscience and no hearts, almost like they are hired assassins. And it's getting worse 'cause don't nobody really care about Black kids killing Black kids. I don't care what they say."

"I couldn't agree more."

"Where are the guns even coming from anyway?" he posed. "All they do is give power to the powerless. And so, their feet run to evil, like it says in the Bible."

"I know."

"I'm worried to death about my three boys," he confessed. "Newburgh is just as bad as Utica, if not worse. I don't know if I can survive another death. I swear to God, man. The pain is always there, burning a hole in my chest. It feels kinda like I got shot too, except I didn't die."

"Well, your sons have you," I said. "That's a huge advantage for them, right?"

"I try to teach them and keep them close, but they're already fighting me on things. We go to church every

Sunday, but I honestly don't know how much it helps."

"What do you mean?" I wondered.

"I mean, I don't know about some of these church folk either," he expressed. "A lot of the stuff they say is too old-fashioned. The kids aren't buying it anymore. If we can't talk their language, then how we supposed to reach them?"

"Well, it sounds to me like you are giving them at least a fighting chance to survive and to be better. Nobody had a father in the house when we were growing up."

"You're right," he reflected. "Me and you didn't have nobody, man. We had to figure everything out for ourselves."

"So, that's something, right?"

"Now I have a good woman too, but God knows that we have our problems there too. Sometimes we're barely holding on."

"I'm not sure that I'm the right person to talk to about relationships," I admitted. "But if you love each other, there must be a way to make it work. Right?"

"It's just hard for us all the time," he acknowledged. "I blame her, and she blames me. But I know that it's really the both of us—we're both broken down inside. Something happened to us somewhere in time, and now every day is a struggle."

"Something like what?" I pressed.

"Like basic respect, I think... I don't know. It just seems a lot of times that she doesn't respect me or what I do. I'm pretty sure that it's not supposed to be like this between us."

"You need to let up off the gas a little bit," I contended. "We can only live one day at a time and do the best we can with what we have."

"I'm trying man. I'm really trying, you know."

"Keep fighting, brother! Your kids and your family are worth the fight."

"Okay, but tell me this, Sammy. Now that you have

beat the odds, and you wear suits to work and everything, does it ever get easy?"

His eyes were pleading for hope that frankly I didn't have to give. I couldn't hide, and I wouldn't lie.

"I can't say for sure, but I'm not so sure that it actually does get much better," I reluctantly divulged. "It's a struggle for everyone, especially for us."

"Then no wonder so many of us are perishing," he said.

He looked broken and dejected.

I felt his pain, which only added to my own.

Chapter 14

I had been dreading Marcus' sentencing day. I knew he was getting a good deal, but still, something about it didn't sit right with me. I fully recognized Marcus' part in taking the life of another young person and that he was a menace to society. I just felt like someone needed to be able to see what happened here through the lens of this baby executioner's plight and that that person probably needed to be me since I was the one standing with him as sentence was pronounced. That meant that I needed to be fully present in the moment.

Thankfully, there were no victim's family members scheduled to speak. I don't think I would have been able to handle all of that. Although the press was present, there was no circus-feel surrounding the proceeding this time around. In fact, there were only a few people sitting in the courtroom. Once again, no one was there for Marcus.

I noticed a very young white woman in the back of the courtroom with a small toddler in hand. The child appeared to be mixed race and had the most beautiful face. The woman was wearing pajamas and a plastic cap on her head. She seemed to be upset. I suspected that she knew one of Marcus's co-defendants. I tried not to stare.

Now that this day had arrived, I just wanted it to be over. All three defendants represented both the shame of a nation and the failures of the church. They embodied hate, ignorance, anger, selfishness, poverty, godlessness, and victimization. Their souls were empty, and their minds mush. And I understood that there were many more out there just like them waiting for their turn to demonstrate their complete lack of regard for their neighbor.

Joe made the same speech they always made about the need to clean up the streets by locking these dangerous offenders up for as long as possible. He also read a letter from the victim's aunt. She just wanted to remind us that her nephew was a good person with people who loved and cared for him and who didn't deserve to die. To the defendants, she wrote:

Our family will never be the same because of your acts against God.

There are no words to describe our pain. You don't even know what

you did. That's what hurts the most. You will never know how much

pain you have caused people who never did anything to you. My

Christian faith dictates that I must forgive you. I am still working on that.

May God have mercy on your souls.

When Judge Mazur asked if I had anything to say before he sentenced my client, I just wanted to pass. There really was nothing left inside of me. We were all just swimming against the current. I didn't see the point in grandstanding like the other two defense attorneys had just done, who I don't doubt meant well.

But I had to say something. I knew that I would be heavily criticized later if I remained silent. I had to remind myself to remember who I was and why I was there.

"Thank you, your honor," I began. "Mr. Williams wanted me to state for the record how sorry he is for his part in causing the death of this young man. If he could live that sad day over again, he would, beginning with not getting into that car. He would do better. He really would. Unfortunately, he can't go back in time. None of us can. It would be so easy for me to stand here and go on a rant about all the different societal ills that have contributed to this wretched moment. But that would serve no real purpose either for nothing I say will change anything about what happened—or do anything for the next kid who will be shot dead in the city of Utica. No parent in this community should have to live in constant fear that their son will somehow get his hands on a handgun or otherwise become the victim of someone else who managed to do just that. No aunt should have to search for words to describe the depth of her pain from gun violence in order to get us to understand just how serious this is. Suffice it to say, we need to do more to help our kids, all of our kids. Because frankly, nothing that we're presently doing is working. There simply are no winners here today."

Judge Mazur spoke a few empty words too before he sentenced Marcus to fifteen to thirty years in state prison. His friends received the promised seventeen-and-a-half to thirty-five years. All three were expressionless and looked completely lost. Once again, I wasn't sure Marcus fully understood what was happening, even though I had methodically gone over everything with him the day before at the jail. I asked him several times if he had any questions, and he said that he didn't.

I had long concluded that Marcus carried a lot of pain that ran deep in the recesses of his psyche. As a result, he was also very tightly wound, which made him unpredictable and dangerous, like a wild animal. There are good reasons why most states have laws prohibiting private ownership of exotic animals such as tigers, bears, and apes. These creatures, however domesticated, simply can never be trusted to not give in to their more basic instincts in any moment. Similarly, most of these kids who are doing these shootings on our inner-city streets are already hardwired predators before they are old enough to shave.

Marcus never thanked me for helping him, not that I thought he would. I don't think that he meant it as a slight; it just never occurred to him. Honestly, I was always more surprised when someone thought to thank me.

Joe approached me just as I was leaving the courtroom. He looked out of his mind and got way too close to me for his own good.

"I can see that you are quite taken with yourself," he said.

"I don't think I know what you mean," I replied.

"I think that you do!" he refuted. "And I for one am not impressed in the least by this Boy Scout act of yours."

"Listen, I apologize if I did something to offend you," I said sincerely. "I was only doing my job. Nothing was personal."

"I take it very personal when someone tries to get me fired."

"How did I do that?" I questioned.

"Nevermind," he rebuffed. "Just know that I owe you one, buddy."

"Are you threatening me?" I challenged. "Because we can settle this like men right now if you want to take it there."

"That's my point," Joe ridiculed. "You people always resort to violence."

"What do you mean by 'you people' exactly?"

"Don't make everything about race, geez?"

"We both know what you meant."

"And we both know that your client is a cold-blooded murdering scumbag who you just

put in a position to kill someone else the minute he gets out."

"This conversation is over," I said. "Please excuse me."

I attempted to walk past him, but he stepped forward to block me.

"So, you feel sorry for these little monsters who just can't resist shooting people from cars?" he mocked. "Allow me to enlighten you a bit."

"Go for it!" I urged.

"We have the gun," he whispered in my face.

"What?"

"You heard me."

"What gun?"

"Ask Trina Williams about the gun she tried to sell the day after the shooting," Joe teased. "The gun her son used to commit a homicide. That's how we caught them. She led us straight to them. Anything for a little crack, huh? And to think that you have the nerve to stand here and be so sanctimonious. What a crock!"

"You mean to tell me that you lied about having the gun and withheld evidence in this case?" I countered.

"What?"

"Did you withhold evidence related this murder investigation?"

"Nothing favorable to your guy's case," he asserted. "It proves he did it."

"Doesn't matter," I countered. "It's still an ethical violation and you should know that."

"No, it's not!"

"Do your bosses know?" I attacked further. "Do they? Does Frank know how you play games with people's lives?"

"I do no such thing," Joe protested.

"Do I have to report you to the court and bring a motion now to withdraw our plea?"

"You wouldn't dare?" Joe hissed.

"I bet this really will get you fired this time."

I watched as all the blood drained from Joe's face. He looked like he saw a ghost. He was speechless as he reassessed his predicament.

I pretended to look around before leaning in toward his right ear.

"Was it good for you too?" I taunted in a sultry voice and walked away.

———•●•———

I think that one of the reasons that I became a lawyer in the first place is because I liked to argue. It ran in the family. The biggest difference between me and my grandmother was that she was often unnecessarily cruel and cutting with her words. Unlike her, however, I rarely made it personal. But our instincts were the same. Oftentimes, it was merely stress release for me, and I always had a comeback for people who came at me, everyone except for maybe my mother.

So, there was no way that I was going to let Joe get the better of me. I don't know what happened in his office with the Frank, but that had nothing to do with me. We were now clearly enemies for life, which was fine with me. He acted like the rules of law didn't apply to them. He was completely unaware of his implicit bias. I told myself that I needed to be careful around him because he couldn't be trusted either - Like a dangerous animal.

Hypocrisy aside, I never understood the rush to wanting to condemn poor people. It's not like the poor in this country lived better lives or were happier than other people. Not to belabor the point, but most of our clients had next to nothing. Perhaps they deserved to be pitied, but not vilified.

Of course, not everyone we represented was from a disadvantaged background. Many just couldn't afford to hire an attorney. In this regard, however, it was always important for us, when dealing with both the district attorney's office and the judges, to make it clear that this particular client was a college student or someone who lived in the suburbs. We always got better deals when we did.

—— • ● • ——

"I saw the clip of the sentencing," Carla said that night on the phone.

"What did you think?"

"I thought you looked very handsome."

"Why thank you, ma'am?"

"I know that was hard for you," she sympathized.

"I tried to suppress all of my emotions and do my job."

"What were you really feeling?"

"Tired. And probably a little sad."

"Sad about what?" she wondered.

"I feel like I'm playing a game that I have absolutely no chance of winning."

"Because that murdering kid is going to prison?"

"No, I was feeling sorry for me, not for Marcus."

"Why?"

"Because every time I manage to bank away a little bit of hope about the state of the world, something happens and I'm back in the hole again?"

"Is it really that bad?" she questioned.

"It's like the jokes always on me," I articulated.

—— • ● • ——

Exactly one week after the sentencing, I was sitting in the visiting room at the jail when Marcus walked in.

"Hi, Marcus."

"Hi."

"Come take a seat," I encouraged.

"What's this?"

He nodded at the stuff spread out on the table.

"Oh, this?" I answered. "I remember you were telling me about the chocolate chip cookies at Dunkin Donuts. So, I got us some. I hope that the chocolate milk isn't too warm. I know that you said that you like it cold. I got it here as fast as I could."

His eyes got big.

"Why?" he wondered aloud.

"I don't know. I just wanted to say goodbye properly. Is that okay?"

He gave me a quick glance. "Yeah, I guess."

He stared again at the small feast set out before him like a kid on Christmas morning. Then he slowly sat down. I encouraged him to go ahead. He took a cookie out of the box and put the whole thing in his mouth in one quick swoop.

"Good?" I asked.

"Yes," he replied.

"Well, all right!" I celebrated.

He reached for another cookie and hesitated, "Um…Thanks," he said.

"You're welcome."

Chapter 15

Carla asked me to accompany her to her sister's wedding in Rochester. She was very excited. I was too, but for different reasons. This was going to be the first time that I was going to meet anyone in her family. I thought this was an important step for us.

The wedding and the reception were at a fancy hotel downtown. Carla was one of her sister's bridesmaids, and she went home a couple of days before the wedding for all the festivities scheduled, including the bridal shower. I drove in the day before and stayed in my own hotel room, which she had arranged for me.

I met almost everyone at the rehearsal dinner Friday night, which was at a country club. In addition to her parents and her sister, Carla had an older brother, Chris. He was a pharmacist. Her sister, Christina, was a nurse and her fiancé, Eric, who was a white guy from Long Island, had just graduated from medical school. Although I felt a little out of place, everyone was very nice.

"Daddy, I want you to meet somebody," Carla said. "This is Sam Hicks."

"Hello, Sam," her father replied and smiled warmly. "Glad that you could make it."

We shook hands. He was a middled-aged, brown-skinned man of average height and weight. His short hair was just beginning to gray on the sides. He wore dark-framed glasses and was well groomed.

"Thank you," I spoke. "It is nice to meet you."

"It's nice to finally meet you too. I have heard good things."

"Same here," I managed to say.

"So, you are a lawyer, right? Legal Aid."

"Yes, I'm in the public defender's office."

"I must say that sounds so fascinating to me," he remarked. "Carla tells us that you go to court and try criminal cases. She said that you are very talented."

"What I am is very busy," I remarked.

"I would imagine that you are," Mr. Jenkins replied. "At one time, I wanted to be an attorney."

"I didn't know that" Carla interjected.

"It was a long time ago, before you kids were born," he stated. "I was always interested in government. I naively wanted to change the world."

"And so, you became an oral surgeon?" she questioned and squinched up her face.

"Yes, and now I'll have you know that I am saving the world one root canal at a time," he joked.

We laughed.

"Sam, do you golf?" he asked.

"No. I have never tried it."

"Well, I can see now that we are going to have to get you with the program," he suggested. "I spend so much money at this club that I have a key to get in whenever I want to. It's like my home away from home."

"I don't think Mom would appreciate you saying that" Carla said.

"Yeah, well she came here and golfed on *my* birthday! If I did that to her, she would have had me hog-tied in the streets."

"I think you both have issues," Carla proclaimed.

"Look, all I'm saying is, Sam, if you want to learn how to golf, then I'm your man," he offered.

"Thank you," I said. "I will keep that in mind."

There were about fifty people at the rehearsal dinner. Over half of them were white. I met most of them. The good thing was that I didn't have to spend too much time with any one person. I wasn't the best at small talk. I only briefly met the bride and groom, who obviously were in great demand. I never got the chance to really meet Carla's mother or her brother.

The wedding ceremony the next day was beautiful. There were 250 people in attendance, which was the maximum that the ballroom could hold. The ceremony was held one floor below the ballroom. The wedding party and the bride made their entrance by walking. down a huge staircase lit by a series of chandeliers. It was spectacular and very romantic.

Carla's Uncle Sheldon officiated. Christina was a lovely bride She looked a lot like her younger sister. But I only had eyes for Carla, who was absolutely stunning in a pink off-the-shoulder sequin gown. I had to catch my breath when I first saw her walking down the stairs escorted by her brother.

I was seated at a table with her family, so I had an up-close view of everything. I sat across from her parents, but it was difficult to hear them with all of the commotion. Carla was at the head table with the bride and groom. There were white and pink roses everywhere. A band was set up in one corner of the room where there was a dance floor. I felt like I had somehow stumbled onto a Hollywood movie set.

This was only the second wedding that I had ever attended. The other one was the wedding of a law school classmate in Boston two years before. It was really nice. This wedding was even nicer than that one was. I couldn't even imagine how much it cost.

Carla's father introduced me to the table as Carla's attorney friend from Utica. She walked over once or twice, but she was mostly busy with her bridesmaid duties. I watched her from afar like a stalker. She was caught up in the moment and appeared to be having the time of her life. I enjoyed seeing her that way. I just sat there and nursed my beer mostly.

I could tell that her mother was very interested in me even though we had not really spoken. I saw her looking at me out of the corner of her eyes several times. Our eyes met a couple of times. She finally worked her way through all of the distractions and came over and sat next to me.

"Sam, I hope that you're having a good time," she said.

"Yes, I am. Thank you."

She was *very* attractive for her age. She wore a full-length mocha-colored dress with an off-the-shoulder neckline and open long sleeves. I didn't think that she looked much like her daughters. Her skin was lighter than theirs, and her features were more European. Her straight hair was pinned up in the back. Her make-up was perfection. All three of her children looked like the perfect blend of their parents.

"You are very quiet," she noted. "For some reason, I thought you would be different, since you're a trial lawyer."

"I get that a lot," I said and smiled. "But I have always been a pretty low-key kind of guy in my personal life."

"I'm glad to hear that," she offered. "Carla has always been attracted to boys who are extroverted and very much out there. She prefers the shiny nickel to the dull dime. That has gotten her in trouble at times, I think."

Her voice faded a little as she thought about what she was saying.

"I can tell that you are different," she complimented. "I'm glad. Puts my mind to ease a bit."

I wasn't sure what to say. A few questions immediately popped up in my head that I didn't think I could ask.

"Thank you," I muttered. "That's very kind of you to

say."

"I'm sorry that I didn't get the chance to meet you yesterday at dinner, but I had so many different things going on. Do you know I never got the chance to eat anything myself?"

"Oh, I completely understand," I replied. "But I was looking forward to meeting you."

"How kind of *you* to say," she repeated and smiled warmly.

She patted me on my forearm. I could smell her perfume. It was amazing!

"Have you always lived in Utica?" she wondered.

"Yes and no. I went out of state for law school. But I was raised by my grandmother in Utica."

"Do you see yourself staying there forever?"

"I honestly don't know. I never really wanted to settle back there in the first place, but it was easier to get a job there."

"I'm in real estate, and I know that the property values in Utica are shockingly low."

"Right, it's a depressed city," I explained. "There is no real industry.

"Rochester wasn't my first choice either," she shared. "My family is from Chicago. A few of them are here tonight. I like big cities with lots of things going on socially and culturally. I am really into the arts. I like places that are vibrant and active. Carla is like me in that way. My other two children are much more…"

"Jackie, they need you in the front," some woman interrupted.

"Okay," she answered. "Sam, it has been lovely talking with you. I hope that we get a chance to talk some more later."

"Yes, I hope so too."

I believed her. Unless I was really missing the mark, it felt like Mrs. Jenkins wanted some answers. She appeared to be on a mission as far as I was concerned, and it must have taken great restraint on her part to have not approached me earlier. Of course, Carla had spoken a lot about her family, but nothing too revealing. I was suddenly trying to remember what she had said about her mother. I was under the impression that they were very close.

Carla eventually made her way to our table. She set next to me.

"So, how are you doing?" she whispered.

"I'm good. How are you?"

I reached out and lightly touched her middle back.

"My feet hurt," she complained. "I told Christina that these shoes were going to kill my feet."

"Take them off."

"I will."

"Has my family been interrogating you with a lot of questions?"

"No, not too bad. I think they just don't want me to feel left out."

"Good," she said and sighed. "I was hoping that they wouldn't pounce on you. They're all worried about me living alone in a strange city. I keep telling them that I can take care of myself."

"It makes sense to me that they would be a little concerned. Utica doesn't have the best reputation."

"Yeah, I guess. Are you going to dance with me?"

"I thought your feet hurt?"

"They should be all right here in a minute."

"Just say when," I encouraged. "I have been saving myself for you."

I had a good time. We danced a lot with her family and friends. We had our first slow dance to a love song, and I was completely caught up. She held me tight. I knew she felt it too.

Carla's parents hosted a small party at their home after the wedding. They had a beautiful home located in the town of Webster, fifteen miles from Rochester, near Lake Ontario. It was only a small crowd, maybe fifty people. Eric and Christina were there for a few minutes before starting their honeymoon.

There were family photos everywhere, and I especially enjoyed looking at pictures of Carla growing up. Apparently, she was a cheerleader in high school. She had never mentioned it. I wanted to know everything about her.

Most of us ended up standing around the kitchen, which was a contemporary space with stone countertops and stainless-steel appliances and plumbing fixtures. There was food on the table and drinks were in another room. I only drank water. I didn't want anything alcoholic because I had to drive back to my hotel, and it had already been a full day.

It was loud, mostly just idle chatter. Carla had changed her clothes. She was wearing jeans and a Syracuse University t-shirt. I finally met her brother Chris, who was polite, but not overly engaged. Carla did most of the talking.

"Chris somehow managed to fall off the bar last night at the bachelor party and came home with a black eye," she advised. "Can you believe it? He's wearing my makeup now. Looks pretty good."

"Nobody noticed," he said.

"You're lucky Christina didn't know. She would have lost her mind."

"Could have happened to anybody," he protested. "I don't see what the big deal is."

"Yeah, it could have happened to anybody, but these things always seem to happen to you," she scolded. "I wonder why that is, Christopher?"

He rolled his eyes and stuck out his tongue.

"Sam, you should know that the women in this family love to sit around and male-bash," he said with a faint grin. "Men-haters all of them, and Carla is the worst one."

"Is that right?" she confronted.

"You should run, Sam," he joked. "Run very fast."

"I suggest you be quiet before I tell mom what you just said," she threatened. "Men haters? Give me a break!"

"Go tell," he urged. "I don't care. I'm not afraid of any of you."

"Christopher, I'm not playing!"

"See what I mean, man," he said under his breath. "Angry all the time."

I laughed. I could tell that they were close in a way that I never really was with my sisters. Clearly, every relationship in my life growing up was impacted by our living circumstances. We seemed to love differently in the Hicks' household than other people did. Arguably, it made us harder, which was necessary for survival. But we were also crippled emotionally because of it. Regardless, I was more than a little jealous of Carla's loving connection with her siblings.

After about an hour of standing around, I was ready to leave. It had been a long day. Now my feet hurt too. I was just looking for the right moment to make my exit.

"Sam, can I get you something?" Mrs. Jenkins asked.

She had changed her clothes too. She was now wearing a navy-blue pant suit and had taken her hair down and put it in a ponytail.

"Thanks, but I'm good."

"You're not driving back to Utica tonight, are you?" she wondered.

"No, I'm going back to the hotel."

"Good. I'd be worried that you might fall asleep at the wheel."

"Yeah, I know."

"Sam, do you work a lot of hours per week?" Mr. Jenkins asked from across the room.

"Uh, maybe something like sixty hours, I'd say."

"That's not too bad," he remarked. "What would you say is the racial makeup of the people you serve? Are they mostly Black?"

"Maybe fifty-fifty."

"Are most of them are guilty?" he asked.

"Guilty of something I'd say," I replied.

"What do you mean?"

"I just mean that sometimes people are not necessarily guilty of the charges filed against them, just of being stupid."

He laughed.

"I think that's probably true," he continued. "A while back, we took on this young girl from the city as an intern. She seemed nice enough. She was paid as part of some city-run program. I just had her doing office stuff, like answering the phones and filing. She lasted maybe a week before she just stopped showing up. She never called or anything. We never did find out what happened to her."

"Ah, that's too bad," some woman standing in the middle of the room chimed in.

"Tell you what I think," Mr. Jenkins spoke. "I think that these people don't really want to work. So, it doesn't make much sense to me to try to force them to."

"I don't know," I reluctantly responded. "A lot of people we represent don't see the point of working every day at some low paying dead-end job if they still can't get ahead. I bet the city wasn't paying her that much. And they don't see the point of staying in school or getting themselves educated if at the end of the day they don't have anything to show for it in the short run."

"Excuse me for saying, but I think that's nonsense," he answered. "We all start somewhere. God helps them who help themselves. Isn't that right? And a handout is not the best way to help anyone because it keeps them dependent on others."

"I don't necessarily disagree with you," I obliged. "But I do think that throwing people lifelines is a good thing to do. It's just that sometimes we fall so deep, and things get so dark that we can't even see what is directly in front of us. The deep water is also the darkest."

"Well, all I know is I had to work hard for everything I have," he asserted. "No one ever gave me anything. My father taught us that and I passed that on to my children. Sounds to me like you work hard too, so you know where I'm coming from. Am I wrong?"

"No, I know I'm blessed," I acknowledged. "I just want to help other people who I can clearly see are hurting and lost."

"Sam, I can tell that you are a good man," he hedged. "I just hope that you aren't wasting your time. You know, time is a commodity that we don't get back. You're only young once, and when it's gone, it's gone."

"I for one like what you said, Sam," Mrs. Jenkins spoke out. "I wish that more people were selfless like you. I think you should be commended."

"Thank you," I replied cautiously. "But I don't really do that much."

It felt like every eye in the room was focused on me, like a pride of lions on a wildebeest. It was intense.

"I'm sure you help a lot of people," she reassured.

"On that note, I think *you* should get back to the hotel," Carla said and turned and rubbed my right forearm. "It's getting late. Come on, I'll walk you out."

She took my hand.

"You're probably right," I agreed. "It was such a pleasure meeting everyone."

There was a small chorus of goodbyes as we turned and walked hand in hand toward the front door.

"You, okay?" she wondered.

"Yes, I'll be all right. The hotel is not far."

"No, I mean are you okay about what my dad just said. I know how he comes off sometimes."

"Oh yeah," I lied. "Don't worry about it. I understand where he is coming from."

"I just don't want you to get the wrong impression," she said. "He's harmless."

"Like I said, not a problem. Please don't worry."

I pulled her close and kissed her gently on the side of her face.

"Excuse me," a man spoke as he approached us from behind.

It was the reverend who performed the ceremony. He was still wearing his suit, but he had taken off his tie. I never saw him again after he prayed at the beginning of the reception. I didn't know that he came to the house.

"I don't believe that we have met. My name is Sheldon Jenkins."

He looked a lot like his brother. But the pastor was a couple of inches taller and very thin. They wore the same glasses. I wondered which one was older.

"Oh, this is my uncle," Carla spoke. "I told you about him."

"Yes, you did," I said and extended my hand. "I'm Sam Hicks. It was a nice ceremony."

"Thank you, Sam Hicks" he replied. "These things always take on added meaning when the people getting married are someone you really care about. Christina and Carla are like my own daughters."

"I'm surprised you are still here," she stated. "Aren't you going to have a hard time getting up for church tomorrow?"

"I'm not scheduled to preach, so I can sleep in a little."

"I'm glad you came back."

"I just had to go pray for one of our members who is in the hospital," he replied. "It took longer than I thought."

"At least you made it," she commented.

"This is your young man, Carla?"

"Yes," she whispered.

She only hesitated slightly that I noticed.

"I just wanted to tell you how impressed I am with you," he began. "I heard what you just said. I don't agree with my brother on a lot of things, and this is one of them. My father was a surgeon, and he gave us a big head start in almost every way. So, your point was well taken."

"Thank you."

"Don't mention it. I pastor a small church in the inner-city of Rochester. My congregation is made up of people who don't have much by the world's standards. We are working-class people struggling to survive at or below the poverty level. But we love the Lord. I have several members who have been to jail and have struggled with drugs and other vices. I have lost count of the number of young Black boys I have eulogized just this year alone, who were murdered on our streets. Several of them I knew personally."

"Oh, I'm sorry to hear that," I said.

"The Bible doesn't tell us to help ourselves, at least not the way Charles means," he instructed. "We are supposed to love other people more than ourselves. And Jesus stressed that we are to especially remember the poor."

"People give to the poor during a natural disaster like a hurricane or something, or at Christmas time, putting money in the red kettle at the mall, but those things are just a drop in the bucket," I boldly commented. "No pun intended."

"Yes, yes, that's how I see it too," he agreed. "The city and the state just throw a little bit of money our way with programs that don't work just to appease their own consciences and to get reelected."

"I see a lot of pain," I said. "That's all that I was trying to say in there."

"I'm sure you do," he acknowledged. "If you see it, then you know that God sees it too."

"Then why doesn't he do anything about it?" I spoke before I knew it. "This whole world seems broken, hardly worth living in."

"I hear people say that a lot," Pastor Jenkins acknowledged. "But we have to be careful about exalting our limited understanding over the knowledge and judgments of God."

The pastor looked a little sad. He looked tired too.

"Excuse me for saying this reverend, but it seems like God has forgotten about the poor himself."

"Forgotten?" the pastor asked and looked dumbfounded.

"That's just the way it looks from my perspective," I shifted. "I'm just a public defender, but things are really bad, and they are only getting worse. Like you said, people are dying every day"

"Yeah, I know," he acknowledged. "But that's why *He* sent us people like *you*."

"*Me*?" I questioned.

"That fire in your belly was divinely sent. You mean you didn't know?"

He leaned in.

I was caught completely off guard. I suddenly felt seriously dizzy. My mind was also searching frantically for something to say in response. But I was left speechless. So, I just stood there, transparent, and exposed.

He just smiled knowingly to himself.

"Listen Sam, it ain't over yet," he spoke and chuckled slightly. "God is still on the throne. Maybe you should read the end of the book. I don't want to spoil it for you, but we win!"

"Right," was all I managed to say.

"I know that you are trying to get out of here," the pastor spoke. "So, I don't want to keep you any longer. I just wanted to shake your hand. It was very nice meeting you, son."

He turned and walked away.

Chapter 16

I got a new case. At first, I was very excited about it. I didn't know all the details, but they said it was a kidnapping. The closest thing that I had ever had to kidnapping was a case where a guy got into a fight with his girlfriend and then forcibly restrained her when she tried to leave. That kidnapping charge ended up getting dismissed, and he pleaded guilty to an assault. So, this was something different for me. I wanted exposure to a lot of different things.

But this case turned out to be much more than I had bargained for. The defendant was Joshua Weeks. He was arrested by the state police after a seven-hour manhunt through the woods near the rural town of Boonville located in the northern part of the county. The search ensued following a complaint received from a woman reporting that she and her twenty-one-year-old daughter, as well as her daughter's twenty-year-old friend, were held at knifepoint in her home for several hours. Both of the two younger women were sexually assaulted.

Apparently, the news coverage of the search was extensive. Somehow, I missed all of it. Typically, I only watched the local news when Carla had a story airing, and she hadn't had anything in over a week. I ended up watching the videos of the manhunt in shock. Only then did I realize just how big this case was going to be. It looked like something you would see in a movie. They showed a police helicopter circling overhead trying to find the suspect, along with a search crew going door to door.

According to the police report, they found Joshua Weeks hiding in an old, elevated hunting blind. He surrendered without incident. Being a typical spring in upstate New York, it had rained the whole time, which had made tracking him more difficult. His only complaints at the time of his arrest were that he was cold and hungry. He was taken to the state police barracks, given lunch, and interrogated for hours. Ultimately, he made a written confession and was thereafter transported to the county jail.

I met Joshua for the first time in the hold room at the county courthouse He was a thirty-eight-year-old, bearded, bald, white guy who appeared to be about 5'10" tall. He was thick and muscular. His upper body, including his neck, was covered in tattoos. I had just enough time to introduce myself and shake his hand before they told me that the judge was ready for us. He showed no expression, and he didn't say a word.

No bail was set for Joshua in city court when he was first arraigned there. The case was presented to the grand jury the next day, and he was being arraigned in county court within a week of his capture. This was a lot faster than normal. It usually took several weeks to get to this point in the process. My guess was that maybe they wanted to have the victims testify there as soon as possible before they had too much time to think about all that had happened. Regardless, I had never seen or heard of a case moving this fast before.

The courtroom was almost empty for the arraignment. I wasn't sure why that was until I remembered that the indictment was sealed. It was also the longest indictment that I had ever seen—thirty-two counts! Most of them were sex offenses. My head was spinning.

Once court was in session, I immediately waived the reading of the indictment and entered a plea of not guilty to each count. Without looking up, Judge Lombardi encouraged me to bring a bail motion, which we all knew would be a complete waste of time because there wasn't a chance in hell that my client was ever going to be able to make any bail he would set.

I asked for a copy of Joshua's written statement as soon as possible. That is when Joe Bartolotta immediately walked over to where I was standing and handed it to me. There was a sly grin on his face, and he seemed pleased with himself. I really didn't understand why.

Joe also gave me a copy of Joshua's criminal record, which was lengthy. He had several felony convictions, including two rapes and two serious assaults against women. He also had an extensive juvenile record. At the time of his recent arrest, he was on parole, having been released from prison just a month ago. Judge Lombardi unsealed the indictment at the end of the arraignment.

When I got back to the office, I headed directly to Teresa's office. The door was opened, and she was sitting at her desk reading.

"I just finished with the arraignment," I said anxiously.

"Oh yeah?" she responded. "How did it go?"

"He's a white supremacist!"

"Really?"

"You're going to tell me you didn't know?" I questioned.

"Actually, I didn't know that," she refuted. "How would I?"

"Well, I can't do this. You need to reassign him to someone else."

"Why?" she inquired.

"You're kidding me, right?" I questioned. "Did you hear what I said? This guy is a hardcore bigot. He looked like something right out of *Mississippi Burning*."

"Did he tell you that he didn't want you representing him?"

"No, not yet," I admitted. "But he will!"

"How do you know that?"

"How can you say that?" I argued. "Even if by some crazy chance, he doesn't have a problem with me, I have a problem with him—a *big* problem! Nothing about this makes sense and I don't understand why you…"

"Sam, are you a racist?"

"What?"

"You heard me. Are you a bigot too?" she pressed.

I was running out of air, and I was trying to catch my breath. I wanted to go into one of my rants, but I wisely managed to hold back.

"No, I mean no… I mean not like him!"

"Then if it doesn't matter to him, then why would it matter to you? Who is the bigger man?"

I paused for a moment to process her point.

"I'm sorry, but I'm not buying any of this," I persisted. "It probably does matter to him. I only saw him alone for a second. He hasn't had enough time to react to me. I'm pretty sure he never had a Black attorney before, and you know that this case is going to be a real bear with the press and all and …"

"Sam, I think you are overreacting," she calmly stated. "You need to slow down and step back and get some perspective. Do me a favor: just go see him. Let's see what happens with him. You never know."

She looked me directly in my eyes. I thought she looked old.

"Okay, I'll go and see him," I reluctantly agreed. "But…"

"Good. You do that," she flatly stated. "But let me remind you that you are not the only lawyer who works here, just the only Black one. Everyone else regularly represents people of different races, people who don't necessarily care for them for questionable reasons. This isn't the dating game."

"Yeah, but this is different," I maintained.

"Oh really? How so? The victims here are not Black, right? They're white. It wasn't a crime where race was a factor."

I refused to take the bait, but the quiet storm rising inside my gut was reaching dangerous wind levels. It seemed that everyone who I worked with thought they understood what it was like to be me and knew exactly what was best for me. I was growing tired of being held to a different standard than everybody else, and frankly of being patronized.

"So, you are telling me that if he doesn't want me, then you will reassign him?" I shifted.

"Go see him, and we will talk," she reasserted.

I walked out angry. I agreed that some of our Black clients weren't exactly tickled pink to have a white public defender, but Black people in this country were used to being treated by white professionals in all fields. This was different, and Teresa knew it. I had never refused any case that she had assigned to me. But me representing a member of a hate group that has targeted Black people for over a century was an obvious conflict of interest. I also feared that I would be rebuked by other Black people as well.

Amy, our receptionist said the press called for me all afternoon. She gave me the written messages on a small note pad. I didn't look at them. I had no intention of returning any of their calls. We almost never spoke to the press about any of our cases. Unlike some private attorneys, who played up to reporters every chance they got, we never thought we had much to gain by doing that.

I couldn't see how visiting Joshua at the jail could possibly go well for me either. Generally, I didn't like to procrastinate, but sometimes the act of doing certain things weighed heavy on my mind like a ton of bricks. This was one of those things. The plan was to go on Saturday. I didn't go until Wednesday.

<hr>

For some reason, Joshua looked different to me when he walked into the visiting room than he looked in court. He wasn't bad looking, but he did have that institutional look, meaning he clearly was uncomfortable in his own skin, like a stranger on foreign soil. None of these hardcore guys could easily blend in society. When I told him to take the chair across from me, he immediately complied and put his head down.

"Hi," I said.

He slowly lifted his head and his eyes met mine.

I didn't notice his eyes before. They were two different colors: one was gray, and one was brown. I had seen that in dogs before, but never in a person. His eye lids were reddened and thick. The added combination of his bald head and his ghostly-white complexion made his eyes really pop, and it felt like they were drawing me in against my will. I was unexpectantly shaking inside, and I fought hard against them.

"Like I told you in court, my name is Sam Hicks, and I have been assigned to represent you," I spoke out and cleared my throat. "These are serious charges against you. They could send you back to prison for the rest of your life. Do you understand?"

He nodded his head. He was staring hard. It felt like he saw through to the heart of me. Suddenly, the air was thick.

I shifted again in my chair.

"Your bail is now set at $500,000 cash or a million dollars bond," I continued. "Do you want me to bring a motion to try to get it lowered a little?"

He just shrugged his shoulders, leaned back, and

crossed his arms. I got a good look at his tattoos.

"Is there anyone in your family who could maybe help you?"

"No," he finally responded.

"Are you okay? Do you need a doctor or anybody"?

"No."

"I have a written statement here with your signature on it that you gave to the state police, do you remember signing this?"

"Yes, I remember."

"Is this your signature?"

I leaned across the table, and he looked hard at the document. He squinched his eyes trying to read. It appeared that his eyesight might not be that good.

"Yeah."

"Did you read this statement before you signed it?'

"No"

"Here, read it to yourself," I insisted. "Take your time."

He took it and began to read it to himself. I welcomed the silence. I was struggling for some reason to settle down. He seemed to be reading at a normal pace. At one point, he looked up quickly and rested his gaze on me.

"Is something wrong?" I asked.

"I didn't say this stuff," he said in earnest.

"What stuff?"

I stood up and walked behind him. I was now looking over his shoulder at the document.

"Here," he said and pointed.

I read aloud:

*I don't want to go back to prison with all these f*****g black n****s*

*and sp**s. I'd rather kill myself then have to live with these people again.*

It is cruel and unusual punishment to force any red-blooded white man

to have to live like this in our own country. It's against the constitution
too. When will America wake up?

"Oh, okay," I said. "The police like to add things to the statements just to make the person look bad to the jury. Don't worry about it. Is there anything else that you see that is out of line with what you said?"

"No, but I know I never said that," he maintained.

"Okay, I got it. Did they read you your rights before you signed it? Did they tell you about your right to remain silent and not talk to them?"

"No."

"But you already knew about your rights," I argued. "This wasn't your first time?"

"Yeah, I knew," he admitted.

"Then why talk to them?"

He responded only with an eerie grin. My still shaking insides were becoming a major distraction for me.

"Did they threaten you in any way?" I forged ahead.

"No."

"Then I don't get it," I pressed.

"It doesn't matter," he voiced.

"Did anyone make you any promises? Is that why?"

He shook his head no.

"Just about the food," he offered.

"Food?"

"To get me food when we were done."

"Did they give you anything to eat?" I asked.

"Yes, they got me McDonald's. I liked it."

I looked at him in disbelief. Nothing was adding up. He was no dummy. I felt like he was playing with me for some reason.

"Okay," I said and shifted once again in my seat. "There is all this stuff about climbing in the widow and using black electrical tape to tie people up?"

Joshua just let the question hover in the air.

"There were three women in the house?" I resumed. "It says here that one of them used to be married to your brother. Is that true?"

"Yeah, she was married to my brother Stevie."

"They are not married anymore? They are divorced?"

"Yeah."

"Did you get along with her when they were married?

"Who me?" he responded and raised his eyebrows.

"Yes," I pushed.

"She's a liar," he said dryly.

"Did she ever lie about you?"

"No."

"What about the other two women?" I asked.

"What about them?" he questioned.

"Did you know them before?"

"Lisa. I knew Lisa. Not the other one."

"You're her uncle."

"Maybe. I don't know."

"Do you remember what happened in the house?"

"No. I was drunk."

"Do you remember anything at all?"

"No."

"This says that you forced your way into the house and tied them up in different rooms. You then sexually assaulted Lisa and her friend repeatedly for several hours. You then ran out of the house into the woods, and the state police found you hiding about two miles away. Do you remember doing any of this?

"No. I don't remember."

"What do you remember?"

He only hesitated slightly.

"Um…faces," he muttered. "And…commotion like."

"Commotion? Do you remember beating your ex-sister-in-law with a belt?"

"Nope."

"Do you remember pulling down your pants and defecating on her bed?"

"No."

"Do you remember choking her?"

"No. I don't."

"Were you angry with her about something?"

"Angry? No, I wasn't angry."

"Then why did you do it?"

"I don't know that I did."

"But you remembered a lot more when you spoke to the police?" I pointed out. "It's all in here, but now you don't remember any of it."

"No, I didn't," he disagreed.

"What do you mean?"

"I only pretended to remember."

"But why would you do that?" I wondered aloud. "Why wouldn't you just tell them you didn't remember anything? Wouldn't that have been easier?"

"No reason. I just did."

"Okay…How much did you drink before all this happened?"

"I don't remember."

"Were you drinking with other people?"

"No."

"Where were you drinking?"

"At my mom's house."

"Was your mother there?"

"No, she wasn't home."

"What were you drinking?"

"I only drink beer."

"Where did you get the beer from?"

"I bought it."

"Where?"

"I don't remember."

"Does your mother live in Boonville?"

"Trenton."

"Is that where you are from?"

"Yes, Trenton."

"And is that where you went to high school?"

"Holland Patent. I played football," he bragged.

"Did you graduate?"

"No."

"How did you get to Boonville that night?"

"I don't remember."

"That's like twenty miles or something, right?"

"Yes."

"And you didn't have a car?"

"No."

"What is the last thing you do remember?"

"Drinking beer at home."

"How long have you had a drinking problem?"

"Um…I had my first beer when I was seven," he boasted. "That's all I can say."

"And from that point, were you a regular drinker?"

"Uh…my father always let me finish off his beers. Sometimes I would steal a can or two."

"Was this the first time that you were drinking since you were released from prison?"

"No."

"Do you remember getting arrested by the state police?"

"Yes, I was in the tree. They had a police dog—a big ole German shepherd. That sucker was big!"

"And you weren't roughed up?"

"No."

"Okay, I think I have enough information for now. Is there anything you want to ask me?"

"Uh…no."

He shook his head and glanced at me quickly before lowering his eyes. I could tell that he was thinking about something, even though his countenance was blank as he tilted his head forward slightly. Clearly, he was used to holding back.

"You sure, anything at all?" I urged. "Most people have questions."

"No," he whispered quietly.

"Okay then. Thank you. I'll be in touch."

"When will I see you again?" he wondered as he stood up.

"Hard to say. I will check-in with you as things progress. You know if you need to see me, all you have to do is put out a slip."

"Okay."

I sat there alone for several minutes jotting down my notes and trying to gather my thoughts. I left the jail still not knowing what to think. Joshua was very different than I thought he would be. I expected him to be over-the-top emotionally and consumed with hate. He wasn't anything like that. I was prepared to defend myself against a barrage of personal insults, not necessarily racial, and demands to do more to help him. It was common for these guys to unleash on us at the beginning. They pretended to be offended at the very idea of being held in custody. It was kind of a fake persona that they all wore like a Broadway actor on stage. Joshua was very constrained compared to most of our other persistent offenders. I couldn't read him, and I found that to be more than a little unsettling.

———— • ● • ————

I waited for Teresa to seek me out. I wasn't being defiant; I just wasn't sure what to say to her. I figured this soup needed more time to simmer and thicken.

"How was your visit with Weeks?" She finally sought me out a few days after my jail visit and was standing just outside my office door.

"Oh, better than I expected, I guess."

"Is he asking that he be assigned a white lawyer?"

"No, not right now," I admitted. "He's kind of a scary dude."

"I'm not surprised to hear that."

"I thought he'd be crazy, but it's like he has no feelings at all. He was not remorseful or embarrassed or overly concerned about the charges. It's almost like he's having fun with all of this."

"Yeah, I get that," she replied. "I think the guys like that who are devoid of emotion or empathy are the most dangerous. They are the serial killers and rapists."

"Well, he's definitely a serial rapist," I reflected. "It's hard to believe that one guy could even physically do all the stuff he did in that house that night to those poor women."

"So, you still want off this case?"

"Uh, I don't know."

"What do you mean?"

"I'm still not really comfortable with it, but this is a pretty clearcut case," I explained. "There is no question about the identity of the assailant because he knew the victims personally and he signed a detailed confession. They have the right guy. I'm not seeing any defense here, so the offer from the DA is going to be pretty steep, something like a life sentence, and we are going to have to take it. So, it probably doesn't really matter who represents him in the long run."

"Right. That's all true, but..."

"And I heard what you said before about representing people who may not like you," I added. "You have a point."

"But I do understand your reservations, Sam," she acknowledged. "Honestly, I really do get it."

"I appreciate it," I said. "I just don't want to be second-guessed or be the reason that the plea is overturned on appeal with someone arguing that I never should have handled this case in the first place because there was a clear conflict of interest."

"I really don't see that happening," Teresa surmised. "But you know where I am if we need to talk."

Chapter 17

Generally, I didn't talk to Carla about my cases. For one thing, she worked for a news channel. I had to be careful about revealing too much. But more than anything, I wanted to keep the ugly stuff that I saw and dealt with daily far away from her. I wanted to protect her, and I needed her to also help me forget. I didn't want my two worlds to collide.

"How come you didn't tell me that you are representing that guy who they were looking for with the helicopter?" she wondered.

She was sitting up in bed, and I was getting dressed.

"No reason," I replied. "I was just assigned the case."

"Have you spoken to him?"

"Yes, once," I replied. "He's quite the character. He's not somebody anybody should mess with."

"He looked deranged in the clips that I saw."

"Let me just say that I think that there is a lot going on there," I expressed. "He would make a great case study for someone."

"You need to be careful," she remarked. "He sounds dangerous."

"I'm not afraid of him. At this point, I'm all he's got."

"But does he understand that?" she wisely questioned.

"I think so," I responded slowly. "He's very intelligent; he's just odd. I think he's a white supremacist or something. He said some crazy stuff when he was arrested, and I think I saw a swastika tattoo on the inside of his wrist. He certainly looks the part. But he doesn't want me to know about that side of him because he thinks I won't want to help him. I don't get it. I think he wants me to represent him for some reason."

"He really wants a Black attorney?" she asked in disbelief.

"Yeah, sometimes I think white people who act racist know down deep that it's all just a bunch of nonsense, but they need it in order to feel good about themselves. Once the door is opened, the hate takes over and becomes ingrained."

I sat down on the edge of the bed and reached for my shoes and socks.

"I don't know if I believe that or not," she countered. "Maybe their actions reveal what has been hidden in their hearts all along. I think you have to believe people when they show you who they are."

"Agreed," I responded. "But I'm not sure that we are any better. I know Black people who hate white people with all their hearts and still manage to work beside them."

"At least we can understand why?"

"Maybe, but it's still wrong, and ignorant," I argued. "It's like an evil trick. They make us want to hate them. And then that hate becomes our downfall."

"So, you think that this guy doesn't really hate you because you are Black?" she asked.

"Um… that's a good question," I said. "I wouldn't go that far. He is definitely out there. He's probably full of irrational hate for a lot of people, including himself."

"Even more reason to be careful," she opined. "He's got nothing to lose by going after you."

I knew that Carla was right. Although I was not afraid that Joshua would try to physically harm me, I knew that he was no different than most of our clients who could turn against us at any moment and try to get us in trouble with the bar association—or worse. Without a doubt, he was as calculating as he was cold.

Obviously, I didn't believe his selective memory loss. I also thought that he specifically chose his victims because he knew that they were two women living alone in the house. The other young woman was just an added bonus. I suspected that there was history with his former sister-in-law or his brother that played an integral part in all of this. I just didn't know what the endgame was for him.

"Did he rape them?" Carla asked and sat straight up.

"Yes."

"Oh…bad?"

"Yes."

"All three of them?"

"Just the two young ones."

"How awful!" she voiced. "I feel so bad."

"Me too."

"I hope you lose," she stated emphatically.

"I have already lost," I replied matter-of-factly.

Joshua's prison record was replete with rules violations, including fights and assaults on staff. I requested a copy of his medical and mental health records from the NYS Department of Corrections as well. I really wanted to see his mental health records. If nothing else, it had to be interesting reading.

He last served a ten-year bid for rape in the second degree stemming from an attack on a woman outside a bar in Remsen, New York. Apparently, he knew the victim there too, and he was able to get a good deal in exchange for his guilty plea. I wanted to see the confidential pre-sentence report from that case to get an idea of his family life, but it wasn't in his prison file and the probation department that prepared it claimed that they couldn't find it.

When I called Joshua's mother, she hung up on me. I

called her right back, and she didn't pick up. I wasn't surprised in the least that she wasn't interested in helping her son. What he did to those women, while living with her, was incomprehensible. She gave birth to a psycho, and that fact probably tormented her regularly. Regardless, I just wanted to cover all my bases.

I filed with the court my typical pre-trial motions, including a motion to suppress the statement that Joshua made as being coerced and illegally obtained. They were just boilerplate, and I didn't expect to win any of them. Again, I just needed to protect myself.

Further, because Joshua clearly understood the nature of the charges against him and he could help in his defense, we couldn't argue in good faith that he wasn't mentally competent to stand trial. Even if he was heavily intoxicated at the time of the attacks, voluntary intoxication was not a viable defense in New York State. In many ways, this was one of the easiest cases that I had because there was literally nothing to say on his behalf.

Local attorneys kept coming up to me asking me questions about this case. For the most part, they just wanted to commensurate with me because the truth is that this was a case that no lawyer would voluntarily want to handle, especially for free. Considering all the public interest, it was just a hot mess. I feared that I would forever be known as the guy who represented one of the worst offenders to ever be prosecuted in Utica.

Notwithstanding, I decided to just take it day by day. Joshua Weeks was not my only client. The work remained a grind, and I was still losing cases left and right. I needed to manage the stress of it all better. I started jogging, which is something I never thought that I would do. Not being the athletic type, I always hated running as a kid in gym class. But it helped. I suddenly understood what people liked about it. I was learning how to wind my body down and to free my mind.

———•●•———

Mama loved her birthday and always threw her own party. She wanted me to come to dinner at her house. She also invited my girlfriend, but fortunately, Carla had to work. I went by myself and brought a gift from the both of us.

There were seven people there when I arrived. They were all women from Cornhill. I was disappointed when my mother arrived with her new "friend." Apparently, she now preferred women sexually, and the two had been dating for about six months. Mama told me about it a week before and thought it was funny. Everyone there was a little uncomfortable and shied away from the couple.

"So how are you doing, Sam?" Janet Hicks asked.

"I'm good. How are you?"

"You know how I do," she remarked and smiled bright.

She looked the same. One thing I can say about my mother is she didn't really show her age. She always wore her hair in long braids that hung down to the middle of her back. She was also wearing a jean dress and brown ankle boots.

"Have you met my friend, Kamika?"

"No. Hi, Kamika," I said. "It's nice to meet you."

"It's nice to meet you too" she replied.

Kamika looked to be much younger than my mother. She was about twenty-five years old and approximately 5'6." She was thin and wore a green camouflage jacket, brown slacks, and a pair of brown Timberland boots. She also had a yellow scarf on her head that covered her scalp completely. I had no idea what my mother was thinking bringing Kamika around Mama.

"Janet, baby you didn't tell me that your son is so handsome!" Kamika remarked.

"He's a big-time lawyer too in the public defender's office. He's my mother's pride and joy. Yes, he is!"

"I bet he is," Kamika said with a silly grin.

Her smile revealed that her teeth were already badly yellowed. No doubt the result of years of chain smoking, which also was evidenced by the nicotine smell she carried.

"Have you heard from Tanya and Tasha?" Janet Hicks inquired.

"No, they never really ever call me."

"They say the same thing about you," she contended.

"Well, they are the ones who moved away, not me," I shot back. "The phone works both ways. They don't really ever call Mama either."

"Mama said that you are going with that pretty Black girl on the news?"

"Yes, I am."

"Is she nice?"

"Yeah, she's nice. She would have come tonight but she had to work."

"You gonna marry her?"

"We haven't talked about that," I revealed "We haven't been together long enough to even think about marriage."

"Well, you better hurry up and start thinking about it before she leaves yo ass," she said and laughed hearty.

Kamika laughed too.

"And you'd like that, wouldn't you?" I followed up. "If she left my ass?"

Janet Hicks was taken aback and just glared at me for a second.

"See, Mama got you all sensitive like that," she contended. "I haven't seen you in a while, and I was just trying to catch up and make conversation. You always so uppity like."

I didn't know what to say. Or rather, I couldn't think of anything that was worth saying to her. My mother was still the only person in the world who could really get to me. No matter how hard I tried to ignore her, she always found a way to reinjure my fragile psyche. I just stood there and waited for the right moment to get away from her.

Fortunately, Mama was my mother's nemesis, and it was her day, so she was in rare form. Mama took an instant dislike to Kamika, who she kept calling "Bruh." Every time Janet tried to take the floor or lead the conversation, Mama shot her down. It wasn't long before my mother and her lover were relegated to the front hall by themselves.

There ended up being around twenty people in attendance altogether, including a couple of small children. The conversation that night was loud and raucous. It went from idle gossip about people in the hood to race and politics. And no one really knew what they were talking about. Mama still hated former President Reagan and did a mean impression of him supposedly lying during a press conference. It was hilarious and spawned other impressions of other famous people by some of the guests. Mama was having a good time, and that's all I really cared about.

One of the hazards that comes when people know that you are a lawyer was that someone was always walking up and asking for legal advice. The problem with that is that being a criminal attorney, I didn't really know a lot about other areas of the law, such as bankruptcy and family court. But people asked me about those things all of the time.

Miss Lawrence from across the street somehow managed to corner me in the kitchen. I was just coming out of the bathroom when she made her quick approach.

"Sam, can I ask you a question?"

"Sure," I said, "What is it?"

She was heavy set woman in her mid-fifties. She raised seven children by herself. I always thought she was a good influence on my grandmother because she was averse to drama and knew her Bible. Mama seemed to really respect her.

"It's about my daughter-in-law Chanice, Rudy's wife. You remember Rudy, don't ya?"

"Yes, of course."

She seemed desperate and was speaking under her breath like she didn't want anyone else to overhear our conversation.

"She died last year," Miss Lawrence announced. "Chanice did. She was eight months pregnant, and she went to the emergency room and told them that she was having a lot of pain. They didn't believe her and just sent her home without doing anything, you know. Come to find out that she was bleeding internally. She died the next day at home. The baby died too."

"Oh, that's just horrible!" I exclaimed. "I'm so sorry."

"I know it is," she replied. "One of the worst experiences of my life."

She began to cry and dabbed at her eyes with a tissue.

"I don't understand the doctors and nurses that they got working in these hospitals," she vented. "I really don't. They are supposed to help people and instead they act like they don't care at all about anybody, especially Black people."

"That's true," I said.

"Just when I thought I had seen everything," she cried.

"I feel like that a lot too," I admitted.

"Do you think Rudy has a case against them?" she solicited. "Now he's got to raise the other three kids by himself because their mama was stolen from them. I just feel so bad for him. He's so lost."

"Sounds to me like he might have a pretty good case," I offered.

"Seems like we just can't win for losing," she expressed. "I help him out as much as I can, but I'm getting older now too and I got this bad knee. I keep the two little ones for him during the day while he's at work."

"I feel so bad.''

She just nodded her head and blew her nose. Her eyes were red and looked tired. Black people generally aged first in the eyes.

"He needs to talk to a malpractice attorney," I offered. "That's not what I do. I tell you what, I'll get you the name of someone."

"You think that you can do that for us?"

"I'll get back to you this week," I spoke. "No problem."

"Okay, I'll tell Rudy. This means so much. Thank you very much."

"You're welcome."

"I have to say that I have already had enough heartache to last me two lifetimes," she reflected.

She gave me a big hug and walked away.

I just stood there for a minute. I was more than a little spent. I didn't really know Rudy. He was rough, and we ran in completely different circles. Still, I couldn't even imagine the depth of his pain and despair. It was all so senseless. This was the stuff that fed both my repressed victim mentality and ruminating anger.

Mama was drinking. I should have guessed. She was known to partake of the sauce from time to time. However, I never liked to see it because it always made her crazy.

"Mama, it's not there," Janet shouted.

"Yes, it is," Mama refuted. "Did you look on the bottom shelf?"

"Yeah, I looked where you told me to."

"I'll look," I interjected.

I found the potato salad in the refrigerator behind the big black pot.

"I got it," I announced.

"Where was it?" Mama inquired. "Was it in the refrigerator where I said it was?"

"Yeah, way in the back."

"See, Janet, this is what I'm talking about with you…"

"It's not a big deal," I quickly interrupted. "I found it."

"I didn't see it," Janet argued.

"That's cause you didn't look where I told you!"

"I did look!"

"Yo mama ain't got the sense that God gave a cricket," Mama criticized and looked at me in disgust. "Tell the truth and shame the devil!"

Even I felt bad for Janet. I knew she was embarrassed. Like I said before: she shouldn't have been there.

Chapter 18

Obviously, there was a lot to dislike about my job. But this had to be the absolute worst. There I was sitting in my car on a rainy, damp day, outside a house in Cornhill looking for one of my clients who didn't show up for court. He was supposed to be sentenced today following his plea to felony assault. He was going to be sentenced to what we called a split sentence, that is, six months in jail and five years of probation. In real time, he would probably only serve four months in jail. It was a terrific deal considering that the elderly man he robbed with a knife literally had a heart attack and almost died. Judge Lombardi was furious when Tommy didn't show up and told me that I had twenty-four hours to get him in or the plea deal was off the table.

It was an old, broken-down duplex. There was a raggedy wooden fence out front that led to a set of stairs and a porch with two doors. There also was dog poop covering most of the stairs and the porch. Tied to the railing was a huge pit bull-type dog with the biggest head that I had ever seen. He started barking like crazy when I first approached. I had been sitting there for about an hour because I was afraid to go anywhere near the dog.

I was just getting ready to leave when a teenage boy walked out of one of the doors. He appeared to be in a hurry.

"Hey, excuse me," I called out through the car window. "Does Tommy Nelson live here?"

"Who?" he asked.

"Tommy Nelson. I'm his lawyer. I really need to talk to him. It's important."

"He's sleep," the boy said.

"I'm sorry to ask, but can you do me a big favor and tell him that I am here?" I begged. "Please, I would really appreciate it."

The boy rolled his eyes, sighed heavily before turning and running back into the house. He returned in less than a minute.

"He's coming," the boy indicated.

It took Tommy about ten minutes to come out. He was wearing a white V-neck t-shirt and black pants. His hair was matted about his head, and he was barefoot. His eyes were red and swollen. I suspected that he was drunk or high—or both.

"Hey, what happened to you today?"

"What?" he asked.

"You were supposed to be in court today. The judge was really mad. What happened?"

"I couldn't get there," Tommy replied defensively. "I didn't have a ride."

"Well, the judge wants you in court first thing tomorrow. He said that if you don't show up then he is going to issue a bench warrant for your arrest, and he is going to make you withdraw your plea and go to trial."

Tommy didn't say a word. He just looked at me as if he didn't have a clue what I was talking about.

"Do you understand what I'm telling you?" I pressed. "If you don't show up again you are going to go to prison for a long time."

"Can I come later? Like next week?"

"No, this is it. You agreed to the deal. Remember, you wanted to be home by Christmas? I worked hard on this deal for you."

He put his head down.

"So, you gonna do this or not?" I pressed. "I need to know right now whether I need to meet you there."

"…Okay…Yeah," he mumbled.

"Don't be late," I urged. "It's at 10:00 a.m. We got a good deal. It would be crazy to mess it up now."

As I drove away, I had no idea if Tommy would show up the next day or not. Most of these guys didn't think rationally. There can't be too many things more frustrating than trying to reason with people who either refuse to be or are incapable of being reasonable. Admittedly, it is unfair to label individuals or to group everyone together. But I just saw it too many times. Most of our clients were actively fighting against their own best interest. It was like they were blinded in many respects.

Fortunately, Tommy somehow found his way to court like he said he would, and his sentencing went off without incident. However, I felt a little like the angel of death whose role it was to stand by and watch as harsh judgment was pronounced on the weak and the wicked. I can't speak for the judges or the people in the district attorney's office, but there was nothing satisfying or rewarding about being there for us.

The fact is that, except for possibly China, the United States has more incarcerated persons than any other country in the world. Even if we accepted, for the sake of argument, that Black people commited more violent crimes in this country than white people, nearly all the underlying contributing factors, such as poverty and the breakdown of the Black family, flow directly from a broken society built, in large part, upon slavery. Middle-class and upper-class people of all races don't generally rob old people at knife point.

The undeniable fact is that Black people, as a race, have not recovered fully from the effects of having been enslaved and purposely held down. Unfortunately, this is true even for those of us who like to tell ourselves otherwise.

———•●•———

I was getting ready to leave the office for the day when someone showed up and wanted to speak to me. Amy didn't get a name. I came out to find a thirty-something white woman sitting in the lobby.

"Can I help you?" I asked.

"Yes, are you Sam Hicks?"

"Yes, I am."

"I'm Virginia Weeks. My brother is Joshua Weeks."

I did a double take. I didn't know that Joshua had a sister. She bore no resemblance to her brother. She was pale skinned, wafer thin with shoulder-length straight hair. She looked very plain, like a stereotypical librarian or schoolteacher of old. I brought her into our small conference room.

"How can I help you?"

"Ah… I wanted to see if there was anything that I could do to help my brother."

"Like what?" I asked.

"I don't really know," she stated. "But I wanted to see what was going on."

"Well, he's at the county jail. There are thirty-two counts in the indictment. The biggest indictment that I have ever seen. Most are sex crimes."

"Yeah, I know," she replied.

"He claims that he blacked out and does not remember what happened."

"I believe that," she indicated. "You should know that I am a primary care physician. I practice in Massachusetts, in a small town outside of Boston. My entire family has addiction issues, including both of our parents."

"I tried to reach your mother, but she wouldn't talk to me."

"No, she wouldn't," she advised. "She wrote Joshua off years ago."

"Then why did she let him live with her after he got out of prison this last time?"

"Good question," she answered. "You'd have to ask her that."

"I have only met with him a couple of times, but he is hard for me to read," I admitted.

"Oh, really?" she voiced and laughed to herself. "My brother is a master manipulator. He likes to play games with people. He is very bright, like my father, who was a ruthless man. But there is something very seductive about Joshua. He's got our daddy's eyes with a black heart. One must be careful."

"Are you here to warn me?" I questioned. "Is that it?"

"No, not at all," she refuted. "I'm sure you already know enough not to fully trust him."

"Then what?"

"I love my brother," she explained. "I know that that might sound strange to you."

"No, not at all."

"I know everything we went through with our father, the beatings, the abuse… Joshua didn't get the way he is overnight or by accident. You probably don't believe this, but he was a good kid. Everyone loved him. But he was overtaken by something dark."

She appeared to be struggling to maintain her composure. Her voice broke a few times, but she never cried.

"Something like what?" I wondered aloud.

She merely shrugged her shoulders.

"When you are poor and uneducated like we were, just about anything can happen," she justified. "I get that he's probably a very dangerous man. They never should have let him out of prison. That's on them."

"You're probably right," I conceded. "Is that what you want? For your brother to go back to prison for the rest of his life?"

"I certainly don't think that he should be put in a position where he can hurt some more women like my poor niece," she expressed. "But I don't want him mistreated either. He's still human!"

I thought I saw a little bit of fire rise in her eyes, which fortunately for her, were less harrowing than Joshua's eyes. But I could tell that she was no wallflower.

"I think I understand," I replied.

"Are you the only lawyer who will be working on the case?" she asked.

"Yes," I answered. "Unfortunately, we don't have the luxury of assigning more than one attorney to a case."

"I see."

"Would you feel better if he had a white attorney?" I not-so-innocently solicited. "I mean, in light of the way he is?"

She had a puzzled look on her face.

"The way he is?" she repeated.

"It's no secret that he is not particularly fond of Black people," I boldly asserted.

I looked directly at her.

"Joshua doesn't have a problem with Black people," she disputed. "Who told you that?"

"I'm sorry," I replied. "But that isn't my impression. I'm pretty sure that he was heavily involved with hate groups in prison."

"I wouldn't know anything about that," she insisted. "But when he was about ten years old, he was best friends with this Black kid from New York City, who was up here for the summer as part of some fresh air program, or something. His name was Myron. I can't remember his last name for some reason... They were thick as thieves the two of them. Joshua cried like a baby when Myron went home. He was probably Joshua's closest friend ever."

"Then I don't get it," I confessed.

"I told you he likes to deceive people. He can't help himself."

We just stared at each other.

"Is there anything else that you think I ought to know?" I said to break the awkward silence.

"Not really," she answered. "But perhaps I can be a resource to you. I mean if you are interested in the truth about him."

"I am very interested. Thank you."

"Please don't tell him that we spoke," she requested. "He is a control freak, and he will be angry if he finds out that I came here."

"Okay, I won't."

"Thank you."

"But I really do appreciate you coming in," I added.

"Here is my card," she said as she reached out. "Please feel free to call me if you have any more questions."

I liked her. I was also truly fascinated by everything she said. But there was something a little off about her too—although I couldn't quite put my finger on what it was. I was just glad that I had a source who I could turn to who could possibly help me fill in some of the blanks concerning her brother. At that point, I was desperate. I was willing to take whatever help I could get.

In the end, there was no denying that this was a once-in-a-lifetime kind of case. I decided that I could either play it safe or seize the moment and run with it. Instead of worrying about what bad thing could happen, I considered that maybe I should take advantage of this unique opportunity to witness human depravity up-close from an entirely different perspective. I really had nothing to lose, and the experience could only serve to make me a better lawyer.

———— • ● • ————

Judge Lombardi wanted to do the pre-trial conference in the courtroom rather than in his chambers like he usually did. I arrived ten minutes early. There wasn't anyone else there yet. I put my file on the defense table and sat down. I wasn't really thinking about anything. Although I couldn't be positive, I thought I saw Joe exit the judge's chambers and walk speedily out a side door that led to the hall. A minute later, he walked into the back of the courtroom through the same doors that I had used to come in.

"Hi, Sam," Joe said without looking at me.

"Hi," I responded.

We sat there in silence. I knew that he was still angry about what happened with Marcus. I didn't care. It's not like we were ever really friends anyway, or that I was interested in improving our relationship. No, that ship had sailed.

The judge walked in a sat down at the bench. He was not wearing his robe, just his suit.

"I wanted to talk to you fellas about this Weeks case," the judge began. "Have you guys talked about a plea."

"No, we haven't," Joe responded.

"Okay, are you prepared to make an offer?" Judge Lombardi asked.

"No, not really," Joe advised. "All three victims are still pretty traumatized by what happened to them. I haven't been able to talk to them and clue them in."

"You should both know that I have already written a decision granting the defendant's motion to suppress the written statement the defendant signed as having been illegally obtained," the judge advised. "I'm going to file it today."

"What?" I said before I knew it.

"Yes, I am granting your motion."

"Without a hearing?" I asked.

"Yes, I don't think I need to hear from the state police. The people can object or appeal if they want to, but that's going to be my decision."

I couldn't believe my ears. I knew immediately what was happening. The district attorney's office figured that they didn't really need Joshua's statement to convict him because the evidence against him was overwhelming. So, they punted in order to avoid having to put someone from the state police on the stand at a hearing to talk about the investigation. It was gamesmanship, nothing more. My blood boiled. So much for the notion that justice is even handed.

The worst part was that Judge Lombardi was part of it. We rarely won suppression hearings before the judges in this county. And we definitely never won any without a hearing. I lost a lot of respect for the judge at that moment. But I'm sure he didn't really care what I thought and that his conscience didn't bother him in the least.

One mark against me was that I was hard and unforgiving toward others who have let me down. I think that it came directly from my mother and from the fact that she never loved me. I just want people to be who they say they are and do what they said they would do. I have been let down in my life more times than I can remember. But I was always harder on myself than I was on anyone else. I've always known that I could be my own worst enemy. Old habits aren't just hard to break, they own us.

———— • ● • ————

In New York State, complaints of attorney misconduct

are made to the Grievance Committee. The committee is authorized to investigate all wrongdoing committed by lawyers against their clients. A lawyer who breaches the rules of professional conduct can be reprimanded, suspended, or disbarred. Typically, the major violations are when an attorney steals money from his or her client or misappropriates it.

I received a letter from the grievance committee informing me that a complaint had been filed against me by a former client. It was my first one. I was really upset. Teresa said I was overreacting again.

The complaint came from Victor Conroy. He was a Black guy I represented on a felony burglary charge that went to trial last year. He had broken into a gas station at night and stole a bunch of petty merchandise, mostly cigarettes and candy. His criminal history consisted of just misdemeanor convictions, although he had been arrested for felonies twice before. He only lived a block from the gas station in question.

Furthermore, there was a videotaped recording of him in the act. He refused to plea to anything and wanted to go to trial. It lasted two days. The jury deliberated for one hour before finding him guilty, and I'm not sure what took them that long. Judge Mazur sentenced him to one to three years in state prison. Victor was a complete jerk and impossible to work with. I secretly wished that he had gotten more time.

The allegation in the disciplinary complaint was "ineffective assistance of counsel," which was just a catch phrase meaning my lawyer was terrible. The committee requested a written response from me within fourteen days. I provided one the next day. One month later, I received a copy of a letter sent to Victor in prison by the committee denying his grievance as without merit. Regardless, I was still very put off by the whole thing.

———•●•———

Over time I had gotten to know almost everybody who worked in the courthouse. If not by name, I knew them by sight. We all parked our cars in the same parking lot and rode the same elevators and had lunch at the same places. It was a regular soap opera too with the sheriff deputies seemingly always on the prowl for new female conquests. A couple of them really liked our secretaries and were always lurking about.

Unfortunately, the rumor mill ran amok. I always thought it harmless until it hit me head on.

"Hi, Sam," she said.

"Hey. How are you?" I responded.

She approached me as I was walking into the courthouse. I couldn't recall her name. I knew that she worked in the probation office. I remembered that she helped me once find a last known address for somebody I needed to talk with. I certainly had never interacted with her before on a personal level.

"Are you still dating Carla Jenkins from Channel 5?" she asked pointedly.

"Um…Yes, I am."

"I always thought that she is a beautiful woman. And I like the way she dresses too. Anyway, me and my husband were having dinner at Roscoe's last Friday night, you know that really fancy restaurant on Route 5 in Verona. It was our anniversary, and he surprised me and took me there. That's where we ran into Carla having a *cozy* dinner with this dashing-looking man. It just got me wondering if you two were still an item."

"He was probably just a friend from work or something like that," I replied.

"Yeah, that's probably it," she voiced meekly.

I could tell that she wasn't buying it. She was giving me a quizzical look.

"It's not really any of my business anyway," she continued.

She shrugged her shoulders after having stated the obvious. I wondered how many other people she had mentioned this to. I bet it was a lot.

"I don't know why, but I always notice these things," she told herself. "I need to learn to close my eyes or look away from some of the things I see."

Chapter 19

Carla's parents hosted a party at their home to celebrate their thirtieth wedding anniversary. She invited me. I didn't mind going. She told me after her sister's wedding that everyone in her family was very impressed with me, but I wasn't sure I believed her. That certainly wasn't the impression that I got, especially from her father.

However, I was very interested in seeing her uncle again. He made quite the impression on me. Generally, I didn't care that much for clergy. Most of the pastors in Utica didn't do much, as far as I could tell. Although I saw a few of them on the news occasionally after something bad happened, I never really saw any church do anything proactively to stop the violence or help people get jobs or better situated. It seemed like all the Black churches were struggling themselves just to stay afloat financially, and the white churches were simply missing in action.

When I was in college, I was required to take a religion class. My instructor was Professor Michael Dukes, a weird, middle-aged white man who wore clogs all year long. He was definitely not a fan of Christianity. He mostly just made fun of Christian doctrine, much of which he claimed was stolen from other ancient middle eastern religions and ultimately used to support and perpetuate ungodly state policies, such as slavery and segregation. I wasn't really swayed much by anything he said, but some of the stuff he had alleged stayed in my head and probably impacted the way I viewed the church going forward, which no doubt was his intention.

We got there early because Carla wanted to help her mother get ready. Apparently, they were expecting nearly a hundred guests. But there really wasn't anything for her to do when we got there. It was a catered affair, and the caterers were doing all the set up. Carla immediately disappeared upstairs, so I hung out alone in the den watching the big screen TV.

"Hi, Sam," Mr. Jenkins said. "I see you found my man cave."

"Hello, sir."

"Oh, please that's not necessary. Just call me Chris."

"Okay."

"Glad you could make it, man. Carla's mom will be very happy to see you. She was quite taken by you."

"It's good to be here," I expressed. "Congratulations on your anniversary."

"Thank you," he replied. "Between you and me, marriage is the hardest thing that I have ever done."

"Really?"

"Don't get me wrong. I love my wife. But it hasn't always been easy because I don't always understand what the hell she is talking about. That's very hard for me because I don't do well when things don't make sense to me. That makes me want to punt."

"I get that," I admitted. "I grew up in a house with all women and me. There was always stuff going on that was beyond my understanding."

"I don't think too many of us guys really get it, if you want to know the honest truth," he remarked. "Women interpret that as our great failure as men, but it's really a product of the fact that we are created different, and we think entirely different."

"So, it's just an issue of communication?" I wondered.

"Men are more primal than woman," he asserted. "It's a fact. That means that it's hard for us to shut down our God-given animal instinct to fight when we are attacked physically or emotionally. It doesn't matter from whom or where the assault comes. Unlike most women, men don't want to understand the threat. We want to defeat it!"

"Dad, do you want me to park in back so there's more room?" Chris interrupted as he rushed in. "Oh, hi, Sam. How are you?"

Carla's brother offered his hand, and I shook it.

"I'm good," I answered. "Nice to see you again."

"Nice to see you too," he said. "You guys hiding out already?"

"Not yet," his father responded. "I was just telling Sam here my highly acclaimed theory on the man and woman dynamics."

"Whoa, it's way too early for all that, don't you think?"

He was laughing and tilted his head slightly, looked at me, and winked.

"It's never too early to educate you young bucks on the ways of the world," the elder Jenkins insisted. "None of you know as much as you think you do."

"Well, okay, Dad, but I'm going to need a beer first."

"Yeah, I guess you're right," Mr. Jenkins conceded. "There's plenty of time for me to hold school later."

"Well, I have to move my car, so what do you want me to do?"

"You can park in the back, off the grass. Just leave room for the caterers to get out please."

It was a nice party, but I knew it would be. Everyone one was friendly. It was a racially diverse group. The food was awesome. Smooth jazz was being played throughout the house. I tried to stay in the background as much as I could. Carla was busy elsewhere, so I was left alone to mingle and find my own way.

At one point, I crossed paths with Christina.

"How's married life?" I asked.

She had her hair pulled back into a messy bun and was wearing a red dress, black tights, and black boots. Dressed like that, she looked a lot like her mother.

"Oh, it's good," Christina replied. "It's been a real adjustment for both of us because this is our first time living together. I always had my own apartment to go home to and regroup. This kind of feels like I am flying solo without a net for the first time."

"Do you think that you're finding out hidden things about him that you didn't know?"

"That's a good question," she remarked. "Let's see… I think I knew Eric well enough. He is a simple kinda guy—what you see is what you get. I am much more needy in the relationship than he is. Our schedules have been terrible. He's at the hospital now. We're like two ships passing in the night. Honestly, I think that bothers me more than him."

"I'm sure that it bothers him too, but we guys just deal with things differently."

"I don't know, maybe," she whispered.

"No, it's really true," I maintained. "Men see in black and white. Women see in color."

"You should know that me and Carla are both like that."

"Like what?"

"I just mean that we scare easily. I think it's because we're both insecure. We tend to see things that aren't always there."

"Insecure? That's funny cause that's not how I see her at all," I admitted and sighed heavily.

"That's because she doesn't like to talk about her stuff or show weakness. That's where we are different. I probably tell Eric too much. Poor guy!"

She laughed to herself.

"Well, I definitely appreciate the heads up," I spoke.

"Apparently, I need it."

"Don't take it personally," she said and smiled warmly. "All men are clueless."

She got no argument from me. I was clueless. Clearly, I didn't know what Carla was thinking most of the time. There wasn't any strife between us, but that was probably because we both tended to avoid conflict like the plague. I know I did.

For instance, it almost seemed like she had been avoiding me all night. She was quiet on the drive to Webster and couldn't wait to get away from me as soon as we arrived. Rather than ask her about it, I told myself that she was probably just tired. But she hadn't really checked on me since we arrived either. She was a lot different with me than she was at Christina's wedding. She seemed distant and her overall mood was downcast and didn't much match the occasion.

In contrast, her mother seemed to be on top of the world. Perfectly attired in a flowy, one-shoulder party dress, she moved effortlessly around the house as if she was walking on a cloud. Once more, however, I only spoke to her briefly.

"Sam, my daughter told me you were here," she said at one point during the course of the evening. "So glad you could make it.

"Thank you," I replied. It's good to see you again."

"I hope that you are enjoying yourself."

"Oh, I am. Everything is perfect."

"How sweet of you to say!" she replied. "This wasn't my idea, but the kids talked us into it. We just had Christina's wedding. I thought it might be too much too soon."

"No way!" I resisted. "Thirty years is quite an accomplishment. You deserve to be celebrated."

"I agree," she admitted. "Before we got married, I told Chris that I would kill him if he ever cheated on me. He believed me, and that's why he is still alive and walking among us."

We both laughed.

"Is that the key?" I wondered. "No cheating?"

"No, it's a lot more than that, I think," she replied. "I'd say being able to accept your partner's weaknesses is key. And let me tell you, my dear husband has a lot more of them than I do."

"That sounds right to me," I said.

"Maybe you and Carla can come to dinner sometime," she continued. "I know that you are both so busy, but I would love to get to have some real time to get to know you."

"I would like that too," I replied.

"Good. I'll work on Carla."

I ended up talking a lot to a man who golfed with Mr. Jenkins and to his wife. Jill Grossman and Fred Rubenstein were Jewish. Fred was a podiatrist. Jill was a sociology professor at State University of New York at Brockport. They were both very liberal and socially active. They were also very interested in my job and asked a lot of questions. I didn't mind at first, but I found it hard to break away from them.

"One of the things that so impresses me about Chris and Jackie is that they have defied the odds in so many ways," Jill said.

"Yes, they have," I agreed.

"They are a true success story. The divorce rate among African American couples is nearly twice that of whites in this country," she continued. "I find that to be astonishing!"

"It only makes sense," Fred added. "Socio-economic, and educational disparity have eroded the Black family. I mean, all these factors contribute to both divorce and crime rates and yet the 'alt-right' persist in the denials of what is really happening."

"It must be incredibly hard for you, Sam, witnessing the unequal treatment in the criminal justice system every day," she sympathized. "The police brutality alone must take a toll on you. I can't see how it wouldn't."

"The way I see it, I have a simple job and that job is to represent my client to the best of my ability," I presented. "I try not to focus too much on the big picture, like the politics behind it. The people who I am defending want me to keep them out of prison or get them out as soon as possible if they are already confined. That has to be the goal."

"Excuse me for saying, but isn't that a bit of a deflection?" Dr. Rubinstein questioned. "As a physician, I can't just look at treating the infection without also looking at the root cause. Otherwise, the infection is just going to come back, and it might be worse the second time around. That's how people lose their extremities, perhaps even their lives."

"What you are saying makes sense," I conceded. "But I'm more like the doctors in the ER. I treat trauma in a lot of people at the same time on an emergency basis. I'm paid by the county. Maybe attorneys in private law firms can take more time and investigate the root causes of their client's criminal and antisocial behaviors, although I bet that most don't. But I just know that I can't go there."

"I'm sorry. I didn't mean to offend you," Dr. Rubinstein stated.

"No, no, you didn't offend me at all," I reassured. "It's just that tackling issues like systematic racism and police brutality are way above my pay grade."

"But what about the psychological trauma of those things on you personally?" the professor asked. "You can't tell me that you are immune to it."

"No, I can't tell you that," I admitted with a straight face.

"Oh dear, that breaks my heart," she declared and

lightly patted me on the shoulder.

The highlight of the evening was when Carla's parents danced to their wedding song, "At Last" by Etta James. All three of their children toasted them separately after and said wonderful things about their parents. It was all very touching, and everyone seemed to be having a great time. It was inspiring to witness a successful Black couple up close.

However, I couldn't help but reflect again on how different Carla's upbringing was than mine. With us, it wasn't as much about race as it was economics. Our worldviews were entirely different based upon privilege and opportunity. I would have wagered to bet that in many respects her sister, Christina, and her white husband had more in common than I had with Carla. Those people were diamonds; I was more like glass.

Truthfully, I felt a lot like a phony who was only pretending to be someone that Carla should be interested in. I always doubted my ability to work through the problems that are inherent in all relationships because I had no real experience doing anything of the kind.

I was never taught how to compromise. For us, it was about submission. Growing up, it was Mama's way or no way. People yelled and screamed a lot, but deals were rarely ever made. Dysfunction was a part of just about everything we did, including the way we related to each other.

It sounded like Carla had a lot of old boyfriends. In comparison, I was still only crawling when it came to matters of the heart. Obviously, I knew that I had deep feelings for her, but at this point, I wasn't even sure that my feelings were fully reciprocated. Sadly, I was mostly content to just stay in this extended holding pattern with her forever.

To be clear, however, I wasn't exactly afraid of Carla hurting me. I was born on a road paved with pain and brokenness. I knew that Carla wasn't the only woman in the world, and I also believed that I could take the pain of losing her. But I was afraid that in the face of a breakup that I would be forced to accept in my heart that I was destined to always be alone, or worse yet, be second class and inferior no matter what I did, or how hard I tried.

We headed for home just after midnight. We talked about the party a little. Her uncle was a no-show. Carla said that he was a little under the weather and decided to stay home and rest. I was sorry to hear that. She claimed that she enjoyed herself, although she still seemed a bit somber to me. She eventually nodded off to sleep. I just played the radio softly. I wasn't tired in the least. My mind was racing. I couldn't shake the feeling of impending doom as my adversary and accuser in my head kept taunting me.

I ended up sleeping at Carla's apartment. She made breakfast for us Sunday morning. Her mood seemed to be much improved, and we joked about me spending so much time with Dr. Rubinstein and his wife, who apparently were notorious for holding people hostage. She said that she needed to do some research for a story she was working on, and I left around 10:00 a.m. I was still tired, so I just laid around all afternoon determined to not think about anything at all.

Chapter 20

Joshua walked in like he owned the place. It sounded like he was humming quietly to himself. He closed the door behind him and smiled broadly. Although I was already uncomfortable, I ignored his odd disposition. He sat down in the empty chair on his own initiative.

"Hi, Sam," he whispered.

"How are you?" I asked.

That was the first time that he called me by my first name. I noticed right away because it sounded like an insult the way he said it.

"Oh, I'm all right," he replied. "How are you?"

His eyes were intense again. Joshua seemed to have mastered the art of nonverbal communication. It was as if there were two conversations going on in his head at the same time because his expressions did not always match what he was saying with his words.

"I'm good too," I spoke.

"Sam, how is Carla?"

I recoiled immediately, and I felt a charge inside as my chest and my heart suddenly began to beat faster. For a second, I couldn't hear myself think. There was just a strange rushing sound of wind in my ears.

"Who?" I questioned.

"She's your girl, right? I saw her on the news."

"I don't want to talk about my personal life with you,"

I insisted. "It's not appropriate."

I was angry but did my best to hide it. Not only didn't I want Joshua to see me sweat, but I didn't want him to have that kind of control over me. He was obviously used to being the one who set the temperature in the room in his interactions with other people. That meant that I had to be bold enough to adjust the gauge when I deemed it necessary.

"I heard that about you," Joshua commented.

"You heard what, exactly?" I pressed.

I tried to look disinterested.

"Nothing bad," he said in a reassuring tone. "They say that you are a straight-up guy. That's all."

"I don't know what you mean by that," I replied abruptly and looked away from him. "But I didn't come here to talk about me. I have a couple of things to tell you."

"Please, go ahead," he directed.

"First, the judge has suppressed the statement that you signed after you were arrested. He said that it was coerced from you since you were in a weakened state having been without food and water and out in the elements for several hours."

"I never said I was coerced," Joshua reported. "Did you tell them that, Sam?"

"No, not exactly," I replied defensively. "But I did make the motion. The judge came up with the rest of it all on his own. But that means that your written statement can't be used against you at trial."

"Well, that's good, right?" he posed. "Good for you."

"Except that the ADA just informed me that they will not be making any plea offer in this case. Either we plea to the whole indictment, all thirty-two counts, or go to trial. If you do plea, then the sentence will be at the discretion of the judge, meaning he can sentence you to the maximum."

"So, it's a game, huh?" he readily grasped.

"I guess you can call it that—a wicked game for sure," I said.

"You know I love games," he said. "And those are my favorite kind."

"Well, we are going to lose either way," I argued. "I can't let you enter a plea to the entire indictment. That would be legal malpractice on my part. No, you have to go to trial."

"Isn't that my choice to make?" he resisted.

"Yes, but you would plea under these circumstances over my objection," I articulated. "Is that what you want to do? Is that what you are trying to tell me? You want to voluntarily go to prison for the rest of your life because that is essentially what would happen?"

"Don't worry, Sam," he urged. "I will never do anything that you don't want me to do."

"Am I supposed to believe that?" I asked defensively. "Because I don't!"

"I have never lied to you, Sam… well except maybe one little white lie."

Joshua pouted and extended his bottom lip like a small child begging for something.

He looked ridiculous. I was unfazed.

"What white lie?" I questioned.

"That's the point. They don't count because they are the harmless kind," he contended.

"I heard about you too," I said before I knew it. "Apparently, you like to manipulate people and play head games."

"I wonder who told you that about me," he stated. "You know, it's really sad when you can't even trust family."

"So, what gives?" I pursued. "You bored or something?"

"That's where you're wrong," Joshua defended and leaned back in his chair as he crossed both arms in front of him. "This life is nothing but a game—the whole damn thing. Take you for example, all you do is hide your true self from people. Nobody knows who you really are, Sam. Hide and Seek is your game of choice. My guess is that you are very good at it too."

"Again, I don't know what you are talking about," I argued. "I don't play games, and I definitely don't play games that hurt people!"

"See, that's where we disagree again," he played his hand and shrugged. "Some of us are just better at it than others. I have to say that my money is on you against this ADA."

"That's another lie because you don't have any money," I disputed. "If you did, then you'd have private counsel, and I wouldn't be here trying to represent you."

"It's called a figure of speech, Sam," Joshua objected. "You never heard of that?"

"Sorry, but I can't trust your words."

"I don't understand where all this hostility is coming from," he protested. "We are just having a nice friendly conversation here, attorney to client. There is no need for all this tension between us. This isn't a prize fight, you know. I already told you that you were doing a good job. I don't know what else you want from me."

"Like I said, I don't play silly games and I'm not sure that you really understand what is going on here," I countered. "This is an election year, and Judge Lombardi is up for re-election. He wants this case in the news every night. It's free publicity for him at your expense. He wants to show the world that he is tough on crime, and they are going to do everything they can to jam you up."

"I don't care what they want," Joshua said with a smirk. "I don't think they know who they are messing with."

"I don't think they care anything about you," I asserted. "The prosecutors and the judges always have the best cards. When they join forces, game over. That's what I'm trying to tell you."

"Sam, let me ask you something, do you think that these poor women who I supposedly kidnapped and had my way with want this trial splashed on the news every night?"

"I seriously doubt it."

"There you go," he declared. "Your move, counselor."

"I'm not going to further victimize these women if that is what you are suggesting!"

"I'm not suggesting any such thing," he disputed. "But I am wondering if you are open to shining light on their darkness the way that they are trying to do to me?"

"I guess that depends," I hedged.

"Well, you might want to think about it," he suggested and yawned big. "In the meantime, I'm exhausted. Is there anything else that you need to discuss with me, Sam?"

"No, I can't think of anything."

"I think you know where to find me," Joshua said and jumped to his feet and stretched out his back by arching backward. "Sam, just please consider that it's nearly impossible to clean the swine or the pen where they play and breed without getting a little dirty yourself."

— • ● • —

I think that we both knew that Joshua won that round too. I'd say that he was beating me handily. Talking with him was like talking to the devil himself. He was creepy, and he made me feel dirty somehow. Not only were his hands unclean, but his intentions were to corrupt. He had no right to stand in righteous judgment of the judge, or the ADA when his own conduct in brutalizing these women was the underlying reason that we were even having the discussion in the first place.

It felt like he was trying to manipulate me in some way to advance his sinister cause. The issue for him was more than reducing his prison time. No, it went much deeper than that. As a result, my guard was completely up when it came to handling him.

But that still didn't mean that he didn't have a point and deserved to be treated with human dignity just like everyone else. The bottom line was that I was his lawyer, and I had to defend him. In so doing, I couldn't just stand idly by and let them run all over him. That simply was something that I could never do.

However, I was very troubled by the things that he said about me personally. My biggest fear about my Aunt Joyce was that she would tell the jail population things about me that could endanger the people in my life, like Mama. I really hadn't considered Carla. I wasn't sure if I should warn her in some way.

Obviously, Joshua was just trying to get a rise out of me. Despite his assertions to the contrary, his weapons of choice were lies and inuendo, which he freely wielded like a medieval sword. The fact is that he couldn't be trusted to tell the entire truth about anything. He somehow had picked up on some of my insecurities. He clearly knew that telling me that I was hiding from the people in my life was going to get under my skin.

In response, there wasn't really anybody for me to hide from. I had never lied to Carla about anything, or to anyone else for that matter. While I admit that I still struggled with low self-esteem and self-doubt, I was upfront about it to anyone who cared to inquire. Honestly, I thought I was doing pretty good because I wasn't just ignoring it. I was fighting like crazy to overcome. I figured that I just needed time to fully recover from what was a moderately damaged mindset and self-image.

I didn't say anything in my monthly case report to Teresa about Joshua being a psychopath. For one thing, I just assumed that everyone already knew this about him. Additionally, I didn't want her to think that I feared him. However, I was, in fact, a little afraid of him. Only a fool would ignore a hellhound standing in front of him with a known propensity to attack with reckless abandon.

To her credit, Teresa did ask me directly whether there was ongoing racial tension with Joshua. I had to admit that there wasn't. She seemed relieved. I didn't want to have to explain to her that Joshua was an equal-opportunity hater. So, I just left it at that.

I felt that I needed to call Virginia Weeks. I didn't know if she was in regular contact with her brother, but I didn't want her to get caught off guard if he accused her of having spoken ill of him to me. But she wasn't really that bothered when I told her. She said that she hadn't seen Joshua in over a year. Apparently, she sent him cards and letters on occasion, but she found that meeting with him was too upsetting.

I gave her an update on the status of the case. I told her everything I knew and answered her questions. She seemed grateful and asked that I let her know if there were any big developments. She indicated that she might try to attend the trial.

Chapter 21

Carla lived on a small, quiet street in east Utica just within the city limits. It really was a nice neighborhood. Her place was an old one-family house converted into two apartments. It was all one floor. She lived in the front.

We had long stopped going grocery shopping together. It just became easier to go on our own because it was faster that way. Also, when we were together, we tended to spend more money. That was the main thing for me. However, we continued to buy things for each other. She was always buying me weird stuff that she knew or heard about and wanted me to try.

I stopped by her place unannounced early one Saturday afternoon, which is something that I had only done one time before. I had just bought her two bottles of this wine that I knew she really liked. I wanted to give them to her rather than bring them to my apartment. She opened the door as soon as I knocked. I was only there a couple of minutes. She had papers all over her living room, and I could see that she was busy. But I could tell that something was just a little off with her- it was just a sense. I only felt slightly rushed.

As I was slowly driving away, I got just a block away when an oncoming white sports car passed me on the left and quickly parked right in front of her place, right where I was just parked. I instinctively slowed down and came to a complete stop in the middle of the street. That's when I saw, through my rearview mirror, a tall, white guy get out of the car. He was carrying a flower bouquet. I only saw him for a couple of seconds as he walked in the direction of her porch.

I made a quick U-turn at the next corner and drove back to her apartment. I parked a few feet behind the white car, but I didn't get out of my car. Instead, I just sat there watching her front door and window. I was tempted to get out of the car several times, but I resisted. My thoughts were holding me hostage. I was there for about thirty minutes, but it seemed like an eternity. I could feel my insides churning faster with each passing minute.

Suddenly, I jumped out of the car as if I was shot out of a cannon. Most of what happened next is a blur in terms of the sequence of events. I just remember knocking on her door and demanding that she open it. She refused and told me to go home, which served only to add gas to my already raging fire.

I recall trying to break the door down with my shoulder and trying to get inside through her front window. I know that I also attacked the white car with a rock, and I was kicking the driver's side front door when the police pulled up. They said that I wouldn't calm down and that they had to handcuff me and put me in the back of the patrol car.

I mostly remember the feeling of being on fire and an all-consuming rage soaring through my body like electric currents that energized me. I wanted to battle. It was a primal aching need, and it was too big and too strong for me to overcome. It felt like this was all happening to me, rather than something that I was actively doing. So, I gave myself completely to it.

When I finally came to myself, I was sitting alone inside a jail cell. That's really when everything stopped moving. It was sudden and instantly I was sinking in a sea of condemnation. I was glad because I wanted to die. I just closed my eyes as tight as I could as my spirit slowly spiraled downward.

"Sam!" Teresa said.

I opened my eyes, took one look at her through the bars, and I began sobbing uncontrollably. Once again, my emotions took over my body and hit me in waves. I was a slave to them- completely beaten into submission and reduced to a shell of a man.

"Sam, you need to calm down," she directed. "Can you please do that for me?"

I cried there for several minutes before I was able to regain my composure somewhat. I was embarrassed beyond words- like my nakedness had just been exposed to the entire world.

"Sam, are you hurt anywhere?"

I shook my head no.

"Can you stand up?"

I complied, but I held my head down."

"I'm going to get you out of here," she said. "But I need to know that you will not try to go back to your girlfriend's apartment. I need you to promise me."

I nodded without looking at her.

"Okay then," she spoke. "I am putting my neck out here because I trust you when you tell me something. I know you to be an honorable person who wouldn't lie to me. Please don't let me down."

I slowly raised my head and looked her in the eye. I was still unable to speak.

It took about an hour for them to release me. A nurse came into the cell and examined me. She was very nice and spoke very gently to me. The knuckles on my right hand were bleeding and both of my wrists were raw from me pulling against the handcuffs. She applied antibiotic ointment and bandages to the injured areas.

They had my car. A patrol car followed me home. Once inside, I slowly walked into my bedroom and lowered my body onto the bed. I began crying again. But it was a controlled cry this time. I eventually kicked off my shoes and got underneath the covers. My head was pounding, and I felt sick to my stomach. But I also was very tired. I quickly drifted off to sleep.

When I opened my eyes, I wasn't exactly sure where I was or what had happened. My throat really hurt and there was a sour smell around. I had apparently vomited on the side of the bed. I sat up and remained motionless. That's when I remembered the rage feeling…and then the rest of it.

I walked into the bathroom and turned on the shower. I felt like I had been hit by a truck. My entire upper body was sore and ached, especially my right shoulder and neck area. I stripped down and stepped inside. The hot water beating steadily against my face felt like heaven.

I always loved hot showers. Growing up, oftentimes the water at home wasn't hot enough or the pressure wasn't strong enough. Once, when I was about ten years old, we couldn't use the shower in the bathroom for about six months because it was broken, and our landlord either couldn't or wouldn't fix it. We could only take baths. But this was perfect. It was relaxing me, and I wished that I could have stayed there forever, or better yet, died that way.

I was putting my bedding in the washer when someone knocked on the front door.

"Who is it? I asked.

"Sam, it's me, Larry."

I slowly opened the door.

"What are you doing here?"

"Teresa called me."

I stepped aside and gestured for him to come in.

"I brought you some coffee and some breakfast pizza from Tony's," he said. "I know you like it."

"Thanks," I whispered.

I took the bag and walked into the kitchen. He followed closely behind. I took the plastic top off the coffee cup and put in one creamer and sat down at the kitchen table. He sat down across from me.

"How are you?" he asked.

"Not good."

"You want to tell me what happened?'

"I saw this guy at Carla's…I just lost it."

"Did you know that she was seeing somebody?"

"I suspected. Someone told me a while back that she saw them having dinner."

"And you just kept that to yourself?" he questioned.

I didn't respond.

"Have you spoken to her?"

"No."

"Well maybe you should at some point—probably not right away."

"I don't want to talk to her," I stated emphatically. "Am I getting fired."

"No, I'm pretty sure that your job is not in jeopardy."

"How do you know?"

"Teresa just wanted me to make sure that you were okay," he replied. "You know that you're her claim to fame being the only Black attorney in Utica."

"I'm not the only one," I disputed.

"That other guy doesn't count. You know he's crazy."

"Am I being charged with anything?"

"No, everybody really respects you," he revealed. "Even Utica PD. They are going to protect you. But you will probably have to pay for the property damage you caused. Did you really try to pry inside a locked window with your bare hands?"

"I'm so embarrassed," I confessed as I covered my face with my hands. "She can fire me. I don't care. I don't want to go back to work anyway."

"Embarrassed?" Larry questioned. "They say that

you're as strong as an ox. Believe me, nobody has ever said that about me."

"You mean stupid as one."

"You're not stupid," he dismissed. "You should've found someone to talk to if you were having problems with your girlfriend. We've all been there."

"I was just trying to handle it, you know," I explained. "I never confronted her or said anything. It's not like we're married. She's free to date anyone she likes."

"I'm not sure that I agree," Larry remarked. "But she owes you some answers. You love this girl. Anyone can see that."

"Not anymore."

"You can turn it off just like that?"

"Damn straight," I stressed.

"You're a mean one, Mr. Grinch," he joked.

"Are you kidding me?" I unleashed. "She has been playing me for God only knows how long! I feel like such an idiot. I keep thinking of them together in bed laughing their heads off at my stupidity."

"You don't know that," he argued. "It's not like you caught them in the act."

"Right, I don't know what they were doing in there, but I'm pretty sure they weren't trading recipes. She's lucky that I didn't get my hands on her boy. That's who I wanted anyway. Not her! To hell with her! I felt disrespected and then, I don't know… I guess, I saw red!"

"You think? Larry teased. "All I'm saying is we don't know all of the facts here. You're lucky you didn't kill somebody."

"Like I said, I'm really embarrassed," I reiterated. "I tried, but I couldn't hold it back. Then I was swept away in it."

"Maybe you need to talk to someone?"

"Someone like who?" I wondered.

"Like a counselor or somebody," he suggested. "You

can't tell me that you didn't scare the crap out of yourself."

"I'm not talking to any counselor!" I said. "It's not like I walk around flipping out on people all the time. This has never happened to me before."

"No, you don't," he remarked. "You have learned to suppress it—to fight against it with your wit. But what happens the next time you can't tell somebody off and get swept away? Do you really want to take that chance?"

I paused to think. My brain was still basically mush. I took a big sip of my coffee. It was cold.

"So, Teresa is making me go to counselling?" I explored.

"Yeah, she's going to talk to you about it."

I slowly inhaled and blew out the tension in a rush.

"Okay," I said.

It felt like the clouds hovering over me just got a little darker.

I think that it's fair to say that I wasn't exactly a believer in counseling. Most of our felony offenders who had been to prison had received some kind of counseling at one time or another to little or no avail. I wondered how many counselors Joshua Weeks had seen over the years. While counseling might be beneficial to affluent people going through a divorce or a mid-life crisis, some problems simply can't be talked away. That's honestly the way I felt.

Moreover, I had never met a Black counselor before. The same way that some people need a male or a female therapist, Black people mostly need trained Black professionals, especially when the underlying issues stem, in substantial part, from generational poverty and/or discrimination. Even then, I suspected that real breakthroughs and victories were a long shot.

Indeed, what was any psychologist or counselor really going to say to the young Black guy who had two or three baby mamas, no job skills, and no meaningful life connection to anyone of substance? Whose heroes were all dead or in prison themselves? Whose broken thoughts and secret shame had become strongholds that were holding him captive like a plantation overseer, or a sheriff at the county jail?

"Oh, one more thing," Larry said as he was getting ready to leave. "Teresa wants you to take a week off with pay."

"A week? You're kidding?"

"Nope, effective immediately," he reported. "You can't go into the office or to any of your courts or to the jail."

"Anything else?" I dared to ask.

"I think that's it," Larry said. "See you in a week, buddy, and call me if you want to talk."

Apparently, everyone thought that I was becoming a workaholic. His suggestion was that I get in my car and go visit an old college friend or somebody. Unfortunately, I felt like I didn't have any friends and that I was all alone in the world. This was rock bottom for me.

I had a better idea. I thought I would get drunk and stay that way all week. I was secretly excited at the prospect. I hadn't overindulged since I met Carla. If I could, I would have gladly gone back to the day before I met her.

Fortunately, I thought better of the idea of medicating my pain with alcohol and resisted the temptation to sink even deeper into the dark abyss. Contrary to Teresa's orders, I went into the office after hours one night when no one was there and brought home a couple of my files. But I mostly just stayed inside my apartment with the lights dimmed and hid from the cold, cruel world.

Mama happened to call me in the middle of my forced sabbatical. She wanted me to pick up some things for her from the grocery store. I knew I needed to get my body moving. I went that afternoon.

"You didn't have to work today?" she asked.

"Uh, no. I took the day off."

"Did you remember the cake flour?"

"Yeah, I got it."

"Good, cause you know I don't like to use regular flour in my coffee cake. I like my cake to be smooth."

"I got it," I repeated.

"What's wrong?" she wondered.

She gave me a hard look.

"Nothing," I lied.

"You look terrible," she insisted. "Did something happen?"

"No, nothing happened?"

"You sick? There's a lot of sickness going around. JT has that bronchitis bad. Eileen's been really worried about him."

"I'm not sick."

"Then what?" she insisted.

"It's nothing," I answered. "I'm just tired."

"How's your girlfriend?"

I tried to show no reaction.

"Carla? Oh, we aren't together anymore."

"What do you mean 'not together'?" she asked.

"We broke up?"

"Broke up? How come?"

"It just wasn't working out," I said.

"Not working out how?" she questioned. "Was somebody fooling around?"

"I'm sorry, but I can't talk about this now."

"See, I knew it" she asserted.

"You knew what?"

"I knew that heffa was no good."

"Please don't call her that," I begged. "We both called it off. It was both of us. Not just her."

"You think you will get back together?"

"No, I don't think that's going to happen," I admitted. "It's over for good."

I felt a sharp sting inside after I spoke. It was the first time that I had considered the finality of the breakup, at least in my heart. I wasn't planning on talking about this. In fact, Mama was probably the very last person on the face of the earth I wanted to talk to about this, other than my mother She was jealous of Carla and couldn't be trusted to be considerate or fair-minded. I knew that she loved me in her way. I loved her too. But I also knew I needed to get out of there as fast as I could.

"I always say that there're plenty of other fish in the sea," she continued.

"I know," I said to appease her. "Well, I really gotta run. I don't want to be late."

"'Cause I know some nice girls," she claimed. "A lot better for you than miss-high-and-mighty."

"No, you don't," I resisted. "There aren't any nice girls in Cornhill."

"Yes, there are," Mama disputed. "Just the other day, I was talking to…"

"Nice girls don't live here," I interrupted. "They get out as fast as they can and go as far as they can because they know that there is nothing here but darkness and despair. We can be poor anywhere. There is absolutely no reason to live here. That's why I tried to get you to move with me, but you wanted to stay so bad. I honestly don't know how you do it. I swear that there is something in the air here that chokes the life out of people. I feel like I can't breathe every time I drive down these streets."

"You done messed around and fell in love with this girl," she deflected. "That's your problem. She's not our kind. I could have told you that it wasn't going to work."

Her words cut me like a thousand knives. I just bore down against the pain that I desperately didn't want her to see. I was good at it. I had been doing it my whole life.

"Yes, I know you're right, Mama," I spoke soberly. "I never had a chance. I see that now."

• ● •

It was just before midnight on Wednesday, and I was lying in bed reading a hearing transcript when my phone rang. It was Carla. I hung up as soon as I recognized her voice. She called right back.

"What do you want?" I answered.

"I want to talk to you," she pled. "Please can we talk?"

"I have been ordered to stay away from you. I could get fired."

"I just want to make sure you are okay?" she said.

"I'm great!" I responded. "Couldn't be better. Are you happy now?"

"Sam, I know that you are angry, but it doesn't have to be this way."

"Why don't you tell me how it should be?" I mocked. "You're the one who had me arrested."

"I didn't call the police," she refuted. "One of the neighbors did. You were way out of control. I just wanted you to…"

"How do you think I got that way?"

"We are all adults," she argued, "We could have just discussed everything like rational adults."

"Who is *we*?" I demanded.

"What?"

"You just said that *we* could have discussed this like adults?" I repeated. "Who exactly are *we* talking about? There is me, and there is you and who? What's his name?"

"C'mon Sam," she said. "Can we please not do this? I thought you were better than this."

"And I thought you wanted to talk. So, talk!"

"Please don't cross-examine me!" she demanded. "I'm not one of your criminals!"

"Tell me his name! I have a right to know his name!"

"I'm not playing this game. I can see now that this was a mistake."

"How long have you been sleeping with him?"

"It's not like that," she answered. "We are just friends. You have no right to accuse me of anything just because he came to my apartment one time."

"I don't believe you!" I barked. "You don't have to continue with the lie."

"I'm not lying."

I already knew anyway," I said. "Someone already told me."

"Let me get this straight," she reasoned. "You heard that I was supposedly seeing someone else, and you said nothing. You just held it and waited for the right moment to embarrass me?"

"That's not what happened," I protested.

"That's really weak, Sam."

"Don't you dare try to turn this around and put it on me," I came back. "If you wanted to be with this white man so bad then you should have just told me like an *adult* instead of running all over town behind my back! I would have gladly stepped aside. Exactly who embarrassed who!"

"I can see whoever I want! You don't own me! We never said that we were exclusive!"

"And you never said that it was open season on tramping around either!" I yelled back. "Please don't make yourself out to be the victim. You knew exactly what you were doing. You're just embarrassed because now everyone knows what kind of person you really are."

"Instead of attacking me maybe you should look in the mirror at the immature little boy who you really are!"

"Is that right?" I urged.

"All you do is hide behind your principles of social justice and high standards, so you don't have to face your own failures. You are such a fake and probably the most judgmental person that I have ever met!

"*Judgmental*?" I questioned.

"What difference does it make that he is white?"

My mind was blown.

"It makes all the difference in the world to me for reasons that you will never understand," I debated.

"That sounds like a personal problem to me," she countered.

"Tell me this: was it just a game for you all along?" I attacked. "This whole time? Were you just slumming it until your true white prince came along?"

"That's not fair, and you know it!" she contested. "Black men have been running after white woman since Juneteenth! I have never looked down on you for any reason!"

"You never let me get close either! You kept pushing me away and pretending that it was me. I wanted to love you and you just …"

I sobbed openly.

"But I never asked you to love me!" she insisted. "That's the part that you don't seem to get! I don't understand why nobody gets that!"

"Well, I get it now. That was my bad. But tell me this: who is the one hiding now?"

We were both silent. I hated this ending for us. I had this sick feeling in the bottom of my soul.

"Sam, I swear that I never wanted to hurt you," she whispered.

"I'm sorry that I was stupid enough to let you hurt me," I blurted out. "I think that we both know that I never would have done this to you. But if this guy is who you want, then you have my blessings. You two lovebirds have at it."

"It's really *not* like that," she claimed.

"Then I feel sorry for you," I reflected. "Whatever your thing is, I would have done just about anything to make it better, if you had let me."

We were both quiet again. This is what we were reduced to; two broken-down ships passing in the light of day. All our dents, dings and scratches were on full display at last. I was severely wounded and no longer functional.

"So, tell me now what exactly you want from me?" I dared ask. "'Cause you're right; I'm not understanding. You called me; I didn't call you. I was hoping to never see or speak to you again."

She remained silent for a moment.

"I just…want you… not to hate me," she wept.

I cried too. I couldn't help it. It gushed out naturally, like an oil well.

"I'm sorry, but I can't promise you that," I whispered.

"I really am sorry," she tearfully said.

"Goodbye, Carla."

"Goodbye, Sam."

Chapter 22

The deal that I made with Teresa was that I only had to see the counselor once. Turns out that there were two counselors in the county building next door who I could see for free. They were both white females. I chose the one with the first available opening. I just wanted to get it over with.

Her name was Kelly Brunetti. She was nice enough. She was thirty-something with a high-pitched voice that I initially found to be very annoying. But she had a bubbly personality, and she made me feel at ease.

She talked to me mostly about anger management strategies, such as identifying triggers and recognizing warning signs. She said that sitting in my car outside Carla's apartment for thirty minutes before confronting her was the worst thing that I probably could have done. I should have removed myself from that situation entirely and addressed her later.

"I tell all of the kids I see that they should never feed the monster inside," she said.

"But do you think that my reaction was too over the top?" I asked directly. "It felt like I was possessed. Am I abnormal?"

"I can't really answer that as we sit here today," she began. "Our thoughts, feelings, and behaviors are all connected. The situation you describe was something very traumatic that you just came upon. It would have shaken anyone. If it was me, I would have probably run away and cried my eyes out. You reacted differently because we aren't the same."

"I literally saw red. I hate to think what would have happened if I got inside her apartment."

"Look, Sam. Sounds like you deal with a lot of stress every day in your job. Everyone has their breaking point. You are only human. We must take care of our mental health so that we are best prepared to deal with the unexpected."

"So, what do you think I should do?"

"Work on changing the way you look at yourself and your problems. It's about learning adequate coping skills like stepping away, getting the appropriate amount of rest and exercise, or changing the situation altogether, if possible."

"What do you mean by that?" I wondered.

"Like maybe this isn't a healthy relationship for you to be in at this time," she asserted.

I nodded my head in agreement.

"Key is probably just changing the way you think, which is obviously easier said than done," she advised.

I was only there for an hour. She did most of the talking. Before I left, she gave me a pamphlet on anger management and suggested that I consider coming back if I found that the instances of uncontrollable rage were increasing. She informed me that if she saw me on a regular basis that she would have me work on an "anger-management control plan." But she wasn't sure that I needed that just now.

"Only time will tell," she pointed out.

———•●•———

Notwithstanding everything, I missed Carla like crazy-much more than I thought I would. That really surprised me because we never really spent a whole lot of time together during the week. But I could literally sense the breakup in the air around me with every breath I took. It was also like the rhythm of my heart had slowed somehow and I was out of step with everything that was going on around me. I craved her on a subconscious level.

I also missed being in the office the week I was out on punishment. Upon my return, I threw myself even deeper into my work. I had two big new cases, and I also volunteered to take one of Larry's trials that conflicted with a family wedding that he had coming up. I didn't want to visit any old college friends. Working helped to take my mind off my pitiful existence.

However, I avoided the people in the courthouse as much as I could because I knew that there was a lot of gossip going around about me. It felt like everyone was laughing at me. Even about that, I knew I was probably just being paranoid and that my mistrust of colleagues flowed directly from the overriding negative feelings that I had about myself. Ultimately, nobody said anything to me about what happened or treated me any differently.

— • ● • —

I won two misdemeanor trials in town court. Both defendants were white. One was a bar fight, and the other was an endangering the welfare of a minor charge, where my client, a young dad, had left his sleeping toddler alone in the car for a minute while he ran into a food mart to buy cigarettes. Both really were just the luck of the draw, but a win is a win. It's not like it happened for us very often.

But the Joshua Weeks case was still the bane of my existence. If we were forced to go to trial, then we needed a defense, and I was struggling to come up with one. I thought again about trying to put on a defense that Joshua lacked the mental capacity to commit these crimes, but that simply wasn't a winning legal argument any way you looked at it. Nor was it true. He was vengeful and devious—the perfect serial rapist!

On a routine jail visit, I got a slip that Joshua wanted to see me. He was probably the last person in the world who I wanted to see. I thought long and hard about ignoring it, but I decided to just bite the bullet and call him out.

"Hello, counselor," he said as he took a seat across from me.

"You wanted to see me?"

"Yes, I did. Thank you for obliging me."

"Don't mention it."

"I have been thinking about what you said about the judge using my case for his own political gain," he began.

"What about it?" I pushed.

"What do you think about beating him at his own game?"

"How do you mean?" I asked cautiously.

"What if we called the newspapers ourselves and told them what is really going on? Or maybe I could do an interview with some pretty young thing and sweet talk the hell out of her? It'll work. What do you think?"

I could hardly believe my ears. "An interview? What kind of interview? I mean, what would you say?"

"I don't know," he stated. "Does it really matter?"

"Yes, it absolutely matters!" I argued. "For one thing, I could get disbarred for going public."

"Maybe I can do it without you then?" he solicited.

"Most people would hate you anyway, so what's the gain?" I presented. "These are awful facts for us."

"You could tell me what to say," he explained. "It's worth a try. What do we have to lose?"

"Who have you been taking to?" I demanded.

"No one," he quickly replied. "I was just thinking that we might as well have a little fun."

"Fun?" I questioned. "Because it sounds to me like you have been talking to someone who doesn't know what the hell he is talking about."

"No, I haven't." Joshua persisted. "It's my idea."

"Well, it's a bad one," I spoke as calmly as I could and still managed to sound like a man who was completely on the edge. "Listen, I don't want you talking to the press or to anyone else. Do you hear me? If I even suspect that you are doing something underhanded to hurt these women more than they have already been hurt, I will get myself off this case so fast that it will make your head spin! I mean it, Joshua!"

"Whoa, let's just calm down here," he said. "I told you before that I won't do anything that you don't want me to do. I was only trying…"

"I know what you were trying to do," I maintained. "But let me remind you that you are looking at a maximum sentence of twenty-five to fifty years imprisonment. That for you, is a life sentence. I, for one, would like to see you have at least a fighting chance of seeing the light of day again."

"How very kind of you," he stated sarcastically. "I didn't think you cared."

I avoided his gaze and ignored his tone, which was condescending.

"But there has to be a better way," I insisted.

"Like what?" Joshua asked in earnest.

"I don't know," I admitted. "I guess I'll just have to think of something. But in the meantime, I'll have none of this taking matters into your own hands. Do you understand?"

"You know, I have to say, Sam: sometimes you are a little too *judgmental* for my liking."

I froze in place. Once again, he caught me completely off guard.

"Okay, you win.," he relented. "I won't call anyone. See how easy that was?"

"Well, thank you for hearing me out," I calmly spoke. "I really appreciate it."

I stood to my feet.

"Hey, Sam?"

"Yes."

"What happened to your wrists?"

<hr>

I found this doctor who said that he might be willing to work with me on Joshua's case. He was a therapist who did some psychotherapy with his patients. I got his name from one of my old professors at Utica College. His name was Chris Scanlan, and he was local. I only spoke to him on the phone, but he said that he had read a little about the case and was open to hearing more.

The problem was that he was very expensive, and I didn't think that the county would want to pay for it. I was right.

"What exactly would he be testifying to?" Teresa asked.

"I don't know exactly," I admitted. "He needs to review all of the prison records and mental health records and meet with Joshua for a personal interview."

"But best-case-scenario, what could he say?"

"That Joshua suffers from antisocial personality disorder or even psychopathy and lacked the ability to control his behavior at the time of the kidnapping."

"And how much will that cost?" she questioned.

"The record review itself will probably be around $2,000. Then there is the patient interview at $500 per hour. This doesn't include the fee for trial prep and trial testimony."

"So, ballpark?"

I estimated, "At least $5,000, I'd say."

She flinched.

"Okay. Let me call the comptroller's office," she said. "We have only paid that much once before and that was where we used multiple experts. No promises."

The look on her face was not encouraging. What I didn't tell her was that Dr. Scanlan didn't sound that optimistic himself. He said it was a long shot, but he was open to taking a closer look, which meant that he could find against us or just decide after doing his work up that he didn't want to testify for us after all. In those instances, we still had to pay him for the work he did do. It was a costly proposition regardless of how you looked at it.

Not for nothing, but this is one of the biggest reasons why rich people get a better defense than poor people in our system of criminal justice. The rich can afford to pay for a better courtroom presentation, including for the expert witnesses they need. Although there certainly are bad attorneys, it's a myth that the attorneys make or break the case. Either there is a viable defense or there isn't. Any competent trial lawyer knows the right arguments to make in court. The importance of having quality expert witnesses, however, cannot be overstated. But not every client has the means to support their defense with experts. What's the old adage? *Money talks.*

Teresa later informed me that the county would only give us $2,000 altogether. Obviously, that wasn't going to do it. Honestly, they gave me more than I expected. But I had an ethical obligation to at least try.

I called Tom Lester one afternoon. He was an Italian American attorney from Syracuse whom I met when he was defending a big drug case in Utica, and I was new to county court. He was in his late sixties and was considered by many to be one of the best trial attorneys in central New York. We conversed one day after his trial in the back of an empty courtroom for over an hour. He was very nice and told me that I could call him at any time.

"You know there really isn't an outright prohibition against lawyers or a party talking to the press absent a gag order," Mr. Lester advised. "We just have to be careful what we say."

"I know, but it just feels wrong to me," I stated. "The only reason to do that would be to impact what happens in the courtroom."

"Well, yes and no," he hedged. "The way I see it, you are only trying to get Lombardi to get off his fat ass and do the right thing. There is nothing wrong with that. It would be a disgrace and a travesty to put these women through a trial where they must relive publicly every detail of the worst events of their lives."

"I don't know that I could live with myself if I added to their pain in some way," I disclosed.

"But if the judge doesn't care about the victims, why should you?" he contended. "It's not like you would be lying to the press. Isn't the bigger question for you, what is in the best interest of your client?"

"No, that's not it at all," I said.

"Then what?" he asked.

"Who am I really?" I articulated. "At the end of the day, I need to respect myself, or what's the point?"

"We can't always hide behind our own set of principles, when the world is playing by completely different rules and the stakes are this high. Your client is the one who will have to spend each day of the rest of his life locked away in some dingy prison cell, not you!"

"Right, because he brutally terrorized three women, not me!" I asserted.

"True, my friend," he replied and laughed. "All very true."

"So, what would you do if you were me?" I posed.

"I'd sing like Frank Sinatra," he expressed. "Confidentially, of course. Nothing on the record."

He chuckled to himself.

My head was spinning.

I didn't sleep at all that night. I kept telling myself to just do the best that I could and not worry too much about the rest of it. But I was really struggling. It felt like I had somehow gotten off at the wrong exit and every road was leading to a dead end. It was true concerning this case, and it was also a true description of the general state of my life. I was completely lost.

— • ● • —

Sal Pitino approached me in the hall. He was the criminal court clerk. It was never a good thing when Sal came calling. He was like the Grim Reaper. He informed me that the Joshua Week's trial was scheduled to begin on October 5, which was just a little over a month away. They had set the trial down to last a week. He stressed that this was a date certain and not to ask to have it changed or moved for any reason.

"I've been told to tell you and Joe that this trial will happen even if World War III breaks out the same day," he said.

I had been expecting the other shoe to drop at any moment. Now that it had, I could only laugh to keep from crying. I was sitting at my desk feeling sorry for myself while wrestling in my head once again with my own private demons. They seemed to be a little louder lately and were rearing their ugly heads with more frequency. I had less confidence in my ability to rise to the occasion this time around and defeat them.

The phone rang, interrupting the battle.

"Sam, it's that lady reporter again wanting to talk to you about your case," Amy said. "Do you want me to just take a message?"

"Uh… no," I replied. "It's okay."

"Really?" she sounded startled. "You really want to talk to her?"

'Yeah, I'll talk," I mumbled. "Put her through."

Chapter 23

I made a deal with Dr. Scanlon. He would do a record review for $1,000. After that, we would meet to discuss what he thought. He said that he might still be willing to help me at trial. But he wouldn't be able to meet with Joshua or testify. This was the first positive thing that happened with this case since it was assigned to me.

We had a pretrial conference in Judge Lombardi's chambers on September 10. In addition to me and Joe Bartolotta, a stenographer was there too. For some reason, the judge wanted to put everything on the record. I didn't trust his motives.

"Gentleman, I want to know how many witnesses you each have?"

"We have seven or eight depending on what happens," Joe advised.

"Who are they?" the judge asked.

"There is a nurse who did the rape kits, the two arresting troopers, BCI Investigator Mark Henry, and the three victims."

"Sam?"

"Three witnesses, your honor. Dr. Virginia Weeks, who is the defendant's sister, Dr. Chris Scanlan, and possibly the defendant."

"Who is Dr. Scanlan?" Joe blurted out.

"He is a therapist. He can testify about the mental

health condition known as psychopathy."

"Was he treating Weeks?"

"You can ask him that yourself," I answered.

"Judge, this is news to me," Joe argued. "The defense hasn't provided the People with a report from any therapist."

"I don't have one," I replied. "This case was fast-tracked for some reason, so we are still working on our defense. Some things cannot be rushed. If you want to consent to a small adjournment of the trial, then I can work on getting you a report."

"Not gonna happen," Joe said.

"There will be no adjournment!" Judge Lombardi interjected. "As far as I am concerned, you have both had plenty of time to get ready for this trial. When can you get that report to Joe?"

"No idea," I replied. "Dr. Scanlan is very busy, and I just retained him. He might not have time to prepare one at all."

"I have a right to know what he is going to testify to prior to trial," Joe insisted. "What if we wanted to interview him?"

"I haven't had a chance to interview the victims yet either."

"What?" Joe exclaimed. "If you go anywhere near any one of them, I will indict you for witness tampering."

"You are not the grand jury so you can't indict anyone," I pounced. "Anyway, you know that I have the right to interview your witnesses before trial just like you do. Geez, sometimes I wonder if you even went to law school."

"I went to a better school than you did!" Joe shouted.

His face was red, his nostrils were flared, and he was breathing hard.

"Prove it!" I incited. "Show us your transcript!"

"That's enough!" the judge yelled. "I'm telling you

that I will not put up with this constant bickering between the two of you. Don't make me pull this car over! I want both of you to refrain from personal attacks. Now!"

"We still want his resume!" Joe maintained.

"Okay, no problem," I said. "All you had to do is ask nicely.

"And to be clear, there will be no adjournments of the trial under any circumstances," Judge Lombardi emphasized again. "I expect both parties to be ready to proceed on the scheduled date. You both have been told more than once. That's it!"

— • ● • —

Obviously, I made up everything that I said in the conference about our witnesses. I wasn't planning to call anyone to testify. But I decided that I would be purposely difficult in the hope that either the Judge or the ADA would make a critical mistake. Neither one was exactly a great legal mind. Also, I enjoyed messing with Joe. There needed to be something in it for me.

However, more than anything, I just wanted all of this to be over. I had been with the public defender's office going on three years. I hadn't been on vacation even once. I suddenly realized that I needed to get away. It didn't really matter to me where I went as long as it was far away from Utica. I promised myself that I would look into doing something as soon as this trial was over.

Dr. Scanlan concluded that Joshua most likely suffered from abnormalities related to psychopathy and/or antisocial personality disorder (ASPD). He believed that my client showed signs and symptoms of these conditions as a very young child. Specifically, he said people like Joshua lack the capacity for remorse stemming from cognitive deficits.

"Are you saying that he can't control himself at all?" I solicited.

"Many people who suffer from these conditions also suffer from impulse control disorders, especially when combined with alcoholism."

"So, alcohol can be a trigger for him?"

Dr. Scanlan further opined, "Definitely, but he's not just a mean drunk. He's an evil drunk."

"Is it possible that he wasn't even mentally present when he attacked these women?"

"Possible but unlikely in my opinion," he said. "He knew what he was doing and took great pleasure in doing these things. But the guy was a time bomb. These crimes, or something like them, was bound to happen eventually. It would be interesting to hear the victims full account of what transpired at the time of the attacks. The statements you gave me are incomplete and unclear."

"I don't need you to testify, but could you maybe help me come up with some question areas to cross-examine the witnesses just to make the picture clearer as to what exactly was going on not just in that house, but also in his head."

"Yes, I think that I can do that," he agreed. "I have to say that your client is truly fascinating. I'm also wondering about his siblings. I believe there are two, an older brother and sister. There are many experts who believe that there is a strong genetic basis for ASPD."

"Yes, I have met his sister," I said. "She's a doctor."

"Really? That's incredible! And the brother?"

"I don't really know anything about him," I replied. "It never occurred to me to ask."

"Hmm… I can't help but wonder," he indicated.

The Observer Dispatch headline read, "Judge Denies Plea Bargain in Boonville Kidnapping Case." Citing an anonymous source, the female reporter alleged that the unnamed victims didn't want a trial, but the judge was making them testify anyway. She wrote that this was the first time in the last ten years that a felony defendant in Oneida county wasn't offered some kind of plea deal. She incorrectly stated that the defendant was facing a possible life sentence. I immediately knew that this was going to be a big problem for me.

I was summoned to Lombardi's chambers.

"I assumed that it goes without saying that talking to the press about plea deals is strictly prohibited," Judge Lombardi railed while sitting behind his desk in his chambers.

"I can assure the court that no one from my office spoke to the press," Joe said.

"I never spoke to this reporter either," I echoed.

"Well, somebody did!" Lombardi blasted.

"How do we know it wasn't one of the victims?" I questioned. "The story was about them."

"If I find out that anyone from the public defender's office or from the district attorney's office has been speaking to the media about this case, there will be hell to pay!" the Judge threatened. "And that goes for the victims and the defendant too. I want this case tried in the courtroom and not in the newspaper!"

It seemed to me that the judge's wrath was really directed at me. He shifted his body toward me, and his face was flushed, and big blue veins pulsated on the left side of his neck and on his forehead. He looked like he was about to spontaneously combust.

"Is there anything else?" he asked as he turned away.

"Yes, your honor," Joe spoke up. "It appears that two of our witnesses are not available for trial during the week of the fifth. We are asking that the trial be moved back a week."

"What day would that be?"

"I believe it's October 12," Joe said.

"Granted," the judge decreed.

"I thought you said that the trial date was set in stone and that there would be absolutely no adjournments," I immediately interjected.

"I changed my mind," he responded abruptly and glared at me again. "I'm very concerned that this article is an attempt to challenge my authority as the trial judge."

The air in the room was thick. I swallowed hard, and I could feel my heart beating hard in my chest. I knew for certain then that this impromptu conference was for my benefit and that I was being reprimanded. Even the stenographer was staring at me.

"Thank you, gentlemen," the judge said in a huff.

We took our cue, and both got up and left. I was incensed as I contemplated the blatant double standard. I get how it looked. The defense had the most to gain by bringing this injustice to light. But there was no way of knowing who talked to that reporter, and it wasn't me. I just couldn't go through with it. I told her that I couldn't comment on the case. She obviously spoke to someone else.

I called the county jail and asked the woman in records about Joshua's visitor list and telephone calls. She had been helpful in the past.

"That's so funny, you are the third person this week to call me about that," she said.

"Really, who else called?"

"You know I can't really tell you that," she answered.

"What did you tell them?"

"You are his only visitor, and Weeks hasn't made or received any calls since he has been here."

"What about correspondence? Has he written to anybody?"

"Let's see… no he hasn't," she reported.

"Hmm…That's interesting," I replied.

"I think it's a little sad that he has no family," she sympathized. "Everybody needs family. I know what he did and everything, but being alone in the world can't be fun."

"He kinda brought it on himself," I stated. I was annoyed.

She didn't respond.

I knew that the jail records didn't prove anything. Joshua was too smart to leave a trail like that. He could have easily gotten another prisoner to make the call to the reporter. Even one of the jail employees could have done it for him. Even if I couldn't prove it, my sense was that he was the leak somehow.

I saw about three or four of Judge Lombardi's campaign signs on my way home. I already knew that he wasn't in any real danger of losing the election, and it was doubtful that the press coverage surrounding the Weeks case would sway voters or have any impact whatsoever on his reelection bid. But it was also highly unlikely that he would have even considered forcing these victims to testify if they weren't poor people from a rural community.

I wasn't going to mention the article to Joshua at all because I didn't see the point. He was just going to deny any involvement. But I needed him to call off the dogs. This trial was going to be torture enough without the judge being hellbent on making me pay for something I didn't do.

"I never spoke to any reporter," Joshua resisted. "It could have been anybody."

"Maybe, but so far it has only served to make the judge more unreasonable," I said. "Remember that we need for him to have a change of heart. This was the wrong way to go about it. I'd say we're pretty much screwed now."

"I told you that I didn't do it!" Joshua exclaimed.

"I know. I heard you," I acknowledged. "But if you are planning to do something, don't!"

I looked him directly in his eyes. I had gotten better at being able to do that. But the moment was rife with tensions, like two teammates disagreeing over game strategy in the heat of the battle.

"I wouldn't wave a white flag just yet if I were you," Joshua maintained. "The bigger they are the harder they fall."

"That's the point," I argued. "They won't let us just surrender."

I was sitting in Larry's office shooting the breeze when Amy came looking for me. Apparently, there was someone in the lobby who wanted to see me.

"She said her name is Jackie Jenkins," Amy reported. "She might be the most beautiful Black woman that I have ever seen in real life! She looks like Whitney Houston!"

I jumped to my feet. I was suddenly anxious. To say that this visit was entirely unexpected is probably the understatement of the century!

"What can I do for you?" I asked as we sat at the table in our conference room.

I was struggling to maintain my composure.

"I apologize for just showing up here like this without an appointment," she said. "I know that I took a chance."

"It's okay," I nervously replied. "It's actually good to see you again."

She looked awesome like usual. She was wearing a black trench coat, wide-leg pants, and boots. Her perfume smelled divine. She wreaked of class and looked completely out of place in the courthouse.

"So, let me just get to it," she timidly began. "I realize

that you are probably very busy. I'm here about Carla. You probably don't know this, but she has been at home in Webster with us. She was there for about a week, and I drove her back here to Utica just now."

"No, I didn't know that."

"A week ago, she called me in a panic and told me that she had just taken some pills and she was scared."

"What?" I exclaimed.

It felt like I had just been punched in the gut.

"Don't worry. She's okay," she said and held up one of her hands. "We rushed here and got her. But we are obviously very worried about her."

"Um…I don't know what to say. I'm shocked."

"The thing is that we have been worried about her for a long time. Carla was date-raped when she was sixteen. She has struggled a lot ever since. She was seeing a therapist for a couple of years before she went to college, but she still hasn't fully recovered."

"Oh my God!" I cried out. "I swear she never said anything to me."

"I know she didn't," she replied. "I tried to get her to tell you, but she didn't want you to know. We fought about that right before the anniversary party."

My mind was racing through the rolodex in my head of our past conversations. I was starting to put a few of the pieces together. There clearly had been signs that I either had missed or simply chose to ignore because I was too focused on my own issues.

"But why would she even consider doing something like that?" I wondered.

"Because it got to be too much," Mrs. Jenkins explained. "She insisted that she had everything under control, but I didn't believe her."

"Oh my God!" I bellowed. "Oh my God!"

She cupped her hands together against her chest before softly speaking, "In the past, she has made idle remarks here and there about wanting to harm herself, but this is the first time, that I know of, where she actually took some steps toward doing something like that. I'm literally out of my mind with worry."

She was clearly fighting to hold her tears back.

"I can't tell you how bad I feel," I said. "I knew there was something, but this is truly unimaginable for me."

"I know," she whispered. "It's my worst nightmare."

"Do you think…do you think what happened with us is the thing that caused this?"

"Yes, I do," she indicated. "She told me what happened. I want to say that I'm not blaming you. I get it. She doesn't know that I am here telling you all this. She would be angry with me if she knew."

"But this makes no sense," I contended.

"Sam, do you love my daughter?" she asked directly.

"What?" I reacted.

"Do you love her?"

I refused to answer. My wounded pride wouldn't let me. Instead, I just froze in space.

"You know, sometimes we fall in love with people who are broken," she reflected. "In fact, I'm starting to think that most of us are broken in many ways."

"I'm sorry, but I don't know what you mean," I replied.

"Love suffers long and is kind," she recited. "It's my favorite Bible verse."

"*You* told me yourself that infidelity is a deal breaker. Your daughter doesn't want me."

"Carla doesn't know what she wants!" she stated emphatically. "Somebody has got to take the lead here. I think that person should be you."

"Look, although I hate to admit it, I'm a guy who tends to lead with my heart wide- open," I said. "She doesn't respect that."

"That's not true," she disputed. "The first time that she told me about you she said that the thing that she liked most about you is that you care deeply about the people you represent."

"And look where it got me," I whined.

"Aww… honey, I can see that you are hurting too," she sympathized. "I feel bad about that. I really do feel for you too."

"No worries," I said and shook it off. "I'll live."

"You know, that's all I want for my daughter too," she pled. "I want her to live.

"Believe me, I really want that too, but…"

"I think that you might be her best chance, if not her only chance."

She looked and sounded desperate.

"I'm not sure she would agree," I stressed. "Carla is a grown woman. She can do whatever she wants. She told me so herself."

I was getting angry again. I told myself that I needed to be careful. I didn't want to offend Carla's mother. I really liked her.

"I understand how you feel," she said.

She reached across the table and put her right hand on my forearm.

"Maybe you can tell me something?" she asked. "What do you want, Sam? For you, I mean?"

"At this point, I don't honestly know how to answer that," I admitted.

"Excuse me for saying, but I don't think that's good enough," she pressed. "I mean, don't you have to know what you want in order to have any chance of finding it? Everyone needs a dream."

"I want someone who will always choose me," I reluctantly disclosed. "That's my dream, if you must know. Is that too much to ask?"

My voice was shaking with emotion. I felt a little like I was being put in a position where I had to defend myself when Carla was the one who cheated and who apparently hadn't been honest with me about a lot of things.

"If you want to be somebody's hero, then you have to save somebody," she articulated.

"We can't really count on being able to save other people," I countered. "That's mostly out of our control."

"Then save yourself Sam," she reasoned. "There aren't any chains on you!"

"I know," I whispered mostly to myself. "I know."

"In the end, I really do think that we are talking about the same thing," she maintained. "Don't you?"

I was raw inside from all the reflux from my stifled pain and emotions flowing freely from my soul into my heart and back again. Like a broken man, I just wanted to go somewhere and hide. I didn't want to fight any more losing battles.

"Sam, I like you," she continued. "I told Carla how much I liked you, which may have caused her to pull away from you in some way—I don't know. But I wanted you to know the truth about her. She's my sweet baby girl and … I thought maybe you could save each other. That's really the only reason that I came here. My prayer is that you two kids can figure it out somehow."

"Okay," I whispered. "Okay, I got it."

"Thank you for hearing me out," she said.

Chapter 24

I was so nervous that I didn't sleep at all the night before the start of the trial. I always got a little nervous before my trials, but this was different. I felt like it was me personally who was on trial and that I was the one who was facing being locked away for the rest of my life. Closer to the truth, however, I was convinced that I was about to be exposed to the world for the fraud who I really was. There was a looming sense of doom that I couldn't shake or ignore.

In terms of preparation, I couldn't possibly have been more prepared. I finished all my witness outlines for cross-examination of Joe's witnesses. My opening statement was written, and I had read through it so many times that I had it almost completely memorized. Dr. Scanlon helped me put together a report as if he was going to testify for us, and it sounded pretty good. I even had my suits dry cleaned and ready for the week. Still, it felt a little like I was preparing for my own funeral.

I arrived at the office early that morning. Nobody else was there yet—not even Amy, whose job it was to open the office every day. I turned on the lights and put on the coffee. Although I had been alone in the courthouse many times before when I worked late, it was still a little offsetting to be isolated like that. There were strange noises coming from the old heating system struggling to do its work. It occurred to me for the first time that the building was probably haunted.

On top of my desk was a small white envelope marked "Personal" with my name handwritten on the front in blue ink. It was near the edge. I didn't see it there at first. I immediately recognized the handwriting, and I slowly opened it.

Sam,

Please forgive this small intrusion as I know that you do not want to hear from me. But I know that this is a big day for you and I wanted to wish you good luck. I am pretty sure that you have yourself wrapped so tightly about now that you didn't even sleep last night. Again, I am sorry for adding to your worries. I also deeply regret that you don't know how great you really are. You are an outstanding lawyer and I just want to say that I hope you win!

Carla

Sitting alone there, I cried for several minutes. I was glad that no one else was there to see me. It felt good though, a kind of much needed stress release. I was stuck and couldn't see my way through. I tried to read the note again, but I couldn't. I quickly put it back in the envelope and put the envelope in the top drawer. I hadn't decided yet what I was going to do with everything Carla's mom had said. There simply was too much coming at me at the same time. I needed to compartmentalize everything, which just happened to be one of my strengths.

On my way out the door to court, I asked Amy about the card.

"A deputy delivered them," she answered. "They were probably left at the security desk on the first floor."

"When?"

"Yesterday, late afternoon. You were already gone. I gave them to Larry to put on your desk."

"*Them*?" I asked. "There was more than one?"

"Yeah, there were two."

"I only got one."

"Well, I don't know what happened to the other one," she replied. "They both had your name on the front and they both were marked personal. That's why I didn't open them."

"All right, I'll look for it later," I stated. "I have to go."

———•●•———

Jury selection was scheduled to begin at 11:00 a.m. Approximately 100 perspective jurors were being screened. Only two were Black. I always felt a little like picking a jury was a bit of a crapshoot. Most people don't really want to serve on the jury and are looking to get excused as soon as possible so that they can get back to their busy lives. I could definitely relate.

We had a final pre-trial conference in chambers at 9:30 a.m. Joe and I arrived at the same time, and we had to wait together out in the hall because Judge Lombardi wanted to wait for the stenographer. We made uncomfortable small talk about the weather. He was the only attorney in the district's attorney office who I couldn't get along with. I was glad when the stenographer finally arrived.

"Good morning, gentleman," the judge began. "You have both tried cases in my courtroom before, so I think you guys know the drill. We will select twelve people initially to put in the box. I will question the jury pool first, and then I will give both of you ten minutes to ask follow-up questions. I want three alternates. You each can only challenge two people. We will keep going until we get our jury. Any questions?"

"No," Joe said.

"No," I echoed.

"I will not allow any cameras in the courtroom. But reporters will be permitted to sit in that back row. Attorneys are prohibited from discussing this case with the media. This is the order of the court!"

Joe looked at me quickly out of the corner of his eye and grinned oddly before turning away. I was only slightly annoyed.

"Sam is the defendant here yet?" the judge asked.

"I don't know," I replied. "He's not in the courtroom. But I will have them bring him up before the jurors are seated."

"That's fine," the judge agreed.

"Also, I am asking that he not be handcuffed in front of the jury," I said. "And for the deputies not to sit too close to us.

"Yes, no handcuffs," the judge indicated. "There will be extra security in the courtroom, so they will hang back."

"Please have all of your witnesses set and ready to go starting tomorrow," the judge further directed. "I told the commissioner of jurors that we can pick this jury in a day and that is what I intend to do. I will not tolerate any unnecessary delay."

This time the judge looked directly at me.

"My witnesses are ready," I reacted. "We have never delayed anything."

"Our witnesses are all lined up too." Joe declared. "There is a chance that my first witness may be a few minutes late because she is a nurse, and she will be working all week at the hospital. But she can be here on thirty minutes notice. I'm hoping to get through all three victims on the first day, but that depends on how long the cross examinations will be."

"As I mentioned, there will be no adjournments of the trial," the judge interjected in a rather stern fashion. "I have set aside the rest of this week. That's four days. If any of your witnesses are not here when they are called, you will be expected to proceed with your case without the witness. Are we all clear with that?"

"Yes, your honor," Joe answered.

"Yes," I acknowledged and nodded.

Again, my feeling was that Judge Lombardi was thinking that I was going to go out of my way to delay things or to otherwise upset the applecart. I'm pretty sure that was why he wanted the stenographer there. He wanted proof that I had been warned.

But I didn't care what he thought about me. In my mind, he had already shown that he couldn't be trusted to do his job or to remain impartial.

The day dragged even though we moved through the selection process at a pretty good clip. I always felt forced to take people at their word when it came to their personal bias and thought it was futile, in most instances, to dig beyond the surface. Most of the prospective jurors denied knowing or hearing anything about this case, something I found hard to believe considering how much press it had already received. But I kept thinking that I just had to make it to the weekend, and this would all be behind me for the most part.

Joshua sat quietly next to me. He hardly spoke or moved at all. I bought him two blue dress shirts, khaki pants, and brown loafers at the Goodwill store to wear in court. It didn't help much. He still looked like a social misfit.

We finished right at 4:45 p.m. We only had two alternate jurors, but the judge decided to just go with that rather than having people come back the next day. We ended up with six men and six women. Both alternates were men, and all of the jurors were white. No one stood out, and their overall vibe was that they were a group of conservative laborers who were primed to convict anything that breathed.

When I got back to the office at 5:10 p.m., everyone was still there, including Teresa. I only made it as far as the main entryway. They all wanted a firsthand account from me of everything. I didn't mind answering their questions, even though I was exhausted and just wanted to go home. Being in court all day was draining.

"Sam, I found that other envelope," Amy advised. "It was on the floor. I left it for you."

I still needed to call Dr. Scanlan. He was planning to come to court tomorrow so that he could hear the testimony of the victims. I hadn't eaten anything all day and I was starting to get a headache. More than anything, however, I just wanted to go to sleep. Hopefully, I would be able to settle down enough to actually sleep.

I immediately saw the white envelope on my desk when I walked in my office. My name was handwritten in blue ink, along with the words, *Personal and Confidential.* I put down my file box and opened it.

Sam,

The three victims in your rape trial are being forced to testify at the trial against their will. They are terrified, but the district attorney threatened them and said they have no choice. They are planning to hide and not show up for the trial. Thought you would want to know.

Anxiously awaiting your next move.

I panicked a little at first. It felt like I was complicit in a devilish scheme. I picked up the envelope again and began looking suspiciously for any indication of the author of this communication. I looked on both sides. There was nothing.

After settling down, I came to two quick conclusions: First, someone was definitely helping Joshua for some reason. My best guess was that it was someone at the jail because his contact with the outside world was severely limited. No doubt, his circle of influence at the jail cast much wider than anyone would have imagined.

Second, the person who wrote the note had to know somebody in Joshua's family. If the information was true, and I had every reason to believed that it was, then it was doubtful that any one of these victims would have spoken openly to just anyone about anything having to do with this awful case. No, it had to be someone in their inner circle, like a family member, who they trusted enough to disclose that they were considering defying law enforcement and hiding out until the trial was over.

Needless to say, I probably would never know for sure who sent me the note. But the undeniable truth was that I wasn't working this case alone. Ordinarily, I would have appreciated the tip, regardless of the source. However, I feared deep down that I was working with the devil himself, which couldn't possibly be a good thing.

Moreover, something about the wording of the note itself led me to believe that Joshua wanted me to know that he was somehow behind it. This was just like him. But there was no way that I was going to willingly get caught up in one of his wicked games.

— • ● • —

I spoke briefly to Dr. Scanlan, and we were all set. He was planning to be in court by 1:00 p.m. I had a couple of little things to do on my other cases, including returning the call of one of the town justices from one of my night courts. It only took me a few minutes to get through everything. I then gathered my stuff and went directly home.

I ate dinner in bed, which consisted of a medium pepperoni pizza and a bottle of beer. The TV was on, but I wasn't really watching it. I refused to think about Carla and fell to sleep almost immediately. Surprisedly, I slept the whole night through and woke up refreshed.

Chapter 25

They taught us in law school that the opening statement to the jury is not legal or factual arguments. Rather, it is just supposed to be a preview of what we expected the evidence in the case will be, a kind of a road map. The jury can be told who will testify and what the witness is expected to say. But we can't talk about the law or explain the elements of the crimes. The prosecutors, in particular, have to be careful that they don't say too much because they don't want to commit an error that could result in a mistrial.

Joe Bartolotta really was a good trial attorney. His opening statement to the jury was excellent. He wasn't overly dramatic, and he didn't overstate his case. His catch phrase was, "The road to justice is paved on one truth after the other, and like Dorothy, the lion, and the scarecrow, we just have to follow the bricks in the road."

The jury was paying close attention to him and overall, he was very effective.

Obviously, I had a lot less to work with. I kept it brief. I mostly talked about Joshua being a product of his upbringing in a dysfunctional family. I suggested that "[i]f we are going to judge him, or anything that he did or didn't do, on June 15, the night in question, then our own humanity dictates that we look at him through a lens that includes everything he is, including his history of being a victim of abuse and gross neglect. Justice requires an honest and thorough look at what happened in that small country house to the victims and how it came to be."

We broke for lunch at 11:45 a.m., right after my opening statement. Joe's witnesses were scheduled to begin at 1:00 p.m. I hadn't really seen any press yet, but obviously the circus was just starting. I expected a full house of spectators for the afternoon, including the news media, for the testimony of the three victims.

I was looking for signs from Joe or the judge that there were witness problems afoot. I saw none. They were both still on their game. In fact, before I left, I saw Joe standing in the hall talking and joking with a group of people. I was suddenly disappointed because it appeared that the anonymous tip might be wrong.

We began promptly at 1:00 p.m. As I suspected, the courtroom was almost full. I was sitting at counsel's table at 12:55 p.m. with Joshua when the judge's clerk indicated that the judge wanted to see me in his chambers. When I walked in the office, Joe was already sitting there alone with the judge. I wondered if they even knew how that looked. But this time it didn't really matter. I took one look at Joe, and I instantly knew that this was about to get really good.

"Sam, we have a situation here," the judge quickly said without looking directly at me. "Turns out that the victims are not here yet."

"None of them?" I asked.

"No," he replied and looked hard at his watch.

"Well, they have time," I responded. "We haven't even started with the nurse yet."

"Yes, but you know that she will be really quick," Joe offered. "It's just the rape kits, which is basically a business record that you already stipulated into evidence. How much time can that take?"

"It still buys you a little time," I asserted. "Do you

know where they are?"

"As of last night, they knew everything and were onboard to be here," Joe indicated.

"Okay then, they are probably just parking or something."

"Maybe," he replied. "I'm thinking that we might have to take the witnesses out of order."

"No way," I resisted. "I don't think that's appropriate. My expert, who I am paying a lot of money, is here in the courtroom right now to hear the victims testify. I can't afford to have him come back another day. There is no way that the county will pay for that. So, my client will be severely prejudiced if they don't testify today. I say we just wait for them to get here."

"You can't tell me what order to call my witnesses!" Joe erupted.

"You need to calm down," I replied. "I'm not shouting at you, am I? This is your order. You can't just switch up now. It's not our fault that you can't find your witnesses."

"Judge, can we have a ruling here?" Joe begged. "We are asking that we be permitted to call a few witnesses out of order in the interest of justice and judicial economy."

"Then I think we should go on the record with this," I argued. "There is no stenographer in here like before, and I'm asking that we get her in here for this. Specifically, I am going to ask that the People go on record as to what, if any, attempts they have made to get the witnesses here and to provide assurances to us as to exactly when they can get them here in court as you ordered. I have made every effort to abide by the court's prior rulings that you will not permit any delays in this trial. It's only fair that the same rules apply to them!"

Joe squirmed in his chair and pouted. He was losing it.

"But your honor, counsel is trying…"

"My understanding, Judge, is that you didn't want your authority challenged," I persisted. "What gives?"

"We will definitely go on the record, Sam" the judge responded. "But before we do, I want a moment to confer with my clerk. I need for you both to wait in the hall. In the meantime, Joe, I suggest that you try to get us some more concrete answers. And do it fast!"

We walked out together. I sat down in one of the chairs. Joe walked away briskly.

I was left sitting there alone for forty minutes. Of course, I didn't mind. I readily grasped that each passing minute was better for me.

Eventually I saw Joe lingering several feet in the background, close to the secretary's desk. He clearly didn't want to be near me.

"Okay, Joe, what can you tell us?" the judge asked while sitting behind his desk.

"They're still not here," he reluctantly disclosed. "We need time to find them."

"I'm inclined to grant you a short adjournment to find your witnesses in the interest of justice. However, I have been thinking more about this case, and I think that this might be a good time to pursue a plea. I'm opened to whatever you guys can work out. We have a jury empaneled, and I don't want to waste any more of their time."

I didn't say anything.

"What about it, Sam?" Judge Lombardi asked. "You think you can talk your guy into pleading guilty?"

"It depends on what it is," I answered.

We both looked at Joe.

"Twenty-two minimum," Joe said. "He pleads to two counts rape first, one count assault first, and three counts of kidnapping."

"Eighteen years minimum," I countered.

"Are you out of your mind?" Joe erupted. "This is a fair deal, and you know it!"

"If it is so fair, then why didn't you offer it before

now?" I squeezed. "Looks to me like you don't have any victims, so you don't have any case at all. Need I remind you that the written confession was already suppressed as being unlawfully obtained by these fine law enforcement officers. You don't have a firsthand account of anything to present to the jury. Maybe, my client should just take his chances. Maybe he completely walks!"

"Did you talk to them, Sam?" Joe demanded. "Is that what happened? Adding a little witness tampering to your resume, huh?"

"I'm going to pretend that I didn't hear that," I threatened.

Joe looked dejected. He was perspiring heavily on his forehead and his tie was askew.

"Twenty years," he forced himself to say through his clenched teeth. "But he has to plea today!"

"Okay, but I need time to talk to him. They have to take him back to lockup so that we can speak in private."

— • ● • —

True to form, Joshua didn't want to take the plea deal. He was greedy, among other things. He could see blood in the water and like a killer shark, he was circling in for the kill.

"You really don't have a choice," I pointed out. "I thought you would be happy. You know that we don't have a defense."

"We don't need one," Joshua contended. "They don't have any witnesses here to testify against me. They can't prove the case. We can just sit back and watch them spin out of control."

"*Today*," I responded. "They can't prove the case *today*. Sooner or later these witnesses will show up and testify against you."

"What if they don't?"

"What do you know?" I demanded. "Please don't tell me that you had something to do with them not showing up."

"I don't know anything," he lied. "I'm just saying that they got no evidence. They automatically lose, right?"

"And I'm telling you that only a crazy person would reject this deal," I insisted. "They will never go any lower than twenty to forty—no matter what. When this trial resumes, you will get the maximum twenty-five to fifty years. Do you hear me? This is your only chance to ever live free again. I'm asking you to choose freedom!"

"Are you sure?" he inquired. "They don't have to let me go now?"

"Positive," I replied. "You're not going anywhere. Joshua, you're too smart to be this stupid."

"All right, if you say so," he conceded and exhaled loudly. "Not a problem."

"You sure?"

"Only a fool doesn't listen to his lawyer," he asserted.

———•●•———

After all that, Joshua pleaded guilty to the six highest counts in the indictment. There was no discernable response from the audience. He didn't have to make a full recitation of everything he did the night in question. However, he was required to affirm that he was knowingly pleading guilty, on the advice of counsel, and that he believed that pleading guilty was in his best interest. Sentencing was scheduled to take place in forty-five days.

Back at the office, my co-workers celebrated like we won the Super Bowl. I was mostly just relived that this torment was finally coming to an end. Nightmares are often caused by stress and anxiety from negative feelings suppressed during the day. With this case gone, that meant that there was one less thing in my life to torment my nights. I was already beginning to breathe a little easier.

Obviously, it would have been an entirely different result if even one of the victims showed up to testify. I never told anyone about the note. I wasn't hiding it. I just didn't have time to confer with someone in the moment. Besides, there was no strategy involved in it for me. I just had to wait and see what happened.

I was hoping that nothing bad had happened to the victims. Joshua seemed to be a little too confident that they were not showing up for my liking. Whoever he was working with had a plan. I just hoped that that plan didn't include causing more harm to these women.

Ultimately, even with the guilty pleas, the case wasn't over definitively. We all knew that anything could happen prior to sentencing. Technically, Joshua could even attempt to withdraw his guilty plea if he wanted to for some reason. But the fact is that I wasn't outmatched, and I didn't make a fool of myself with the whole world watching- both of which were big parts of what had been keeping me up at night.

It was just after 7:00 p.m. when I got to my apartment. It was completely dark inside. I liked the quiet and the calm. Rather than turning on the lights, I opted to bask there in the emptiness of solitude. I changed my clothes and then just lay on my bed. I wasn't hungry, and I wasn't tired. I wasn't happy or sad either. I was numb, like my brain had been anesthetized. I didn't sleep or allow myself the luxury of thinking about anything. I easily retreated to the place in the back corner of my heart that I had long ago reserved just for me, and I hid out there for the rest of the evening.

Chapter 26

I didn't know anything about the city of Rochester. It was about four times the size of Utica. I had only been downtown once before for Christina's wedding. I really had to follow the directions that I was given closely because I found it to be confusing. It wasn't a stress-free drive by any means.

I was looking for North Clinton Street. The deeper I drove into the city, the worse it got. I quickly recognized the depressing urban blight and desolation. I felt the pain and the heaviness of the spirit of poverty and death that openly dwelled there. This was worse than Cornhill because it was bigger, and the feelings were more intense. I was getting a little nervous because my meeting was scheduled for 1:00 p.m., and it already was 12:50. I relaxed only when I saw the small sign for "First Tabernacle Church."

It was a small white building on a corner lot that had been converted into a church. There was a small parking lot to the right that was protected by a chain link fence in the back and on one side. There was only an old van parked there. I knocked on the door twice and waited. It slowly opened.

A heavy-set, light-skinned woman smiled warmly and invited me to come in. She had a Spanish accent. I thought she might be the housekeeper because she wore plastic gloves and had a cleaning rag in her hand. There didn't appear to be anyone else in the building. She led me down a narrow hall to a small office.

"Sam," Pastor Jenkins said and grinned. "How good to see you again, man."

"Me too," I replied as we shook hands and hugged briefly.

He was wearing a blue Buffalo Bills sweatshirt and jeans. He looked a little older than I remembered.

"I have to say that I was very surprised when you called," he said.

"I know," I acknowledged. "Thank you for agreeing to meet with me."

"No problem," he replied. "I'm flattered that you came all this way just to see me. Have a seat, and tell me how I can help you?"

I was suddenly very nervous. My throat felt dry, and it was hard for me to swallow.

"Um… the last time we spoke was at Carla's parent's house, you said something that I haven't been able to get out of my head. You said something to me about the 'fire in my belly being divinely sent,' and I was wondering if maybe you could explain to me what you mean by that?"

"Oh, that's all," he said and laughed to himself. "I assure you that I wasn't trying to entice you or scare you in any way. I guess I need to be more careful what I say to people."

"Oh no, I didn't think that" I assured. "I have just been thinking about what you said a lot."

"Sam, there are several times in the Bible where it says that Jesus was moved with compassion to do something. It was usually something to do with healing the sick or feeding the poor. We know that it was the Holy Spirit that was moving him to do those things. I just happen to believe that the things that we are most passionate about as individuals in this life are an important part of God's overall plan for all of his people."

"I have never heard that before," I admitted.

"But you know that you are different, don't you?" he pressed. "The inequities and misfortune you see around you in the world affect you tremendously, just like Jesus. Am I wrong?"

"No, you're not wrong," I cautiously conceded.

"That's all that I meant," he said. "You just need to follow that fire you feel inside and see where it takes you."

"How do I do that?" I questioned. "I'm not Jesus."

"And that's the million-dollar question, isn't it?" he asked and breathed hard. "Myself, I wanted to go to medical school. My father was one of the first Black surgeons in this area. I was an excellent student. Frankly, I did better in school than both of my younger brothers who did go on to practice medicine. But when I was in college at Colgate University, I went to a Campus Crusade meeting one night and fell in love with Jesus and the word of God. I tried to ignore it, but I couldn't. Eventually I dropped out of school completely to pursue ministry."

"Wow, that's amazing!" I expressed.

"Well, my father didn't think so," he said with a chuckle. "It basically broke my parents' hearts, although they eventually came around."

He looked dejected, closed his eyes, and lost himself in the moment for a couple of seconds.

"I have never been supported by the church, and I have had several different jobs over the years," he continued. "I eventually had to get a job driving a school bus in order to support my family. It's a far cry from operating on people's hearts in some big fancy hospital, I know. But I don't regret following my destiny in Christ Jesus."

"That's a great story," I said.

"Maybe. I don't know," he hesitated. "I'm not trying to say that you are called to the ministry. That's between you and God. What I am saying though is that being an attorney is just what you do. It's not who you are. You won't be happy until you figure out who you really are. But I think that you already know that."

"Yes, I know… I'm definitely lost. Thanks, this helps."

"You don't have to thank me," he said. "Just follow your heart, son, and don't try to figure everything out upfront. It will come. I promise. You are still so young."

"I don't know about that," I joked. "I feel like I'm a hundred years old."

"Oh yeah? Imagine how I must feel then," he stated and laughed again.

There was a very calming presence about Pastor Jenkins. Most of my nerves had pretty much faded away already.

"I imagine that it must be hard pastoring a church today, especially in the inner-city?" I inquired.

"I know a lot of pastors who are just calling it a day and quitting the ministry altogether," he informed. "The pressures are ever increasing, and people today are so entitled and needy."

"I know about needy people," I sympathized.

"I suppose you do," he obliged. "Some mornings I can hardly get out of bed because my heart is so grieved. I honestly don't know how much more I can take. Recently, I officiated over a funeral for a young girl. She was just seventeen years old. I didn't know her. She just graduated from high school. She was shot and killed about four blocks from here. All she was doing was standing with some friends in front of a convenience store. Now she gone forever, and for what?"

"I don't understand it either," I echoed. "I mean, how did we get here? I thought this is supposed to be the greatest country on earth."

"Can you believe that it was the third shooting that week in this community?" he questioned. "I know a couple of people who are on the City Council, and I know the mayor. None of them are bad people, and they all mean well. But they cannot solve what is essentially a spiritual crisis in our city by secular means alone."

"It's like people of color have been cursed somehow," I said.

"These Black kids who you represent in court everyday have completely given themselves over to a *reprobate mind*," he contended.

"What's that?" I wondered.

"It just means that they have lost any desire that they may have ever had to please God," he explained. "Sadly, they are self-serving in everything they do. They love the violence for the sake of violence and actively pursue lawlessness. They're like demoniacs."

"I agree that most of them don't care anything about God or church," I commented. "It's an old fashion notion to them—probably to most people today."

"The Bible predicted that it would come to this."

"It does?" I questioned. "Do you think that there is anything that can be done?"

"Jesus is the answer!" he proclaimed. "He's always been our only hope. Maybe things had to get this bad in order for many who have completely lost their way to sincerely want to turn around and seek him."

"I don't know," I said.

"Me either," the pastor conceded. "I also don't really know if a true believer can ever drift so far away that he or she becomes reprobate, but I do know those who have ever given their hearts to the Lord Jesus Christ cannot be cursed," he offered. "According to Scripture, Christ redeemed us from curses."

"Well, it doesn't look or feel like that," I argued. "No offense, but if what you're saying is true, then churches have failed to do their jobs. Innocent kids are dying everyday who never had a chance. I know that I asked you this before, but where is Jesus in all this?"

"He is still as compassionate as ever," he stated definitively. "But unfortunately, you can't force people to believe on him. There is a thing called *free will*. Too many people of all creeds and have bought into the devil's lies. He got the jump on us, and now we are too far behind to reach most of them."

"Sounds like the church needs to step up," I concluded. "And not with just food distribution outreaches and prayer vigils after somebody's kid has just shot and murdered somebody else's kid! These young boys doing all these shooting don't have stopping sense!"

"I couldn't agree more," he said. "It's time for our pastors and leaders to come outside of the church walls and take back what has been stolen from us. The Bible tells us to visit those who are in prison, but most churches don't do that. Nobody's got time for all that. I don't have to tell you."

"No, I see it all the time," I divulged. "A lot of our clients never get any visitors. I mean never—and they have been incarcerated for years. It's like they have been completely forgotten and have fallen off the face of the earth. It's really sad."

"These streets are a battleground," the pastor reflected. "We can't be afraid to look the devil in the eye and shout out the word of God directly in his face as we fight for our children."

"I have to say that I'm not sure how that would look, as a practical matter, I mean," I admitted.

"For one thing, I really think that the focus should mostly be on reaching the kids, the little ones who are still in the elementary schools and middle school—and maybe even younger," he proposed. "After his birth, we don't see Jesus again in the Bible until he was twelve years old in the temple questioning the doctors. I would like to see more programs that target the younger group who have not yet reached that age of accountability under Jewish custom.”

“It’s interesting to hear you say that,” I remarked. “I have never considered that before.”

“That means that we would have to go into the homes, which is something that no one really wants to do because the families are all screwed up today,” he advocated. “It’s the family situation that is at the heart of our problems because the enemy of the church has targeted our families and children.”

“That’s true,” I answered. “All the fathers are in jail, and the kids are running through the streets without restraint.”

“And by the time you get them, it’s too late,” he argued. “The damage has already been done.”

I nodded. “So true.”

“What if we taught the little five-year-olds that they are too good to ever sell or use drugs?” he continued. “Too smart to join a gang? Drill into them that all this crazy stuff is beneath them! What if we told our young girls that the boys who sell drugs or who run the streets are not good enough for you because God made you special?”

“I couldn’t agree more,” I declared. “It’s way too late by high school. I know that a very high percentage of kids in Utica are living below the poverty line—something like 40 percent. They need support, confidence, and vision.”

“Yeah, *vision,*” he repeated. “I like that!”

We were interrupted by Sonja, the woman who opened the door for me and brought me in. Turns out she was the pastor’s wife, and I was ashamed of my earlier assumption about her. I didn’t remember seeing her at the wedding. They apparently lived within walking distance of the church, and she made us lunch. I felt bad that she went through all that trouble for me. I wasn’t expecting that at all.

“No trouble at all,” she said. “My husband has been very excited all morning that you were coming. We don’t get a lot of visitors who make him smile."

She lit up as she spoke and quickly gazed over at him. I was truly touched by this wonderful couple.

We ate right there in the office on TV trays. She made chicken and rice with vegetables. We had fried ice cream for dessert. Everything was delicious. I wondered how the pastor managed to stay so thin while eating food this good. He apparently had a healthy appetite.

We engaged in small talk while we finished our lunch.

"I heard that you and Carla broke up?" he blurted out at one point.

My heart sank. I knew that the subject was bound to come up. But I still wasn't ready to talk about her.

"Yes, we did," I answered and looked away.

"I'm really sorry," he stated. "Might I be so bold as to ask you what happened?"

"Um… let's just say that I found out that she was entertaining another suitor."

"Aww, I hate hearing that," he sympathized. "Do you want to talk about it?"

"There really isn't anything to say," I responded. "It is what it is."

"Really?"

He looked skeptical with both eyebrows slightly raised.

I didn't answer him.

"So, it's like that?" he remarked.

I was trying hard not to make eye contact.

"It's just that I keep thinking about her being with a *white* guy," I reluctantly disclosed. "I know that his race shouldn't really matter, but it's the thing that's eating at me the most. It just makes me sick to my stomach because *white* is the one thing that I can never be, no matter what. More than embarrassed or even hurt, I feel *emasculated*."

"*Emasculated*?" he repeated with added emphasis. "Really? Well, that's not exactly a word that I hear every day."

"Well, it's honestly how I feel," I finally came clean.

Our eyes met full force and mine pleaded for him to help me erase some of my pain.

"Sam, let me just say that I think men need respect from their woman probably more than anything else—even sex—which is exactly why so many women choose to withhold it for their own reasons. The male-female relationship is contentious by design because we are made different."

"Maybe it was my fault," I conceded. "Maybe I couldn't give her what she needed."

"Look, I love Carla with all my heart," he began. "But my guess is that she never told you what she really needed, so how could you possibly know?"

"I probably could have tried harder too," I confessed. "Maybe listened better."

"I don't think that it's a matter of how hard you tried to make it work," he said. "Resist the temptation to make excuses for her. She is carrying a lot of pain. You know what they say about how 'hurt people hurt people.'"

"I would have done just about anything for her," I disclosed. "That's why I completely lost my mind when it all went down. It felt like my soul was on fire."

"Maybe, your soul actually was on fire," he surmised. "Maybe it's time that you face your own sense of racial inferiority once and for all."

"What?" I questioned. "Face my racial what?"

"You think white men are better than you."

"No, I don't," I responded instinctively. "I don't want to be white!"

"That's not what I'm saying," he contended. "Think about it for a minute. They have everything that we don't. They have all the power in American society, including most of the money and fame. They have the long straight hair that most little Black girls envy. They wear the white hats, and we look like criminals even when we are just walking down the street minding our own business!"

"I didn't realize that I thought like that," I insisted. "I mean to that extent anyway. Even that is embarrassing."

"All Black people have secretly thought like that at one time or another because that's the lie that we have been told over and over again," he explained. "I don't think we actually wish that we were born white. I know that I don't. But we want what they have. And what they ultimately have as a race, that we don't have, is a sense of positive self-worth."

"Oh, I get it," I exclaimed. "It's like *white privilege* and the idea of a black curse in a nutshell. They kind of work together because they both stem from institutionalized white dominance."

"And I think we can both agree that white people are not morally superior in any way. After all, they enslaved an entire race of people out of hate and for selfish gain. It was pure evil."

I nodded my head up and down.

"But you will never truly be free until you denounce that lie and see yourself as *the head and not the tail*."

"Wait a minute, the *head*?" I questioned. It was a knee-jerk reaction.

"The Bible teaches that God's people are above and not beneath others," he explained. "That's how much ground Black Christians in this country have lost."

"I definitely have never seen myself that way," I admitted.

"You see, Sam, more than being a Black man, you are a child of God. We all are *one family* if we confess him. It doesn't matter what color we are. Together we are the *light* of the world."

"The *light*," I repeated mostly to myself.

"I really don't think that Carla could ever do better than you," he complimented. "You are one terrific young man!"

"Thank you," I responded meekly.

"But it's not how I see you that matters, is it?" he provoked. "It's how *you* see yourself!

"Right, seeing is believing," I echoed.

"The mind is powerful so it's important to believe the right things," he said.

"So, you think people can change the way they think down deep just like that?" I pressed.

"No, I don't think that at all," he admitted. "It may take a lifetime to break free of some mental strongholds. Especially the ones that have been imbedded since childhood. But we must always strive get to the point where we see ourselves the way that God sees us. And I assure you that *he* looks at the *heart*, not our outside appearance."

"I want to be free," I articulated. "But nothing has been working."

"That's because you've been trying to fight everything in your own strength," he observed. "That, son, is the recipe for failure."

"But that's the only way I know how to fight," I explained. "I have never really had anybody to lean on or help me before."

"I don't know about that," he refuted.

"You're trying to tell me God has been with me?"

"You're not supposed to be here. You're where you are today when others just like you are dead and buried in graves."

"Then what am I missing?"

"Probably just walking with him, acknowledging him in your life in all you do."

"Like going to church and praying?" I wondered.

"No, it's much more than that," he articulated. "The Bible says that 'if you confess with your mouth that Jesus is Lord and believe in your heart that God raised him from the dead, you will be saved.' Tell me this, have you accepted Jesus as your personal savior?"

I was both startled and embarrassed by the question, which ignited a slow churning burn deep inside me much like a chemical reaction.

"Umm…I don't know?" I answered meekly. I felt ashamed and guilty. I bit my lower lip and looked away from him.

"That's a fair answer," he said. "Thank you for being honest with me about that. But you know that there is a way that you can know beyond a shadow of a doubt. Do you want to know for sure?"

"Yes, I do," I said.

My palms were sweating, and all my insides were agitated. I felt uncomfortable sitting there in that old wooden chair that provided little support to my back, and I began to nervously fidget about. But I also sensed a change in the atmosphere. Like something big was coming.

"Let me ask you this then, do you believe that you are a sinner lost in this world without Christ Jesus?"

I began to shake uncontrollably. I knew what an altar call was. I had seen many over the years. But I had never felt anything like this before.

"Yes," I whispered from my heart.

"And do you believe that Jesus is the Savior of the world and that he lived, was crucified, and rose from the dead?"

"Yes."

"And do you want him to forgive you for all of your sins and cleanse you of your unrighteousness?"

"Yes."

"For the living God of the Bible to be your God?"

"I do," I agreed.

"Last, will you be his son and serve him with your whole heart?"

"Yes, yes I will!"

"Then that's all that there is to becoming a Christian, if you truly believe," he declared.

"I do believe it," I muttered. "I know it's true."

"Then you are born again!"

Our eyes met, and I was overcome with emotion. I couldn't wipe the tears away fast enough. He was smiling and handed me a tissue.

"Thank you," I said. "Thank you so much!"

"You're very welcomed," he stated. "I honestly can't wait to see what God has planned for you. Always remember that he has set you free for a reason."

"So…what's next?" I asked.

I couldn't believe that this was happening to me. I felt a sense of excitement more than anything else. This unexpected moment was life changing. I felt it deep inside, through to my bones. I wanted more.

"Find a good Bible-teaching church and start attending there regularly," he instructed. "Not all churches are the same so be careful. Some of these denominational folks unfortunately are caught up too much on tradition and have a lot of error in their teaching."

"Okay."

"And I just hate that we have inserted so much politics into our faith," he lamented. "So, be careful because the devil wants nothing more than to steal your joy by polluting your mind with that kind of junk!"

"Okay, I'll do that."

"And Sam, one more thing, and this is very important," the pastor warned. "Be sure to study God's word for yourself to find out who he says you really are. I think you'll be surprised to see that the Bible has a lot to say about overcoming the bad thoughts in our head."

"Right."

I was trying to process everything as quickly as possible. I felt like I had somehow caught a huge break with this unexpectant opportunity to completely unburden myself, and I didn't want to waste it.

I forced myself to speak up. "Um…so what do you think I should do about Carla?"

"Do you love her?"

"Yes, I think I do."

"Then forgive her and move on, man," he preached.

"Just like that?" I questioned. "I'm still really angry at her."

"We all need to be forgiven for something—just like you just asked to be forgiven by God," he explained. "God forgives us, and we forgive others who trespass against us. That's how it works."

"That's going to be hard for me," I confessed. "It's going to take some time. I think that I was born angry. You would understand if you knew how I was raised, if you knew my mother. There are huge holes in my soul."

"Yeah, we all have those," the pastor dismissed. "I have found that some people just clean up better than others. But it's who we are when we get behind closed doors where no one else can see us that really matters."

"I feel like I have a right to be angry about the hand that I've been given," I articulated. "I'm not just talking about my relationship with Carla. I mean, don't you think that Black people have a right to be angry?"

"Our anger is not an excuse to sin," he lectured.

"I know, but what do you do with it?" I wondered.

"Process it, and try to see it for what it is," he replied and sighed heavily. "We ought to be self-controlled and sober-minded. The Bible teaches that God himself feels anger, but that doesn't change his nature, or how he loves us."

"I'm just saying that that's where the real struggle is for me," I explained.

"I hear you, but I disagree slightly," he said. "Our battle is not against ourselves, and it's certainly not against other people. Really, it's against the devil."

"The devil is fighting me personally?"

"Perhaps one of the biggest lies of all is that the devil isn't real," he explained. "I would think that in your line of work that you know that there is a tangible, evil force in the world all around us. There is a mastermind behind all of it, and he is in control of most of the world's systems, like the court system. I suspect that you probably have come face to face with him, or one of his demons, a time or two. Am I right?"

"Maybe once or twice," I intentionally understated the reality. "Trust me. I know he's real. I have literally been locked in a jail cell with him more than a few times."

"He's smarter and stronger than you too," Pastor informed. "That's why you feel like you can't get ahead or like you are always losing ground. We simply can't defeat the devil by ourselves, no matter how hard we try."

"So, we…?

"We have to resist him as much as we can," he instructed. "Forgiving the people who have sinned against us is one way that we do that. We can't let him separate us from our brothers and sisters in Christ."

"Okay, I think I understand."

I breathed in hard, and slowly blew the hot air out of my lungs.

"Sam, I know it's a lot," he acknowledged. "The real reason God's people can't be cursed is because the devil can't possess what God has blessed. The rest of it is just a game. Just pray to God and ask him to lead you in his truth."

"Okay, I will."

The pastor slowly stood to his feet and walked over to me and put his hand on my shoulder.

"And please understand that I'm not saying that you should try to get back together with Carla," he softly spoke. "I obviously don't know everything that happened between the two of you and only you guys can decide that for yourselves. Forgiveness is not the same thing as trust. And you really need trust in order to have a healthy relationship with a life partner."

"Absolutely," I concurred.

"But you will never be able to move on with her, or with any other woman, for that matter, until you forgive her," he advised.

"Alright."

"While you're at it, forgive your mother too, along with yourself. I'm sensing that forgiving yourself is a big part of it for you."

"I don't know how to thank you," I said. "This was a lot better than what the counselor I saw had to offer!"

He smiled warmly.

"Just follow your destiny in him," he encouraged. "I promise you it's a good one."

Those three hours just flew by. I especially enjoyed listening to him talk about his life and the goodness of God. He suggested that I get on the road ahead of rush hour traffic. He prayed for me before I left. When he put his hand on my chest, it felt like I was on fire. I was soaring high as I pulled out of the parking lot, and I stayed that way all the way home.

I fully embraced the birth of my Christian faith. I bought my first bible! I made a few phone calls looking for suggestions for good churches, and there were a few that I was hoping to visit. I had no interest in any of the Black churches located in or around Cornhill. That just seemed like I would be going backward. But I was even more leery of white evangelicals who were too political for my liking.

I was seriously considering taking a trip to Jamaica. I found an all-inclusive resort that was relatively inexpensive that sounded perfect. I just wasn't sure about going alone. I feared that it would be a lot like me sitting on the beach watching other people vacation. There were several single's resorts available too, but I felt like I was too old for those kinds of places.

I was very worried about Carla. I really wanted to reach out to her and make sure that she was okay, but I still didn't know what I wanted from her after that. While I agreed with everything Pastor Jenkins said about us, that still didn't mean that I was settled about her. It also occurred to me that there was a chance she was with this other guy now, and, if that was the case, I was better off not knowing. I considered just sending her a return note saying that I forgave her everything. But that seemed lame.

My intention was to pray about it like the pastor had suggested, however, I didn't have the humility to tell him at the time that I didn't know how to pray. I had never prayed for anything before in my life. And I never once saw or heard my grandmother pray at home. She was mostly just all talk when it came to a lot of stuff. Although she was religious, she didn't truly seek after God, at least not when she wasn't in church. I knew that I really needed to find a church soon.

There was another shooting in Utica. According to the news, one seventeen-year-old Black kid was dead, and another kid was in critical condition. I watched the telecast bewildered. It occurred to me that maybe Pastor Jenkins was wrong about me after all. There wasn't any fire in my belly that I could discern. I was mostly just tired.

I had another case with Joe Bartolotta. It seemed like I couldn't get away from the guy. It was a drug case. Typically, these were difficult cases for us because either the police found drugs on the person or in a common area he shared- like a car. It was nearly impossible to put together a good defense in these situations. Accordingly, the plea deals in drug cases were rarely generous to us.

Joe and I unintentionally walked out of the courtroom at the same time after the arraignment. Although we generally avoided each other, we both made the effort to be professional.

"I was a little disappointed that we didn't get to hear from your witnesses at the Weeks trial," Joe halfheartedly said.

"Oh really?" I questioned. "Why is that?"

"Because I really wanted to cross-examine that sister of his."

"Why?"

"Because she is just as bad as her brother, maybe worse," he expressed.

"That's not true," I resisted.

"She used to beat the crap out of him when they were young," Joe purported. "She controlled everybody in the family, including the mother and the other brother. She probably still does. According to probation, she's supposedly like an enchantress or some craziness. You know, she stabbed a teacher in the chest with a pen when she was just in the fourth grade. Luckily, he didn't die. I have never heard of anyone like her. Can you imagine someone like that treating patients? All of her juvenile records are sealed, which is how she was able to go to medical school in the first place."

"She presents well," I claimed and shrugged.

I tried to sound like I was aware of everything he just said and wasn't that impressed. I couldn't bear it if he knew that I was hanging on his every word.

"Maybe, but I would have impeached the hell out of her if you had put her on the stand!"

"What happened with the victims anyway?" I asked offhandedly.

"Oh, they got spooked by the media being in the courtroom. That's Lombardi's fault."

"But you found them?"

My heart raced inside my chest.

"Yeah, they didn't go too far," Joe advised. "These aren't the brightest people in the world. It wasn't too hard to find them."

———•●•———

I called her. I couldn't take it anymore. It took me all day to get up enough nerve to do it. I felt like an idiot.

"Carla?"

"Hi, Sam,"

"How are you?" I asked.

"I'm good. How are you?"

"I'm good too… um… the reason that I'm calling is… I just wanted to let you know that I got your note and… I want to say thank you."

"I heard your guy pled guilty."

"Yeah, he did."

"Well, that's what you wanted, right?"

"Yes, it is. I'm just glad that it's all over and done with."

"It must be a big relief for you."

"Until the next one," I said dismissively. "There are plenty more where that one came from."

We were both silent.

"I hope that you at least get a little break," she eventually said. "You deserve one."

"I'm thinking about going to Jamaica."

"Jamaica? I love it there!"

"Yeah, I desperately need to reset. I'm hoping that a little fun in the sun will do the trick."

"I think that's a great idea."

"I'm a little concerned that I will be a bored though. I mean, what is there to do at night by yourself?"

"Just go all out during the day," she suggested. "You'll be surprised how tired the heat makes you."

"Hmm… that makes sense. I never thought of that."

"I think you'll love it!"

"I'm still deciding."

"I really hope you go."

I took a deep breath. I felt like I was on thin ice and needed to choose my words carefully.

"Carla, I just wanted to apologize to you if I said or did anything that made you think that I hate you or something. I don't hate you."

"Oh, I know that," she acknowledged. "I think we both probably said things that we didn't mean."

"I could never hate you."

"I don't know," she remarked. "Maybe you could."

"I seriously doubt it! What makes you say that?"

"There are some things about me that you don't know."

"Everybody has stuff," I maintained.

"I just thought that if I told you that you wouldn't see me the same."

"Whatever it is, I wish that you would have told me."

"Me too," she admitted. "I know that I probably made a mistake, but I didn't know what else to do."

"You could have trusted me," I asserted.

"I didn't trust myself," she explained. "People make assumptions about me all the time that I have to live up to. It's exhausting!"

"I'm sorry if I did that," I said. "I didn't mean to."

"I think you know now that I'm not who you thought I was."

"I don't know what you mean?"

"Just that I'm far from perfect."

"You and me both."

"No, Sam," she resisted. "You still don't get it. I was in a mental hospital. Something happened... I'm really screwed up!"

"I don't care about that," I contended. "Apparently, you don't know me either."

"You say that now, but..."

"I don't care," I interrupted. "Everybody goes to the hospital when they get sick. Why would that matter?"

It sounded like she was crying.

"Listen, Carla," I spoke. "Whatever happened, I'm sorry that you got hurt. But a rose is still a rose as far as I am concerned. You're gonna have to let it go."

"I'm trying."

"I know you are. But what if you closed your eyes and imagined that none of the bad stuff ever happened and just let yourself go all the way in that direction to freedom? I know that's what I've been trying to do. It seems to be working."

"It's just been really hard for me," she asserted.

"Just give yourself a break," I maintained. "We all have to fight our way through sometimes."

She didn't say anything.

"There is something else that I want to tell you," I said.

"What is it?"

"I'm saved! I gave my life to Jesus."

"What? Are you serious?"

"I have prayed the salvation prayer a couple of times before when I was a kid going to church with my grandmother, but I never really believed. God didn't make sense to me when all I saw was pain all around. So, I blamed him and turned my back on him. I have been trying to fight everything on my own—and failing miserably at it, I might add."

"But what made you turn to God now?"

"I was talking with a guy, and he helped me to see that this is what has been missing in my life."

"What guy? Like a pastor, you mean?"

"Yeah, you know him. Pastor Jenkins."

"Uncle Sheldon? You talked with my uncle?"

"Yes, he's the guy," I disclosed. "He's great!"

"Are you kidding me? How did this happen?"

"I just called him, and I met with him at his church."

"Oh my God!" she exclaimed. "I can't believe this! He did the same thing with two of my friends in high school. He got them saved at my house."

"Really?"

"Yeah, my dad was furious."

"Why?"

"I don't know," she said. "Those two have a weird relationship. Mostly sibling rivalry, I think."

"Oh."

"He is so amazing!" she remarked and laughed to herself. "This is crazy! Wait until I tell Christina. She's going to lose her mind."

"Yes, he's awesome," I agreed.

"But you don't really know him," she considered. "Why did you reach out to him of all people?"

"Um…I felt something when I first met him at your parent's house that one time. I was really drawn to him."

"Hmm, I somehow missed all of that," she reflected.

"So, after everything happened… I don't know, I just really wanted to talk to him about my life. I was at a point where I didn't know which way was up. So, I called him."

"When did this happen?"

"About two weeks ago."

"And you went to Rochester? To his church?

"Yeah."

"You met with him alone?"

"Yeah."

"And he prayed for you?"

"He led me in the Sinner's Prayer."

"Well, I'm happy for you," she expressed. "I really am."

"Thank you," I replied. "I just feel so much better about everything. There is a growing peace inside that wasn't there before. I really needed to let it all go. I'm talking about the anger and the bitterness that I have been carrying for basically my whole life. It's been slowly eating away at my soul and killing me softly."

"Uncle Shelly did that for you?"

"No, God did it," I advised. "I'm being changed from the inside out."

"I hear it in your voice," she reflected. "You sound different. Maybe, that's what I need."

"Yes, maybe you should talk to your uncle too," I suggested. "I still don't understand it exactly. I know very little about the Bible. But I want to know everything. I'm just so grateful to God for transforming my thinking by opening my eyes."

"So, are you going to stop practicing law and open up your own church now?" she joked.

"I don't think so," I said with a laugh. "Can you imagine that? Me trying to preach to somebody?"

"Matter of fact I can," she complimented. "You're such a good speaker."

"Thanks, but I think that there's much more to it than just being a good speaker," I replied. "That's probably one or the reasons that many Black churches have missed the mark in such a big way. We like a show too much. And they are too easy to fake."

"You're probably right," she whispered.

"Um…Can you do me a favor?" I awkwardly changed the subject.

"What?"

"Can you maybe… be patient and not give up on

yourself? You have your whole life ahead of you. I thought you said before that you wanted to see the world. You are bright and super-talented. So, go see the world, Carla!"

"Thank you. I appreciate it."

"You're welcome."

We were both thinking. I felt anxious.

"I need to ask you something else, and I apologize for putting you on the spot," I cautioned. "But it's something I really need you to be honest about."

"Okay?"

"Do you think that…. Um, do you think that… you could ever love a man like me? It's okay if the answer is no, but I…."

"Is that really your question?" she challenged.

"Yeah…I'm sorry. I know it's weird…"

"Oh, Sam!" she uttered in what sounded like disbelief.

"See, I'm messed up too," I affirmed.

"Sam, let me ask you something," she shifted. "What did you just say? I am 'bright' and 'talented?'"

"Yeah."

"But you didn't say that I'm beautiful. You have never really told me that I am beautiful. Can you tell me why?"

My mind raced to try to recall a time that I complimented her on her appearance. I thought to myself that that couldn't possibly be true. Honestly, I really hadn't noticed, or intended the slight. I just always thought it was a given.

I stammered, "Um… I don't know… I guess…"

"I have never liked it when all guys can talk about is how I look," she divulged. "You somehow picked up on that without me having to tell you and you never did that."

I didn't know what to say.

"My biggest fear is that I will never meet anybody like you again who *listens* to me with his heart," she revealed.

It was my turn to cry. My heart and my soul were filled with a combination of emotions that I had never experienced before. I had cried more in the last month than I had cried in my whole life. To my dismay, I was starting to get used to it.

"Thank you for telling me that," I expressed. "But you are probably giving me too much credit."

"No, I don't think so."

"…Well, I probably should let you go," I spoke slowly.

"Yes, it's getting late."

I paused.

"Please feel free to call me if you ever need anything," I encouraged.

"Same here."

"Okay, I will."

"Okay."

"Have a good night."

"Good night, Sam."

Chapter 28

I went down to the lockup in the sheriff's office in the courthouse to talk to Joshua before his sentencing. It was a small, enclosed space with a wooden bleacher bench bolted to one wall. He was seated there. He wasn't wearing the clothes that I bought for him. He was back in the orange jumpsuit. It suited him better. He seemed to be in a pretty good mood.

"Hi, Sam."

"Hello, Joshua. Your sentencing is today. Do you have any questions?"

I sat down next to him. Perhaps I had gotten too comfortable around him. I didn't know.

"Nope. I've been sentenced before. Did you forget?"

"Right," I acknowledged. "The judge is going to ask you if you have anything to say. I advise against you saying anything. The press is there and anything you say will be used to make you look like a monster and be used against you for parole years from now."

"But I am a monster," he said. "I'm a product of my upbringing? Isn't that what you said?"

"I don't know *what* you are," I replied. "Did I offend you somehow?"

"No, not at all," he said matter-of-factly. "It's a good thing that my feelings aren't easily hurt."

"Yes, a good thing," I chimed in.

"Sam, what happened to you?" he questioned as he leaned in.

"What do you mean?"

"You look different."

"Different how?" I solicited.

"I can't rightly say. Brighter, I think."

"Well, I don't know. It's still me."

"I don't think so," he disputed. "You just don't want to say."

"Just keeping it professional," I professed.

"Fair enough," he said.

We looked at each other, eye to eye. It was like I was looking at him for the first time. I could see his pain. I never really saw that before. There was a lot of it, just past the iris and pupil of both eyes, clear as day—an approaching dark, greenish cloud of debris. I felt sorry for him. He knew he was lost in this world without hope. I knew the torment firsthand.

Joshua spoke first, "Anyway, is this the part where we say our goodbyes?"

"Yes, I guess it is."

"I wish I had something to give you to remember me by," he said.

"That's really not necessary," I resisted. "You're not exactly an easy guy to forget."

"Would it sound like a lie if I said that I have enjoyed our time together?"

"Maybe a little," I answered.

"I thought so," he said.

"Just being honest," I quickly replied.

"That's you, Sam, honest to a fault."

"What can I say? The truth will set you free."

"Oh, I know what I can do," he pivoted. "I want to tell you something. It might help you sleep a little better at night."

"What?"

He leaned in and calmly whispered, "Black people are easy."

He was straight-faced and looked only slightly smug, which I knew took some effort on his part to pull off.

"*Easy?*" I repeated.

I stared back at him.

"Like children who believe that fairytales are true," he continued. "They fall right off to sleep to it every time."

"I don't get it," I resisted.

"Think about it," he mocked. "You're a smart *boy*."

"Excuse me?" I objected.

"Oh, my!" he exclaimed with both eyes and his mouth stretched wide open and his hands cupping his jaw and cheeks. "Did I really just say that? Don't let it bother you. I'm just getting back into character for when I am back on the farm. You know it's not personal. Such fun!"

• ● •

The courtroom was only about half full. I recognized most of the people as being courthouse staff. The press was also well represented. The sentencing itself was uneventful. It felt like any other. It certainly sounded like all the others. Everybody said the usual things, including me.

I didn't see her at all until after sentence was pronounced and the court session was adjourned. I was watching as Joshua was handcuffed and led out of the courtroom when she walked up behind me.

"Mr. Hicks," she said.

"Yes," I replied as I turned around.

I was instantly shaken, and, to my dismay, my startled reaction gave me away. I recognized her immediately—only now she looked more sinister to me. There was clearly something dark and ominous in her eyes too that I had somehow overlooked before or, most likely, had been purposely hidden from view when we first met. I thought I saw her smile to herself at my reaction.

"Twenty years is really the best that you could do for my brother?" Virginia Weeks complained.

She looked disgusted.

"Under the circumstances I'd say that it is the best that anyone could have done," I replied.

"Maybe so," she countered. "But I still wish that we could have afforded to hire a real lawyer to defend him."

"Oh, me too," I answered. "I wish that too."

—————•●•—————

Mama's older sister passed away suddenly. She lived in Crystal Springs, Mississippi, where they were raised. Although I had heard a lot about her, I really didn't know Aunt Liza. Mama sounded more than a little depressed when she called to tell me the news, so I decided to go by the house and check in on her on my way home from work.

She was sitting alone in the darkened living room drinking a cup of coffee and watching television when I arrived.

"You, okay?" I asked.

"Yeah, I'm all right."

"Are you sure that you don't want to go to the funeral?" I inquired. "I know that you don't like to travel that far, but I'll take you if you want. It won't be that bad. I promise."

"No. I appreciate that kindly, but I don't want to go," she insisted. "I don't want to see her like that."

"Okay, if you are sure."

"I am," she responded. "I was just sitting here thinking about how Liza used to take care of us when Mama and Papa were in the tomato fields. She used to have us all over Copiah County. She liked to take us to the cemetery, of all places. For some reason she loved it there. And this one time, we were playing this voodoo game where we were trying to call people back from the dead using a spell. That's when my brother Jimmie Lee jumped down from this tree and Liza took off like lightning so fast down the way, and she just left us by ourselves, I tell you. And she didn't even think twice about looking back!"

She was laughing to herself as the faded memory of it all ran in her head. Obviously, I had heard this account before—maybe a hundred times. She used to love to tell us stories about people putting roots on other people in Mississippi and such practices.

"I think that's crazy," I said.

"Liza was crazy! But she was a good sister to me, you know?"

"I'm sure she was," I offered.

"So how are you doing with your breakup from your girl?"

"I'm good," I replied calmly. "It has forced me to do a lot of thinking about my life. It's time for me to grow up, I think."

"I been thinking about it too, and I think that I owe you an apology," she spoke. "I should have been more understanding before when you were telling me about it."

"No, it's okay," I said. "Don't worry about it."

"It's just that I know that there is no pain like the pain of the heart," she said solemnly. "Lord knows I didn't want that for you."

I felt a slight jab to my gut. I couldn't say anything in

response.

"I came up north when I was just seventeen years old. I wanted a better life for myself than what we had working the fields in Mississippi for white folks. But I never really found it. For some reason, it just never really happened for me. Son, I really do think that you deserve to be happy. All these years, you have been the only light in my life. I swear before God, the only one! I just wanted to make sure that you know that 'cause I don't always say the things I feel on account of I got damaged along the way."

"I know, Mama."

"Just, please don't give up on finding someone who can love you right," she begged. "Don't end up like me. More than anything, all I want is for you to find your way."

"Thank you," I whispered and choked up a little.

"You're welcome," she obliged. "You know, Black people should be among the most blessed and grateful people on the earth because God himself looked down from heaven, heard our cries, and set us free. My mama used to say that all the time. Her name was Liza too. Now they're both gone."

She teared up.

"She was right," I stated.

"She surely was right," Mama regrouped and acknowledged. "But look what we did with the freedom God gave us? We gave it right back to the devil. Now we are in a real mess all over again."

"But it's not over for us yet, is it? God is still on the throne. He has never stopped loving and saving us, right?"

She gave me a quizzical look and paused momentarily before answering, "Amen, brother!"

"If you get the name of the funeral home, we can send flowers," I advised.

"Yeah, that sounds good. I'll ask my sister Noreen for it."

———•●•———

I was exhausted from my day on the beach. I got sunburned for the first time in my life. I fell asleep under an umbrella, and the sun moved. Of course, I knew I tanned in the summer like everyone else, but I just never heard of a Black person getting sunburned. The front of both of my legs and my feet got burned a little even though I had put on sunscreen as advised. Clearly, the Jamaican sun was no joke. I took a cold shower and that seemed to help a little, but the affected areas were sore to the touch and starting to peel a little.

It was already 7:30 p.m. Dinner was at 8:00 p.m., so I had to hurry.

"You ready?" I asked.

"Yes, just let me finish my makeup."

She was wearing a pink top that left her stomach exposed and a long beige skirt. She slowly turned away from the mirror. She really was a rare beauty, truly breathtaking!

"Oh my God!" I exclaimed with utter exuberance. "You are simply beautiful! Stunning! Bravo!"

"Cut it out!" Carla reacted and rolled her eyes. "That's why I didn't want to tell you."

We both laughed.

Because we were all created in the image of God,
Things like skin color and race don't define who
You are as a person, unless you are African
American
    and believe that they do.

ABOUT THE AUTHOR

Ed Thompson is a lay minister in Syracuse, New York. He is also a trial attorney in New York, having practiced law in Syracuse for more than twenty-five years. He is a former federal prosecutor and a former assistant public defender. Additionally, Ed received a master's degree in biblical studies from Alliance Theological Seminary in 2020. Previously, Ed received a BA degree from Ohio Northern University in 1982 and a JD Degree from Albany Law School in 1985. He is the author of four legal fiction titles, including Cursed Black. Presently, he resides in Baldwinsville, New York, with his wife and daughter.